He looked so clueless and innocent, but what if it was all an act?

Basil turned to her. His face was pale. His expression was stricken. His eyes were glazed. He opened his mouth, but no words came out.

She hurried toward him. "What is it Basil?"

"M—Maxine." His voice trembled with emotion. "She won't wake up."

Philomela's eyes focused on the woman supine on the couch. Compared to the classy lady she had seen two nights ago at Fireside Pizza, this one was almost unrecognizable. No longer was Maxine a picture of perfect beauty. Her hair resembled a broken bird's nest, her clothes were in disarray, and the makeup on her face was streaked as if disturbed by a struggle. But it was the expression on her face that shocked Philomela. It registered either agony or terror. Or was it an expression of shock? Death had not come peacefully. Then she saw why. Blood oozed through the front of her white silk blouse, spread to her black suit jacket, and seeped onto the tan cushion of the sofa. She had been stabbed.

Philomela stupidly stated the obvious. "She's dead."

Basil gently stroked Maxine's hand as if trying to stimulate the flow of blood. "Here's the knife." His free hand reached toward the floor.

Philomela grabbed his arm and stopped his fingers from grasping the knife. "Don't touch anything, Basil. This is a crime scene. Fingerprints are important."

"Blimey." He looked up at her, aghast. "The knife was lying beside her when I came in the room. I automatically picked it up. Then I dropped it on the floor. I didn't believe what was actually in front of me. I thought it was a foolish prank."

Everyone's favorite amateur sleuth, Philomela Nightingale, visits her sister in the town of Saltaire. While coping with a thieving museum volunteer and a charlatan psychic, the two women become involved with an identity theft, a hit-and-run car accident, and a murder. The search for clues is overshadowed by a ladies fashion-show and a compulsive shopper and, this time, Philomela's powers of observation and intuition might not be strong enough for her to help the police solve these three serious puzzles.

KUDOS for *Showman or Shaman*

In *Showman or Shaman* by Benni Chisholm, Philomela Nightingale goes to Saltaire, Canada, to visit her sister, where she ends up involved in museum theft, identity theft, and murder. As she begins to investigate, Philomela soon discovers that things are not as they seem, and the most likely suspects appear to have solid alibis. Who can she trust, when everyone is a suspect and some people are not who she thinks they are? Chisholm tells a charming tale, filled with delightful characters and intriguing mysteries. Just when you think you have it figured out, she surprises you—again. ~ *Taylor Jones, Reviewer*

Showman or Shaman by Benni Chisholm is the story of Philomela Nightingale, a magazine publisher from Calgary and an amateur sleuth. She gets a call for help from her sister Procne and flies to Saltaire to help Procne solve the mystery of some thefts at the museum where she volunteers part time. But when Philomela gets there, she discovers there is a lot more going on than simple museum theft. Procne's neighbor is supposedly a shaman, but Philomela has her doubts. Something just isn't right. Then the owner of the boutique dress shop where Procne works is murdered. And both Philomela and Procne are suspects, along with almost everyone else in town. It will take all of Philomela's sleuthing skills and ingenuity to get them out of this one. The story is cute, clever, and intriguing, the plot strong and the characters endearing. A delightful sequel to Chisholm's *Odd Odyssey*. ~ *Regan Murphy, Reviewer*

ACKNOWLEDGEMENTS

A sincere thanks to…

Ty, for coining the name, "Showman or Shaman."

Haley, for gracing the cover.

Viola, Alan, and Spencer, for being the inverse of a certain character in the novel.

The two seaside towns that inspired the fictional Saltaire.

The staff at Black Opal Books who are not only capable, but extremely pleasant.

SHOWMAN or SHAMAN

Benni Chisholm

A Black Opal Books Publication

GENRE: MYSTERY-DETECTIVE/WOMEN SLEUTHS

SHOWMAN OR SHAMAN
Copyright © 2017 by Benni Chisholm
Cover Design by Jackson Cover Designs
All cover art copyright © 2017
All Rights Reserved
Print ISBN: 978-1-626945-88-3

First Publication: JANUARY 2017

Published by Black Opal Books **http://www.blackopalbooks.com**

DEDICATION

To Merritt and our magical offspring—
Rob, Doug, Mary Jane, Jessie.

PROLOGUE

Thursday morning:

S omething was amiss! Philomela Nightingale dropped her hands on her lap and reread the disturbing email.

Hi, Philomela:
The weatherman said you had a big snowstorm. I hate to brag, but we have green grass, yellow crocuses, and purple heather.
My part-time job at Whimsical Woman is good. I just bought a smashing new outfit.
The Historical Museum is not so good. I suspect a male volunteer of theft and don't know what to do about it. Selene, my psychic neighbor, might help, but she's a bit airy-fairy.
Your input would be better. Could you possibly come to Saltaire for a visit?
Toodles, Procne

Philomela was astounded. Her kid sister was asking for advice, something she never did. The kleptomaniac volunteer must really trouble her. A niggling thought made Philomela wonder if the request had something to do with Procne's psychic neighbor. Like the proverbial curious cat, Philomela placed her right hand on the mouse and googled, "Selene." Up came six items about the mythical Greek moon goddess and one item about a modern-day shaman. Philomela clicked the latter. A webpage with a violet surround appeared and a photo of a woman with wispy blonde hair and gentle gray eyes gazed out at her. Adjacent to the photo, a blurb praised Selene's sensitive, intuitive nature. At the bottom of the page, a blue link offered free advice.

Philomela knew free advice was worth exactly what it cost, but she clicked the link anyway.

Good grief. Free advice would be hers after she filled out the included form and honored the Celestial Beings with a gift of $49.00.

What a rip-off. Should she do it?

Yes, for the sake of her sister, she should.

On the form she typed Rae—her seldom used second name, Nightingale—her always used last name, and 7 July, 1960—her birth date. She clicked PayPal to cover the $49.00 then pressed submit. A minute later a violet printed message popped up on the monitor.

Rae,

Westerners suffer from guilt feelings due to lessons learned about Adam and Eve's banishment from the Garden of Eden. These negative feelings rest deep in the subconscious. They cause subtle and not-so-subtle problems. With help from the Celestial Beings, I will be happy to eradicate all your bad feelings.

Selene

Like the proverbial cat, Philomela's curiosity was satisfied. There was no question about her sister's neighbor—Selene was a money-grubbing charlatan. Procne lived beside a fraudulent psychic and worked with a thieving volunteer. No wonder her kid sister needed help. Philomela flexed her fingers, clicked the reply icon, and tapped the keyboard.

Hi, Procne:
Our new snow sparkles like diamonds. Brent is as excited as a kid with a new toy because he and his friend John leave early Saturday morning for a week of heliskiing.
The February issue of The Integrator *is almost ready for publication. If my esteemed employee will take charge for a week, I hope to fly to Saltaire on Saturday afternoon.*
Cheerybye, Philomela.

She hit the send icon and the email disappeared in cyberspace. Five minutes later she received a reply.

Hi, Philomela:
Send your flight information and I'll meet you at the airport.
Toodles, Procne

CHAPTER 1

Saturday 4 p.m., Mountain Standard Time:

Philomela sat in the 737-600 and thought of the reasons for her flight—a thieving volunteer and a money-grubbing shaman. She worried about Procne working with one and living beside the other. Fortunately, her sister was aware of the thief. But did she know about her neighbor's less-than-honest internet activities? Philomela suspected the two people were just weirdly wired. She hoped they were not involved with more dangerous activities. It was a dilemma.

Brushing a few cookie crumbs from her green pantsuit, she hoped the scattered debris would not cause extra work for the airplane's cleaning crew. She glanced up at the ceiling and felt her usual amazement—how could a large tin can with air vents, reading lights, windows, wings, and engines, fly so high in the sky? Even more amazing were the human beings who willingly sat inside and expected to come out alive at an airport thousands of miles from where they started.

And here she was—one of those amazing human beings.

Her eyes shifted from the ceiling to the oval window at her side. Gazing down at the sparkling peaks of the Rocky Mountains, she thought of Brent who would soon be heliskiing in powdery snow. She peered past the tree line down to dim valleys sprayed in dark green and draped in white. In a few months, the wintry scene would be replaced by the sights and sounds of spring—deciduous leaves, alpine flowers, green grass, singing birds. It would be a re-enactment of the Greek myth where Persephone departs from her husband, Hades, for an annual six month visit with her loving mother, Demetrius.

Those mythological Greek gods and goddesses knew very little of the great white north's weather conditions. They didn't have to cope with the drama of four seasons—spring's cheery brightness, summer's blazing heat, autumn's peaceful calm, winter's freezing cold. Nor did they have to contend with taxes and death. Being immortal, they probably paid no attention to the one constant of life—change.

Her own life had seen many changes. During the past decade most of her changes originated with Brent Lark, her type-A personality husband. Thanks to his desire to fly in a helicopter to a mountaintop and risk life and limb skiing down avalanche-prone snow, she now flew guilt-free to Saltaire. She hoped he would complete his adventure by coming home alive and intact. Looking around the fragile plane, she hoped she would, too.

Brent's many attempts to persuade her to heliski with him had been easy to resist. Normally, she happily kept pace with him, but expending excessive energy flailing down steep powdery snow was not on her radar screen. More importantly, *The Integrator*, her eclectic magazine, hit the newsstands and mailboxes every two months, and it needed lots of work before the February issue could be published. When Brent's friend, John, agreed to go with him, her qualms about declining the heliski invitation dissipated.

Philomela's memory cells moved to Procne's email. Was it coincidence or serendipity that Janice, Philomela's reliable full-time employee, had completed an article about a shaman two days before Procne's email arrived? Philomela didn't know, but she did know Janice's article brought her up to date on modern-day psychics. She also knew that her late nights of work had whipped the magazine into good shape. If necessary, Janice could add a few final touches and make *The Integrator* ready for distribution by the first of the month.

The magazine, though not a fortune-maker, covered its expenses. It also kept Philomela in stylish shoes. What more could she ask? She enjoyed her work, practiced a healthy lifestyle, and loved her energetic husband. Life was good.

Thoughts of her happy marriage abruptly contrasted with those of her sister's troubled one. For nineteen years that disastrous relationship had been held together by Procne's positive attitude. Over the years Larry's verbal and physical abuse increased. Finally, much to Philomela's relief, her sister declared, "Enough."

Philomela was proud of her sister. After the divorce, Procne distanced herself from the philandering bully by moving from the bustling city of Vancouver to the sleepy town of Saltaire. Their two children now lived in university residence in the big city and on special occasions took the ferry to visit their mother.

With only a high school education and no real experience in the work-a-day-world, Procne used her positive attitude to start a new lifestyle. She settled into the Saltaire townhouse, volunteered at the local historical museum, and then, with newly acquired experience and increasing self-confidence, applied for a part-time job in a lady's dress shop. The only person surprised when the owner hired her was Procne.

Philomela was not surprised at all. Her sister's positive attitude, willingness to work, and innate flair for fashion was obvious to everyone who met her. Philomela suspected these qualities would lead Procne to bigger and better things. Doubtless, she soon would become a full time employee in the dress shop.

Gazing down at the snowy mountains, Philomela thought of last Christmas. Was it just four weeks ago that she and Brent had entertained Procne and her two children in their Calgary home nestled above *The Integrator* office? The get-together had been so jolly that Procne suggested they meet again in June in Saltaire. That timeframe was now fast-forwarding six months early. But this get-together would consist only of the two sisters.

Philomela recalled explaining to Brent why she wanted to fly to Saltaire. They were eating lunch in their kitchen above the magazine's office. He listened to her and continued to eat her homemade soup. When she finished talking, he held his soupspoon in mid-air and nodded his head. He understood the sisters' relationship very well. "Philomela, that's the right thing to do. Right now your kid sister needs your encouragement and practical good sense." He dipped his spoon in the soup bowl, slipped it into his mouth, and savored the thick, warm liquid. "Is this Garbage-Soup?" he asked.

"Of course not." Feigning indignation, she vigorously shook her head, swishing her red hair back and forth. "This is Kitchen-Sink Soup."

"Ah, yes. Everything's in it except the kitchen sink. I think it's also known as Weekly-Clean-the-Fridge-Soup."

She burst out laughing. "You're getting too smart for your own good."

He finished his lunch, leaned back in his chair, and looked pensive. "Soon you and Procne will laze on a sunny beach and John and I will swoosh down a snowy mountain."

"You and John may swoosh down a snowy mountain, but Procne and I will not laze on a sunny beach. Not on Vancouver Island at the end of January."

Brent's guffaw was—as usual—contagious.

The airplane started its descent and Philomela's thoughts shifted from past to present. Gazing out the window, she watched snowy mountains give way to the Fraser River's muddy estuary. She admired sky scrapers of the coastal city whose eponym originated with Captain Vancouver. Seeing boats on the dark blue Georgia Strait, she checked her seatbelt in readiness to land on Canada's large westerly island. The island had been named after the same intrepid English sailor as the city.

She looked forward to seeing Procne. She even looked forward to helping unravel her weird problems. Once everything was solved, the two of them would enjoy a few days of peace, quiet, and laughter.

CHAPTER 2

Saturday 4:30 p.m., Pacific Standard Time:

Procne Ellis strode into the arrival area of the airport and glanced up at the monitor. The plane was five minutes late. She suspected it was bucking warm Chinook winds blowing from west to east. She flicked her dark hair behind her ears, went over to a wooden bench, and sat down to wait.

She was thankful Philomela could take time to come to Saltaire. Her older sister's companionship was always a joy, no matter the circumstances. Though Procne usually ignored her advice, she knew Philomela had a knack for handling awkward situations and fixing complex problems. And right now Procne had a serious volunteer problem.

When the theft at the museum first surfaced, she had been in a quandary. Feeling extremely uneasy, she spent three days trying to figure out what to do.

She thought long and hard about asking Selene Hamilton for help. Knowing her psychic neighbor would lend a kind ear, be sympathetic, and offer advice, Procne also knew the advice would verge on the airy-fairy and be of little practical use. She hated to worry her down-to-earth sister, but as a last resort she decided to send an email asking Philomela to come for a visit. How lucky that she could leave her magazine in her assistant's capable hands. How fortuitous that the timing of her trip would coincide with Brent's heliskiing trip. Procne hoped Brent would have a good time in the cold and snow on top of the mountains. She was confident Philomela would enjoy Saltaire's spring-like weather.

Earlier that afternoon, Procne went out on the deck of her townhouse and checked the thermometer. The temperature was a balmy twelve degrees above freezing. Not too shabby for the month of January. She hoped the good weather would last until Monday morning when she planned to take Philomela to the Historical Museum. There her sister would meet Basil Devonshire, the infamous volunteer who organized volunteers and supplemented his income by dubious means.

It was unlikely they would see Simon Fraser, the curator, because he usually took Mondays off. Thoughts of Simon brought a flush to her face. There was no reason for the girlish reaction—the curator was kind and polite to everyone. And, of course, he was married.

Sitting on the wooden bench in the arrival area, she recalled reading the advertisement in the local paper: *Volunteers Wanted at Historical Museum.* Her first thought after reading the advert was that working in an old, dusty, musty, boring museum would be just the thing for a newly-divorced empty-nester. Before she could change her mind she phoned the listed number. The man who answered had a deep, resonating voice.

"Saltaire Historical Museum. Simon Fraser speaking."

"Are you the discoverer of the mighty Fraser River?" The question popped spontaneously out of her mouth and for a second she felt like a clever, self-assured wit.

"No." His voice rang loud, clear, and intense. The intensity increased when he added a factual date. "That Simon Fraser died in 1862."

Her self-assurance fell like the steep rapids in the famous river. Her clever-wit status dropped to that of half-wit. Trying to regain some intelligent credibility, she made things worse by stuttering, "I'm P—P—Procne Ellis. I'm interested in volunteering at the Historical Museum."

"Great!" the voice boomed with such loud enthusiasm that she moved the phone away from her ear. "I didn't catch your name. Would you mind repeating it?"

"Procne Ellis." This time she didn't stutter.

"That's what I thought you said. Procne…and Philomela. There's a Greek myth—two sisters committed murder and the gods took pity on them. They turned one sister into a nightingale and the other into…"

"A swallow. My mother liked the names of the mythological sisters so she passed them on to her daughters. My older sister, Philomela, is a nightingale in more ways than one. Her mythological namesake was turned into the nightingale and our paternal surname is Nightingale. I'm the swallow."

"Procne, your parents made a grave mistake in naming you. Swallows don't have good voices. Yours is lovely."

She burst out laughing, the first belly laugh she'd had in ages. Already she liked this man. That startled her because since her divorce, all men had been eliminated from her life, except of course her brother-in-law, Brent Lark, and her son, Harold Ellis.

Getting her laughter under control, she said, "There are many versions of the myth. Maybe I should go along with a lesser one in which Philomela has her tongue cut out and becomes a swallow, and Procne is turned into a nightingale."

"Maybe you should." Simon chuckled then changed the subject. "When will you be available to come for a guided tour of the museum?"

"Wednesday morning would suit my busy schedule." Her nose twitched as she gazed at her desk calendar. It was empty of any pen or pencil squiggles—no appointments or social engagements were in the offing. Like Pinocchio, her nose seemed to grow longer.

"The museum opens at ten a.m. How about Wednesday at ten-thirty?"

"Perfect."

At the designated day and hour she approached the red brick building whose main floor housed the History Cafe, Jewelry for You, and Polk and Swindell Law Firm. Several condominiums comprised the three upper levels and the basement housed the Historical Museum and public washrooms. She didn't know if the building was new or expertly renovated, but she did know it was one of the more attractive structures on Main Avenue.

Actually, she liked all the buildings on Main Avenue, especially the earthy grocery stores, quaint boutiques, quirky coffee-houses, and enticing restaurants. In fact, she liked everything about the town—its peaceful ambience, its proximity to the sea, and its friendly people.

Pausing at the window display of Jewelry for You, she admired an assortment of bling, especially a sparkling bracelet. Then she turned and her heels clicked past the sandwich sign, *Historical Museum.* She walked down the steps of the outside stairway, stopped on the bottom landing, and gazed at an OPEN sign hanging on the window beside a partially open doorway. The door was held ajar by a shiny brass seal—appropriate, she thought, for a seaside town. She stepped inside and looked around.

A tall muscular man leaned on a counter. His brown hair was thick with gray streaks at the temples. Conversing with a lady who sat on a high stool behind the counter, he must have heard her, for he turned and looked toward the doorway.

"Procne Ellis?" he asked.

"Yes."

"I'm Simon Fraser, the one who did *not* discover the famous river." A grin exposed his white teeth as he walked over to her and extended his hand.

She shook his hand, looked up at his clear blue eyes, and suddenly felt as if she were in a tilting sailboat. With great effort, she averted her eyes. Like an expert sailor, she slowly returned to an even keel.

Her rumination of Simon Fraser ceased, interrupted by airline passengers flowing into the arrival area. She leaped from the wooden bench and hurried toward the stream of moving people. She scanned various individuals and soon saw her sister's mass of red hair.

With squeals of delight, they met with open arms. Dark hair blended with red. They separated, chatted excitedly, and strolled to the luggage carousel. A few minutes later, with Philomela's small bag rolling behind her, Procne led the way out of the terminal. Side by side, they walked across the parking lot, passing cars that gleamed in the late afternoon sun.

"The air's so soft and soothing," Philomela said. "And look at the cars. Not a dollop of dust or a drop of dirt on any of them."

"They got washed in yesterday's rain." Procne giggled. "You haven't abandoned your alliterating habit." She clicked her remote and the lights of her car flashed brightly.

"Actually, alliteration hasn't abandoned me. Annoying, isn't it."

Several minutes later, Procne drove her white Mazda along the main road and listened to her sister comment on the surroundings: "Green grass, fancy flowers, leafy leaves. This definitely isn't Calgary in January."

"Welcome to winter in Saltaire." Procne pointed to three large trees with broad green leaves. "Those are arbutus trees. They drop their dead leaves in summer, not in autumn."

She turned onto a side street and, a block later, slowed at what seemed a stately house. Chatting about her two children and her part-time job, she maneuvered the car down a ramp to a basement parking area. A few minutes later, riding up one floor in a small elevator, she asked Philomela about Brent's heliskiing trip.

"It's an adventure—a risk-taking adventure. For him, it's a long awaited dream that's finally come true."

"Guess he'll be able to knock heliskiing off his bucket list," Procne said.

"Unless he wants to do it again."

They reached the main floor and stepped into an open-air vestibule containing three doors, a stairway leading down to the car-park, and a metal gate exposing an outside interlocking brick sidewalk. Procne walked to the door closest to the elevator and unlocked it. She dragged her sister's suitcase inside. "Welcome to my castle."

Philomela stepped inside and, with nary a pause, strolled along a short hallway. She passed a laundry room, two bedrooms, a dining alcove, and, in a sitting area, stopped and stared through a wide expanse of windows. "What a spectacular view. That water must be the Pacific Ocean. I see hills and only one snowy mountain."

"The mountain is Mount Baker in Washington State. It has snow all year round. The hills are islands, the close ones are Canadian and the more distant ones are American. This part of the ocean is called the Salish Sea."

Procne took her sister's arm, ushered her away from the large windows, and led her back down the hall to one of the bedrooms. "This is my daughter Jane's room. The main color is feminine pink and the bed is comfortable." She plunked Philomela's suitcase on top of a low cedar chest then left her to unpack and freshen up.

Several minutes later, Philomela reentered the sitting area and again stared through the windows at the expansive vista. She glanced at the adjacent kitchen, moved toward it, and watched Procne put a corkscrew in the cork of a wine bottle.

"Oretega." Procne held up the wine bottle. "It's a light, fruity white wine that comes from a local winery." She poured some liquid into one of two stemmed glasses, sniffed it, and took a sip. Then she filled the other glass and handed it to Philomela. "It's not vinegar."

They carried their glasses to the sitting area, curled up at each end of one of two sofas, glanced at the fireplace and out the window. Then they gazed happily at each other.

"I'm so glad you're here." Procne's lips curved up at each corner. She raised her glass in salute and Philomela responded in similar manner. Procne took a sip then set her glass on the coffee table. "I suppose you want to hear about the wayward volunteer."

Philomela nodded, sipped her wine, then leaned toward the coffee table and set her glass on it. She waited for Procne to elaborate.

"Well, his name is Basil Devonshire. I confess that when he first phoned me, I was intrigued with his English accent. Also by his brilliant vocabulary—it sort of reminded me of you. Meeting him in person, I found him to be good looking and an interesting dresser, in an English sort of way. He wears corduroy suits. I soon learned he is well organized, excellent at scheduling volunteers, and sometimes rather abrupt. He often corrects people to the point of rudeness. Those traits are not softened by a sense of humor. He has none."

"When did you first start to worry about him?" Philomela asked.

"About a week and a half ago, after overhearing a conversation."

Philomela plucked her glass from the coffee table, took a sip, and waited for her sister to continue talking.

"I was admiring the bling in the shop window of Jewelry for You. From the corner of my eye I saw Basil come out of the History Cafe. His longish white hair and olive-drab corduroy suit were hard to miss. He was accompanied by a woman. Right away I recognized the black chignon hair style and smart black coat with large buttons that belonged to Maxine Springer. I turned to say, 'Hello,' but before I could speak, Maxine looked Basil in the eye and clearly stated, 'Pay the money you owe me within a week or I'll ask your wife for it.' He glared at her. If looks could kill, she would have died on the spot. He said, and I quote, 'Don't you dare mention the loan to Grace.' At that same moment, I saw Jean Greenfield, the owner of the History Cafe, peer out the front window. She obviously wondered what was going on. Then I heard Basil say to Maxine, 'You greedy bitch.' Wanting to be miles away, I tried to shrink into the jewels in the shop window. I saw Basil's reflected profile in the glass as he headed behind me for the museum stairs. He looked angry. He marched down the stairs and Maxine, who looked equally angry, spun around on her stiletto heels and clicked off in the opposite direction. I thought I might have witnessed a lovers' quarrel."

Philomela took a slow sip of wine, set her glass back on the coffee table, and looked pensively at her sister. "It sounds more like a failed financial transaction than a lovers' quarrel. Perhaps it signified the end of a friendship. Do you remember Shakespeare's play, Hamlet?"

"Yeah. Sort of."

"In the play, Polonius gave his son wise advice. 'Neither a borrower, nor a lender be, For loan oft loses both itself and friend, And borrowing dulls the edge of husbandry.'" Philomela continued to look pensively at her sister. "Perhaps Maxine's loan to Basil made her lose both her money and her friendship with Basil. Basil's debt to Maxine may have dulled his ability to manage his own finances."

"You mean Basil might think money grows on trees, so is happy to take money from anyone and pretend it is his own?"

"Possibly." Philomela shrugged. "But, Procne, three questions worry me, and they're pertinent. They all have to do with money. Why did Maxine loan money to Basil in the first place? Why did he treat the loan as a gift instead of a debt? And why did he not want his wife to know about the loan?"

"There must be some logical answers," Procne replied. "Maxine and Basil are smart people, and they're both very community minded. He's a retired bank manager who does a good job as the volunteer coordinator at the Historical Museum. She's an astute business woman who owns two successful dress shops—Upscale Garments and Whimsical Woman."

"Good grief. He deals with you at the museum, and she deals with you at Whimsical Woman. Did they see you?"

"I don't know how they could have missed seeing me."

"Perhaps they were too distraught to see anything but each other."

"Maybe. But, Philomela, what troubled me more was

last Monday when I caught Basil stuffing money from the museum's donation box into his pant pocket. He definitely saw me then."

"What did he say?"

"He said he was checking to see if volunteers were encouraging people to donate. He dumped a handful of coins back in the box. I didn't see him return the wad of bills."

"Did you tell the curator?

"I didn't dare. Simon and Basil have worked closely together for more than three years. I'm the newcomer, the outsider. What do I know?"

"Yes." Philomela nodded. "The curator might consider you an up-start and a trouble-maker. What about your boss at the dress shop? Basil's theft from the museum might be related to his not repaying Maxine's loan."

"Maxine certainly was angry with him."

"What about Basil's wife?"

"Grace is a pleasant, unassuming woman. She attends teas and likes to shop." Procne bit her lower lip, deep in thought. "Do you think I should mention the theft to Maxine?"

"How well do you know her?"

"As well as any employee knows her boss. She's always pleasant and helpful. She's also well organized and efficient. In marketing she's amazing—so creative and so innovative."

"She sounds like a perfect business woman. But, as you mentioned, you're the newcomer. Maxine and Basil and Simon have known each other for years. You were right to hold your tongue."

Procne was pleased with Philomela's assessment of how she had reacted to the theft. "You'll meet Basil on Monday. I can hardly wait to hear your impression of him."

"The entire situation is awkward," Philomela said, "for all three of you."

CHAPTER 3

Sunday Morning:

Bending her knees in half-hearted squats and raising her arms in high-reaching stretches, Procne recalled Philomela's words. '*The entire situation is awkward—for all three of you.*' She paused in mid-stretch and wondered if her concern was greater than that of Basil's and Maxine's. No. Recalling their conversation outside the History Café, she concluded that their concerns must be greater than hers.

A sudden brightening prompted her to look out the window at the eastern horizon. The sun peeped above a hill on a distant island and quickly evolved into a brilliant yellow ball. The sight perked her up and renewed her energy. She vigorously completed her exercises.

By the time she finished showering and dressing, the joy of having her sister here in Saltaire filled her entire being. In the kitchen, her fingers deftly placed bacon strips in a frying pan while her thoughts fast-forwarded to tomorrow morning when Philomela would see the museum and meet Basil Devonshire. Philomela's first impression of the volunteer would be interesting.

With Basil in mind, her thoughts sped back to the first time he had phoned her. She could almost hear his clear, upscale English accent. "Basil Devonshire here. Am I speaking with Mrs. Ellis?"

"Yes, I'm Procne Ellis." After the divorce she had been tempted to revert to Nightingale, but because of the two children she ended up retaining her married name.

"I coordinate volunteers and create monthly schedules for the Historical Museum."

"Simon Fraser said you'd call."

"I'll get down to business straightaway. Would you be free on Monday mornings?"

"I think so." She knew full well no social engagement or doctor or dentist appointments cluttered her immediate future.

"It's a three hour shift. Could you be at the museum from ten a.m. to one p.m.?"

"Yeah, that'll be okay."

Basil cleared his throat. "Did Simon explain your duties?"

"Briefly. I sit at the front counter, greet people, and get them to sign the guest book."

"It may sound simple, but the guest book is important. Part of our funding is based on the number of people who visit the museum. You will also have to answer questions. The most frequent question is: 'Where is the loo?'"

She giggled. "Very historical."

He either failed to catch her jest or simply ignored it. "Another question often asked, especially by the physically challenged, is: 'Where is the lift?'"

"Not elevator. You're definitely English." She grinned, knowing he couldn't see her.

He paid no attention to her remark. "When Simon is not in his office, you must answer the phone."

"I can manage that." She made her voice sound as prim as his.

"A list of phone numbers is available if a volunteer needs help. On Monday morning, I'll reiterate all this in more detail. Be there at ten a.m. sharp." He ended the conversation with an abrupt goodbye. She suspected that whoever doled out humor genes neglected to give him one.

Basil slipped to the back of her mind and the cook-top came to the fore. Attending to bacon spattering on the front burner, she took the spatula and flipped four slices to their other sides.

"G'morning, sis."

Procne glanced over her shoulder. "Philomela, you're up. Did you sleep well? Will bacon and eggs be okay?"

"I slept very well. Bacon and eggs will be perfect. I just recovered from a cold that Brent generously gave me, so my appetite's back to normal."

Procne put the bacon on a paper towel and cracked two eggs into the frying pan. "I know a sure-fire cure for colds."

"Really?"

"Buy a new outfit."

Philomela chuckled. "Is that as good as chicken soup?"

"Better."

"What can I do to help?"

"Pour yourself a glass of orange juice."

Philomela did as ordered and set the glass on a place-mat on the eating counter. She climbed on a high stool, glanced out the window at the rolling Salish Sea, then turned to her sister.

"Apart from the wayward volunteer, life seems to be treating you well."

"I'm free of Larry." Procne waved the egg flipper as

if smacking her ex. "I'm well rid of him. What more can I say?"

"The snapdragon stage is behind you."

Procne's eyebrows formed two questioning arches. "Pardon?"

"Your head no longer snaps and your body's no longer draggin'."

"Philomela, that's awful. Did you dream it up?"

"It came as an email joke. But it fits you perfectly."

Procne rolled her eyes and grinned. Then her expression turned shadowy and, with no preamble, she asked, "Have you and Brent thought about retirement?"

"Certainly. Last year I spent my retirement money on a round-the-world-trip with Janice, my esteemed employee. This year, Brent is spending his retirement money with his friend John on a heliskiing holiday."

"Seriously. I think you two should retire on Vancouver Island."

"Good grief, Procne. Why would we do that? Brent and I love our jobs. We love Calgary. The city's so vibrant, so youth oriented."

"And so cold in winter. You'd love Saltaire, Philomela, even though it's full of goldie-oldies and the sidewalks roll up at six-thirty in the evening. The year-round weather is temperate and the beauty is incomparable. Brent could commute back and forth for a year or two and you could start a magazine similar to the one in Calgary."

Philomela studied her sister with apparent concern. "Procne, are you lonely?"

"Not at all." With a flourish, she set two plates of bacon, eggs, tomatoes, and toast on the eating counter. "I love my abode, the town of Saltaire, and the people in it...well, most of the people."

Philomela nodded and glanced out the window at the forever-moving water.

"Is the tide coming in or going out?" she asked.

"Coming in. You're changing the subject."

"That boat out there is being buffeted by a breeze."

"Philomela, do you hear yourself?"

"I know. Alliteration. I'm still addicted."

"The subject is not alliteration. The subject is semi-retirement. Think about it for a minute." Procne filled two red mugs with coffee, set them on the counter, and eased herself onto the high stool beside Philomela. She quietly concentrated on eating. A few minutes later, she set her fork on her plate and turned to her sister. "Well? What about semi-retirement?"

"I'm thinking about it."

"Keep thinking. Tomorrow, you'll see the museum and meet Basil Devonshire. But this evening, we'll forget all about him. We're going to walk to a restaurant for a casual dinner with two of my neighbors. We'll go Dutch because out here people pay their own bills. That way no one feels indebted to someone else."

"Very logical. Which of your neighbors?"

"Shaun O'Reilly and Selene Hamilton."

"Shaun sounds Irish," Philomela said, "and Selene sounds like a Greek moon-goddess. Are they married?"

"No, they each own their own townhouse. I think they're just friends. But who knows for sure?" Procne shrugged. "Shaun's in the investment business. He helps retired people buy and sell stocks, bonds, and other investments. He's an ideal salesman, good looking, friendly, and smooth. Selene sews clothes and does alterations for my boss. She also relieves as a clerk at both of Maxine's dress shops. I like her, even though she's a bit airy-fairy."

"You said in your email that she's psychic. Does she help heal people? Or does she just prophesy and offer advice?"

"Actually, she does all three. A healing circle meets twice a week in her townhouse. Other people ask her for advice regarding their futures. She often startles people by saying unexpected things about past or future happenings. For example, when I first met her she blurted out that fashion would play a major part in my life. At that point, I was immersed in Saltaire's history. The last thing in the world I was thinking about was clothing. Three days later, Sheila Trust, another neighbor, told me a part-time clerk was needed at Whimsical Woman. As you know, on a whim I applied and—voila—to my surprise Maxine hired me. So, you see, Selene's prophecy came true."

"Selene may have noticed your flare for clothes and simply projected that observation into your future."

"Maybe." Procne shook her head somewhat dubiously. "But an awful lot of her futuristic statements have come true."

Philomela studied her sister a moment. "A healing circle is worthwhile. Good thoughts and prayers are beneficial in helping the sick get well. Do many people ask Selene for help regarding their health or for the health of loved ones?"

"Yeah. They phone at all hours of the day and night, asking for help. She believes her psychic ability is a gift from God, so she gives readings to everyone free of charge." Procne resumed eating.

"Mmm. So she's not a money-grubbing charlatan?"

"Gosh no. Anything but. Mind you, a lot of clients show their appreciation by giving her presents. You know, food, wine, gift certificates, money."

"Is that how she pays for her townhouse?"

"I think she had a small inheritance from her parents and a savings plan from a former job. She used to design clothes and, at one time, she made costumes for a dance studio and a theater group."

"Those jobs sound like fun but not very lucrative. Does Selene advertise on the internet?"

"No. She has a computer, but she's almost computer illiterate. People learn about her by word of mouth. Thanks to her savings, her present earnings from clerking and sewing, and her gifts received for psychic advice she manages quite nicely." Procne jumped down from her high stool and started to clear dishes from the eating counter.

"Does Sean look after her investments?"

"I think he'd like to, but they were all locked in before she met Sean."

"Could there be two Selenes?" Philomela gazed quizzically at Procne. "Your neighbor and another one? One who isn't quite so generous with her talents?"

"Two Selenes?" Procne stared at her sister and scrunched up her nose. "What a weird question." She shrugged her shoulders and put plates, cutlery, and glasses into the dishwasher. She had no idea what Philomela meant by, '*Someone who isn't quite so generous with her talents.*'

CHAPTER 4

Sunday Morning, later:

While helping her sister tidy the kitchen, Philomela thought about Selene Hamilton. This evening they would be together—she could hardly wait to meet the charlatan face to face. It would be interesting to see how the psychic handled herself. It would be more interesting to see if she realized that the physical Philomela and the emailing Rae were one and the same person.

When the mundane kitchen tasks were finished, both sisters donned fleecy jackets and went out the door of the townhouse. In the open air vestibule, Procne opened the metal gate and they stepped onto the interlocking brick sidewalk. Philomela breathed in the soft air and looked up at the blue sky. The clouds had dissipated, leaving only a few cotton-ball puffs near the southern horizon. The sun shone like a cheery messenger bringing warmth from heaven to earth.

"Brent emailed last night," she said. "He wrote that it was twenty degrees below freezing up on the ski-hill and twenty-five degrees below freezing in Calgary."

"Lucky us," Procne said. "We're in Canada's Riviera."

"Yes. It's very pleasant here." Philomela smiled at her sister. "I could get used to it."

"You mean semi-retire?"

Philomela laughed. "Who knows?"

They strolled along the sea-walk and glanced at seagulls soaring above their heads. Procne pointed to a seal in the water gazing up at them with limpid eyes. They met several people, some riding scooters, some walking alone or in groups, and several being led by a small or a large dog. Everyone cheerfully remarked on the warm morning and the bright sun. Stopping beside a bronze man sitting on a bench, Procne touched three winter-pansies clutched in his metal hands.

"Someone places fresh flowers in his hands every day," she said.

"Does anyone know who the someone is?" Philomela asked.

"The someone who does it knows."

Philomela chuckled. "Would Selene know who does it?"

"Maybe. If there was a good reason to know it."

They resumed walking in comfortable silence. Nearing a marina full of large and small boats, Procne stood still and, like a pedantic teacher, asked, "Did you know a boat is a hole in the water into which the owner throws money?"

"I've heard that before. The money pays for moorage, maintenance, fuel, etc."

"Philomela. You just earned a gold star."

They walked a short distance farther then stopped on a boardwalk. Leaning on a wooden railing overlooking a tidal flat, they gazed at three stone Innukchucks—the Inuit markers that came to the world's attention during the 2010 Vancouver Winter Olympics. They watched four ducks swim in a neat row then dive in unison and disappear. The ducks stayed under water for a long time and finally all four popped up and floated on top of the water.

"Those birds are amazing," Philomela said. "They must have huge lung capacities."

Procne nodded agreement then pointed to a large, motionless bird. "See that blue heron. He looks like a statue staring into the water. I wonder how long he'll have to wait until his next meal appears."

Leaving the Innukchucks, ducks, and heron, they climbed several steps to a residential street. Side by side, they walked past townhouses and condominiums and ended up on the interlocking red brick path leading to Procne's townhouse.

"Look at the big black cat sitting in the window," Philomela said.

"That's Hecate. Selene loves animals, especially cats. Our strata council allows two quiet pets, so Selene has two cats. The other one's a mix of colors, sort of a camouflage of brown, black, beige, and cream. She calls that cat, Artemis."

"Selene must know Greek mythology. Artemis is a huntress. Some versions of the Artemis myth say the goddess has three forms: Artemis who is a virgin huntress on earth, Hecate who dwells in the lower world and in the dark sky, and Selene who is a moon-goddess. This mythological trinity imparts an important trait to humans—the uncertainly of good and evil."

"Good and evil are uncertain?" Procne frowned, seeming to doubt that statement. "The only uncertain thing about good and evil is exactly when they might occur." She giggled. "While you were learning Greek mythology, I was raising two kids and trying to please yukky Larry."

"You did well. You have two great kids."

They spent the afternoon in Procne's townhouse, peacefully lounging, chatting, and reading. From the freezer, Procne brought out a frozen ring of large shrimp and a spicy sauce. She set them on the eating counter and said to Philomela, "This will be our appetizer. Not too much. I don't want to spoil Shaun and Selene's appetites for dinner."

CHAPTER 5

Sunday, Late Afternoon:

At four-thirty, Philomela sauntered to the guest bedroom. She reddened her lips and slipped into her reliable, chocolate-brown dress. On more than one occasion, it had earned the moniker—Fantastic Frock. It always came out of her suitcase unwrinkled and ready to wear. Its rich color minimized spills and, when necessary, the fabric withstood washing and drip-drying. As if that weren't enough, Fantastic Frock was made of stretchy material that fit her figure and was comfortable to wear.

To complete her ensemble, she put on a pair of pearl earrings and a pearl necklace. The pearls, though of dubious origin, turned the dress from quite casual to rather dressy. Looking at her reflection in the full-length mirror, she smiled with satisfaction. Though she looked a bit like a little brown wren, she felt ready for any social event.

Sauntering into the living room, she stopped in her tracks and stared at her sister. Procne was a picture of glamor, adorned in black tights, black and gold top, clunky gold earrings, and an arm heavy with bracelets.

Her attire proved what Philomela always knew—her sister not only had a flare for fashion, she also had the height and figure to show clothes to advantage. Philomela noted that, unlike herself who tried to move regally in flat-heeled walking shoes, Procne flitted around like a butterfly in a pair of high-heeled, black leather boots.

On the dot of five o'clock, a series of knocks sounded at the front door. Reminiscent of a tall pixie, Procne sprinted to the front entrance.

Philomela heard her open it, welcome her two guests, and chat gaily as she led them past the dining area to the sitting room. Philomela, standing near a sofa, recognized the psychic immediately. The round face, wispy fair hair, and gray eyes were exactly like her picture on the website. Philomela gazed at the woman and, much to her surprise, felt no sense of apprehension. She wondered if it was due to the psychic's peaceful facial expression. The expression seemed to radiate from within, but then again it could be a result of talent as a brilliant actress. Her round face and wispy blonde hair were accentuated by silver earrings twinkling like stars beneath her earlobes. The computer website's violet surround was absent, but the psychic's ankle length, silver-blue dress enhanced both her slim figure and her other-worldly appearance. A smoky blue knitted cape draped over one arm completed her appearance of etherealness. As she dropped the cape on the arm of a sofa, silver bangles jingled on her wrists. The sound made Philomela think of music created by fairies.

Selene may be a shaman, she thought, *but she's also a showman. Or, more correctly, a show-woman.*

Procne introduced the newcomers, and Philomela gently shook Selene's right hand. The palm and fingers were so delicate and fragile that Philomela was afraid she might injure them. Shaun's handshake, on the other hand, was firm, almost painful. She was relieved when he let go, yet at the same time his curly blond hair and cherubic face brought out her mothering instincts. His youthful appearance was robust and healthy, and he looked cool and casual in smart khaki pants, ivory shirt, and tweed jacket. His energetic appearance and loud voice were friendly, though in sharp contrast to Selene's quiet fragility. The two guests sat down beside each other on one of the sofas.

Procne served grapefruit juice to Selene, Scotch to Shaun, and set two glasses of wine on the coffee table for Philomela and herself. Philomela brought serviettes, prawns, and spicy sauce from the kitchen and passed them around. She then placed the hors d'oeuvre platter on the coffee table and sat down on the sofa across from their guests. Procne sat down beside her.

"If you want more prawns," Procne said, "please help yourselves."

"In my youth," Shaun said, "I played guitar in a rock and roll band. Mostly we played in bars and were paid with drinks. Not the healthiest way to live. To be honest, I almost starved to death." He grinned appealingly. "I'm much better at helping people make good investments in the stock market than I was as a musician." His grin widened to a warm smile as if inviting them to partake of his services.

Philomela returned his smile then gazed at the ethereal woman sitting beside him. The psychic's gentle face suddenly paled, and Philomela wondered if she was going to faint. "Are you okay, Selene?" she asked.

Selene clasped her hands together in her lap. "I'm fine. Unfortunately, a woman I just envisioned is not. She's not breathing."

"Good grief!" Philomela looked around, almost expecting to see the breathless woman. Then she again stared at the psychic. "Do you know the woman?"

"I didn't see her face. She was lying on a tan colored sofa. She may be passing to the other side."

"Can you help her?"

"No, not at all. I don't know if this vision has already happened, or is happening, or will happen."

Philomela continued to stare across the coffee table at the psychic. Her appearance was light and airy but her contribution to their social conversation was extremely strange. Philomela bit her lower lip then cleared her throat. "To be honest, Selene, I find your…out-of-this-world talent…dreadfully disconcerting."

Selene laughed gently, and the sound reminded Philomela of tiny sleigh bells amid a shower of softly falling snowflakes.

"Psychic abilities run in my family," Selene said. "My mother and grandmother had the gift so we accept them as part of life. I confess that during my youth it was more a curse than a blessing. I didn't want to know about future happenings, especially bad ones."

"I can imagine." Philomela experienced a feeling of empathy. "Coping with unpleasant situations in the here and now is bad enough. Dealing with ones that will happen in the future must be terrible, especially for a young girl. For that matter, most adults would be unnerved by a scary presentiment. One way or another, they'd probably turn it off." Selene nodded in agreement and Philomela pointedly asked, "Do you advertise your psychic talents on the Internet?"

"Never." Selene's reply was firm and clear.

"Do you have a computer?" Philomela asked.

"Yes, but I seldom use it. Mind you, I occasionally go on the Internet to obtain information on a particular subject."

"Do you use emails or Facebook or Twitter?"

"I seldom use emails. I know nothing about those other things."

Philomela was reminded of a Shakespearean quote. "Methinks she doth protest too much."

"People hear about my work by word of mouth from friends, family, and acquaintances." Selene glanced at the dapper man sitting beside her. "Shaun says the Internet would bring a wider audience to me, and more people would be helped. He even offered to set up a website for me, but I'm uncomfortable with the idea. Technology has its good qualities, but it isn't my strong point. For me, personal interaction and mental telepathy are far more important."

Philomela lowered her head and surreptitiously studied Selene. She wondered if the woman was an out-and-out liar. Was her gentle, kind demeanor a clever performance? Philomela thought of the website, the emails, and the blue link requesting forty-nine dollars. The person sitting across from her was no shaman. A shaman was recognized by his or her sincerity and honesty.

"I'll be happy to set up a website—if Selene ever changes her mind." Shaun smiled at Philomela then branched out on a rock and roll story. His manner and words came across as smooth, amicable, and humorous.

Philomela listened to his amusing anecdote. Like an experienced comedian, he held her entranced. She realized this ability would make him a natural-born salesman. At the punch line of his story, she chuckled then shifted her gaze back to the ethereal woman sitting beside him.

"Selene," she said, "does your unusual talent give you an advantage when betting at a horse race?"

"None whatsoever." Selene chuckled softly. "Gambling at a casino is the same. No advantage."

"Is that because you purposely don't take advantage of your intuitive abilities?"

"Partly. And partly because I never receive prophetic warnings for myself. I have to learn everything from experience."

"Is there a reason for that?"

"I think so. It prevents me from unintentionally abusing my talent."

"That makes sense." Philomela nodded agreement. "Do you ever hold séances for other people?"

"Only if someone insists on chatting with a deceased family member. I don't like being a medium. It's exhausting. I prefer having spirit guides send information to me." She gazed up at the ceiling and her eyes grew moist. "My brother died several years ago, and he is one of my sprit guides, or if you prefer, one of my guardian angels."

"I stand in awe of people like you who are attuned with both the ordinary and the non-ordinary." Philomela spoke with genuine sincerity, though she doubted that the woman sitting across from her was either genuine or sincere. She appeared open and honest, but obviously that was a front. And was she truly attuned with the spirit world? "I have to confess," Philomela said, "I belong to the class known as, 'I'm from Missouri, give me proof.'"

Selene nodded with obvious understanding. "All of us are born with psychic abilities, but most people lose them while growing up. Many sensitive people attribute their prophetic feelings to an overactive imagination and ignore them." She sipped her grapefruit juice then offered Philomela a drop of intuitive proof. "You, Philomela, are sensitive to others and you pay attention to your intuition. You could easily develop your psychic powers."

Procne giggled and looked at her sister. "Philomela, a few days ago I told Selene that you inherited our Scottish Granny's second-sight."

So, Philomela thought, Procne had planted that thought in Selene's head.

Procne giggled again. "I, on the other hand, inherited Granny's passion for clothes."

"That's true, Procne, you have a fantastic flare for fashion. But I don't have true second-sight. I only get gut feelings." Philomela turned to Selene. "Brent, my husband, calls my feelings woman's intuition."

Selene gazed up at the ceiling as if searching for a response. Apparently finding one, she smiled at Philomela. "Intuitive insight comes in a flash and seems irrational. The flash comes from an unknown source and can be described as lifting the veil for a glimpse of beyond the beyond."

Philomela knew her own vague flashes of insight were always accompanied with a contraction of her abdominal muscles. That was why she called them gut feelings. She looked directly into Selene's gray eyes. "I've read that second-sight is an impression made by the mind upon the eye. Or by the eye upon the mind. Either way, it allows a person to perceive events that will happen in the future."

"Foresight is one definition of second-sight," Selene said.

Shaun groaned. "Come on now, girls. If foresight is second-sight, what is first-sight?"

"First-sight is ordinary sight," Selene quietly said. "Ordinary sight comes first, and foresight, or nonordinary sight, comes second."

Shaun shook his head and threw his arms up helplessly. "It's all too much for me." Then, as if the question just occurred to him, he asked no one in particular and everyone in general, "Do you believe in fate?"

Philomela answered his question with another question: "You mean predestination?"

"I guess so."

"The doctrine that says everything is determined in advance?" Philomela asked.

"Yeah, that's what I mean."

Selene answered his initial question. "I believe some things are predetermined, but most things depend on what a person does throughout his or her lifetime. What a person sees, does, and doesn't do, make up his or her destiny."

"Cause and effect," Philomela said. Selene nodded and when no one else commented, Philomela expanded on the old adage, "Heavy smoking and poor eating habits will eventually cause ill health."

"Cause and effect," Selene murmured.

"Come on now," Shaun said, "that's not psychic. That's basic fact. It's like a person who doesn't save for retirement will have a problem retiring. "

Philomela nodded.

"Drink up everyone." Procne clicked her index fingernail on the face of her wristwatch. "It's time to go. I hate to cut this fascinating conversation short, but our reservation is for six-thirty." She drained her glass and leaped to her feet.

The others followed her lead and stood up.

CHAPTER 6

Sunday Evening:

For six blocks, Philomela and Procne walked briskly behind Selene and Shaun. Along the way, Philomela counted six streetlights, two cars, and three other meandering pedestrians. She remembered Procne saying that Saltaire's sidewalks rolled up at six-thirty. This must be what she meant.

Philomela liked the feeling of peaceful inactivity, but it changed abruptly when they entered the restaurant.

Fireside Pizza's bright lights, warm fireplace, buzzing conversation, and sparkling laughter provided a warm welcome. Though every table appeared to be occupied by diners, a pleasant waitress led them to an empty table at the back of the room. She picked up the reserved sign and smiled at Shaun, the only male in the group. All four sat down and she handed out menus. Shaun whispered to her.

"No." Procne leaned forward and loudly interrupted their quiet exchange. She shook her finger at the waitress. "Don't let the gentleman pay for us. We all agreed to have separate bills."

The waitress appeared to be at sixes and sevens until

Shaun helplessly shrugged. "I bow to the power of a higher authority. Separate bills it is."

With method of payment decided, all four diners haphazardly glanced around at fellow patrons then seriously buried their noses in the menu. They commented on a few items then, in friendly accord, each ordered a locally-made cider. Selene ordered a big salad, and the others each ordered a medium-size pizza, three different varieties. The ciders were delivered first.

Shaun took a sip and his eyes widened in surprise. "It has a nice flavor. I didn't expect it to taste so good."

All four sipped their drinks and chatted about generalities. After the food was placed on the table, the three pizza eaters shared slices with each other. Amid laughter, they agreed to disagree on which pizza was the tastiest, which had the best consistency, and which was the healthiest. The discussion provided no conclusion but at the end of the meal every plate was empty.

Selene lowered her head and quietly said, "I give thanks to all the plants and animals that provided us with the ingredients of this delicious meal." She raised her head and smiled at her dinner companions then leaned back in her chair.

Philomela was reminded of mealtimes when her father thanked God for the food about to be eaten. Back then it was called *grace*. Selene's rendition, though similar, came after the food was eaten and gave thanks not to an almighty power but to the plants and animals that had comprised the sustenance. After all, some of the plants and animals had given up their lives to provide their food.

Shaun, moving on after Selene's expression of gratitude, beckoned to the waitress. When she drew close, Procne reiterated her previous pronouncement, "Separate bills, please."

Shaun shook his head with mock helplessness. "My

female friends are very independent." He smiled at the waitress. "The pizzas were delicious, good enough to warrant a return visit."

She acknowledged his compliment by beaming a smile at him. A few minutes later, she presented four separate bills.

As Philomela placed the exact amount of cash plus a tip on her bill, she peripherally saw her sister wave her arm. Looking up, she realized Procne was greeting four people who had just entered the restaurant. Philomela particularly noted a tall, slender man with mostly white hair. One of the female newcomers returned Procne's wave and walked over to them.

"Is the food good tonight?" the newcomer asked.

"The pizzas were delicious," Procne replied. She introduced Sheila Trust to Philomela and explained that Sheila and her husband Tom were fellow townhouse owners. "They live in the penthouse above Selene and me."

"We live in the attic." With an expression of childish innocence, Sheila grinned at Philomela. "Poor Shaun lives in the basement."

Procne giggled at what apparently was a longstanding joke. "Tom's president of our strata council," she said to Philomela. "Being a realtor he knows all the ins and outs of everything. Sheila works at Upscale Garments, and she's the one who told me Maxine was looking for a sales clerk at Whimsical Woman. As Basil would say, Sheila works in the posh shop, and I work in the tarty one."

Sheila's facial expression changed to that of a prim school teacher. "The classic shop and the casual shop," she corrected. "Not posh and tarty." Abruptly reversing her teaching role to that of a groveling one, she twisted one hand around the other and gazed at Philomela. "As you doubtless know, Procne is one of the volunteers who keep this town alive and well. Volunteers help run the Community Center, the Movie House, the Quake and Shake Society, the Hospital, the Adept Adult Day Center, plus all four museums—marine, history, aviation, and agriculture."

"Good grief," Philomela said. "Your spiel sounds like a radio advertisement for the town."

Sheila burst out laughing. "I guess it does."

"Volunteers really are the backbone of the community," Selene said, confirming Sheila's description. "Saltaire would collapse if volunteers went on strike."

Sheila nodded and glanced across the room at her three dinner companions. "I must go and rejoin my group. It's nice to meet you, Philomela. See you anon." With the elegance of a model, she glided away.

"Is Sheila going to buy one of the dress shops?" Selene asked.

Procne turned sharply to her neighbor. "What do you mean?"

"I've heard rumors."

"I guess that particular rumor is rampant. On more than one occasion Sheila has asked Maxine to sell. To tell the truth, she would like to buy both shops. But Maxine isn't interested in selling either of them."

Philomela surreptitiously studied Selene. Her question had appeared as a non-sequitur, out of the blue. For some reason it seemed important, but Philomela could not fathom why.

"Philomela," Procne said. "The Trust's dinner companions are Melvin and Maxine Springer."

Philomela looked questioningly at her sister. "Your boss and her husband?"

"Yeah." Procne nodded her head and Philomela gazed at the smart looking couple.

"I knew Melvin at university," Shaun said.

"Really?" Procne seemed surprised. "Did you know him well?"

"We were acquaintances. We took a few courses together. He was a handsome football player, though a mediocre student. We never became good friends, mainly because I disliked how he treated people."

Procne leaned toward him as if anticipating some juicy gossip. "What did he do?"

"Well, he got a first-year arts student pregnant then dropped her like a sizzling potato."

"Yuuk," Procne said. "Not nice. What did the girl do?"

"She quit university and got an abortion."

"Well," Procne said, "maturity must have changed him. Now he's kind, thoughtful, and considerate. He's always nice when he comes to the shop. He does accounting for Maxine, and he helps us when any heavy lifting has to be done."

"Mm. I wonder where he invests his accounting revenue." Shaun gazed thoughtfully at Procne. "Does a dress shop have much accounting?"

"Lots," Procne replied. "Clothes have to be ordered and wholesale merchandise has to be paid for. Retail sales have to be deposited in the bank. Lost and damaged items have to be recorded, and water and electrical bills have to be paid. Then of course there's the almighty provincial sales tax and the federal goods and service tax. Not to forget our annual income tax. Whew. The list also includes salaries, rent, and who knows what else? Thank goodness, I don't have to look after all those things."

Philomela was surprised at her sister's knowledge of the intricacies of the retail business. The list of accounting tasks was familiar to Philomela because managing a small magazine and managing a small dress shop obviously had many similarities. Her thoughts shifted from the list of business expenses to the Springers and Trusts who were chatting with a waitress.

"Maxine Springer," Philomela said aloud, "is a classy-looking lady. Her chignon hairstyle and black and white outfit are gorgeous, very glamorous."

Procne nodded. "She's always perfectly coifed and perfectly dressed."

"Very upscale." Philomela gave her sister a conspiratorial grin. "Not whimsical."

Procne giggled. "As Basil would say—Maxine doesn't tart up. She's posh."

As if knowing they were discussing her, Maxine glanced in their direction, smiled, raised her hand, and daintily waved her blood-red finger tips. Procne returned the wave with her pale gold finger tips.

Philomela shifted her gaze from the glamorous owner of the two dress shops to her husband. His more-salt-than-pepper hair and his smart pin-striped suit made him look like an advert for expensive Scotch whisky. In his youth he probably turned many a young girl's head. Suddenly Philomela's peripheral vision glimpsed a shiver of Selene's shoulders. Glancing sideways at the ethereal woman who was also looking at the newcomers, Philomela saw her shoulders quiver again. "Are you cold, Selene?" she asked.

"No, not really." Selene smiled, sat up straight, and placed cash on her food and drink bill.

Philomela wondered about the psychic. She seemed so gentle, completely incapable of taking advantage of gullible people. But did she hoodwink those who physically visited her as well as those who contacted her on the internet? Right now she managed to portray the exact opposite of a charlatan—a trustworthy, sensitive person. Philomela considered her a puzzle, an enigma, a real conundrum.

Later that evening, in her niece's pink bedroom, Philomela readied herself for sleep. Before climbing into bed, she brought out her iPad and found two email messages waiting for her. She read the black print of the most important one first.

Dear Philomela:
The powder snow is perfect, the ski guides are knowledgeable, and the weather is great. The food isn't as good as what you cook, but at least it's edible. John and I met all our fellow skiers. They are interesting people. They've come to this heliskiing ski resort from around the world. You'd enjoy them. I wish you were here.
Love, Brent.

They'd been apart two days and already she missed him. For the sake of her sister, however, she would push that conscious thought aside and focus on the reality of being happy. With Procne, being happy was easy. However, Philomela wasn't sure how future contacts with Selene and the thieving museum volunteer would affect her. Tomorrow she would find out about Basil Devonshire. She bent over her iPad and typed a reply:

Dear Brent:
If the food isn't as good as my cooking, it must be terrible. Glad the skiing is great and your fellow skiers are interesting. Procne is fine and all is well in Saltaire. We went with two of her neighbors to a pizza place for dinner. Good food and fascinating people. Wish you were here. I miss you a lot.
Hugs, Philomela.

Her eyes focused on the second email. Because of the violet print and being addressed to Philomela's seldom used second name, she immediately knew who it was from.

> *Rae*
> *Why have you not contacted me? The cosmic forces are strong and are watching over you. They know you are sensitive and need help. Your guardian angel wants to speak to you and impart important advice. Please reply immediately before the cosmic forces of good fade away.*
> *Selene*

Philomela harrumphed. She had already paid forty-nine dollars via PayPal to the Celestial Beings, and Selene didn't even mention receiving it. Glancing at the blue printing below the violet message she frowned and murmured aloud, "Another blue link benignly beckons." Her voice oozed with sarcasm.

She clicked on the blue link and a line of black print appeared—*Intense spiritual guidance will be yours for only $49.00.*

Selene's money grubbing effort was so obvious it was almost amusing. For a moment, Philomela mulled over the idea of showing this email to her sister. Sharing a giggle about it would be fun.

A sober second thought prevailed. She knew the disturbing overtones of the messages would upset Procne. The suggestion that her seemingly likeable neighbor was a cheat and a liar would cause her shock and dismay. Besides, the psychic's obvious dishonesty could be an unpleasant reminder of how Procne's ex-husband used to behave. Philomela concluded the webpage and emails should be withheld forever from her sister, or at least until a later date.

In the meantime, there was much to ponder. Could

there be another shaman called Selene? A twin sister perhaps? Perhaps the webpage originally had been designed to help people then gradually sank into a money making machine that defrauded the weak and gullible. Or worse, it may have been planned to suck innocent people into a web of evil intrigue.

She shook her head, shut off her iPad, and climbed into bed. Still thinking of the duplicity of Procne's neighbor, she turned out the light. It took her a long time to fall asleep.

CHAPTER 7

Monday Morning:

Adorned in the green pantsuit she had worn on the airplane, Philomela followed her sister downstairs to the entrance of the museum. She glanced at her wristwatch—nine fifty-seven. They were three minutes early. Walking through the open doorway, she noticed a man sitting on a high stool behind a counter and reading a newspaper. He lowered the newspaper and stared at them.

"Good morning, Basil," Procne said.

"Good morning, ladies." He dropped the paper on the countertop, eased off the stool, and walked around the end of the counter. Procne introduced Philomela, and he politely shook her hand. "It's a pleasure," he said. Then he turned to Procne. "Did you attend the air-force's Freedom of the Town parade on Saturday morning?"

Procne shook her head. "No, I didn't."

He frowned, raised his chin, and stared at her. "Most Saltaire residents show appreciation of our armed forces. Two arms of the military are located nearby. Are you aware of that?"

"Yeah, I know the Pacific Naval Fleet is based near-by."

"During World War Two, young airmen from all the British Commonwealth countries trained at our local air-port." He continued to stare at Procne as if assessing her understanding of his statement. "A large crowd attended Saturday's Freedom of the Town parade."

Philomela appreciated Basil's short history lesson but her general impression of the man was less flattering. He looked pompous and sounded pedantic. His attitude wor-ried her because his purpose seemed mixed—less to im-part information and more to reprimand her sister. Or, Philomela thought, he perhaps intended to belittle Procne in order to discredit her knowledge of his thievery. Then again, he may resemble totalitarian leaders by being power hungry, wanting to control more of her life than just the museum-volunteer aspect.

"Most of Saturday I worked at Whimsical Woman," Procne said. "And my sister arrived late Saturday after-noon."

"You mean the shop wasn't closed for the parade?" Basil frowned. "Maxine is usually more community minded than that. Chasing the almighty dollar obviously took precedence."

Philomela was shocked. If he had paid his debt to Maxine, perhaps she could afford to close her business for an hour or so. Philomela's thoughts flitted wildly but, like Procne, she remained silent.

"Philomela." Basil turned to her and smiled, but his smile failed to reach his eyes. "Whilst Procne brings the guestbook up to date, I'll guide you on a tour of the mu-seum." He beckoned with his hand and she followed him to an area filled with shelves holding exquisite wooden bowls, plates, and goblets. "This is a wood-turning dis-play. Next month the area will show the handiwork of local weavers. The display here is changed every month."

They walked on and passed a closed door. "That's the curator's office," he said. At the next door, which was open, he ushered her inside. "This is the staffroom." She gazed at a mix of autumn-colored sofas, easy chairs, and a round table surrounded by straight-backed chairs. He walked to a bookcase, bent down, and studied electronic equipment situated on a lower shelf. He adjusted a few knobs. Classical music filled the air. "The sound system is here," he said, stating the obvious.

Recognizing the melody of Chopin's "Military Polonaise," Philomela followed Basil to the far end of the room. They stopped near the round table.

"We hold our monthly board meetings at this table." He resumed walking and, with guide-like purpose, stopped under an archway and waved his right hand at a small, utilitarian kitchen. "When needed, coffee, tea, and food are prepared in here."

Saying no more, he led her out of the staffroom. He paused in front of a variety of displays—an old pharmacy, an ancient ship model, some century-old clothing, and an old kitchen containing a few items she remembered well.

"I must be a museum piece," she murmured. "I still use my mother's meat grinder, and it's exactly like the one on that counter."

To her surprise, Basil gave her a smile that actually reached his eyes. A minute later, in a tiny area where three short rows of chairs faced a TV screen, he explained that pertinent videos were played here. Then she followed him up the stairs and around a corner. With a flourish, he pointed at an elevator door.

"There is the lift. It enables physically challenged people to have access to all floors. The main level of the building contains the History Cafe, Poke and Swindell law office, and Jewelry for You. The lower level has the museum on one side and the male and female loos on the other."

"For a small town, this museum is incredible. I can see why Procne likes volunteering here."

As they returned to the main entrance, Basil explained the importance of encouraging visitors to sign the guestbook. "We need to know the number of visitors for funding purposes. We also encourage people to drop loose change and bills into the donation box. If they prefer, they can make larger tax-free gifts." Nearing the counter, he stopped walking and stared at Procne who was watching a white-haired lady sign the guestbook.

"So your grandson is visiting for seven days," Procne said.

"That's right," the woman replied.

"And you want him to enjoy his holiday."

"Of course I do."

Philomela gazed at the young boy whose down-turned mouth and slumping posture portrayed anything but enjoyment. Old stuff obviously bored him to death.

Procne apparently recognized his disinterested body language, for she countered his lack of enthusiasm by walking from behind the counter and squatting down to his height.

"What do people do in a museum?" she asked.

The boy gazed at her as if she were an idiot. "They just look."

Philomela stifled a giggle.

Two vertical lines appeared on Procne's brow. "Just looking can be pretty dull."

The boy's eyes widened and Philomela realized he was surprised that an adult would admit such a thing.

"Come with me, young man." Procne stood up from her squat, took hold of his hand, and led him over to a model train. "See that red button? Why don't you press it?"

Surreptitiously following them, Philomela heard the phone ring behind her. She glanced back and saw Basil answer it. Not hearing what he said on the phone, she focused on the young boy. He stared at the red button guardedly, as if expecting it to explode. Then he took a deep breath and bravely raised his right index finger. He gently touched the button. Nothing happened.

"Press harder," Procne ordered.

The boy pressed harder, and the train started to move forward. Philomela saw his eyes light up as he watched the miniature train chug from the station, go over a bridge, through a tunnel, around a mountain, whistle at a crossroad, return to the station, and chug to a stop. She watched his shining eyes look questioningly up at Procne who grinned and nodded in response. He pressed the red button again.

Philomela was impressed with her sister's ability to capture the boy's attention. Procne had other talents besides wearing and selling fabulous fashions. The boy, sometime in the future, might recall this museum and its train with fondness. Perhaps he might even become a museum curator.

Philomela strolled back toward the entrance area where Basil now conversed with the grandmother. Not wanting to interrupt their conversation, she paused and listened to him explain how the museum was funded. The woman responded by opening her purse and dropping a ten dollar bill in the donation box. Philomela saw Basil's lips curve into a crescent moon.

The woman joined her grandson and Procne strode over to the counter.

"Procne, could I have a word?" Basil moved toward her.

She nodded and studied him quizzically.

"I hate to ask this of you, especially since you have company. Whilst you were entertaining the young lad, Wendy phoned. She has the flu and will be absent tomorrow morning. Could you substitute for her?"

Procne knit her brows together, placed her top teeth on her lower lip, and glanced questioningly at her sister. Philomela responded with an affirmative nod. "Okay," Procne said. "Philomela and I will man, or should I say woman, the museum tomorrow morning."

"You are the salt of the earth. I thank both of you." He gallantly bowed his head, first to Procne and then to Philomela.

So, Philomela thought, *Basil isn't always abrupt, bossy, or stealing money. He has the ability to be polite, gentlemanly, and appreciative, though probably only when it benefits him.*

His disagreeable qualities reminded her of the dual personality of the fictional Dr. Jekyll and Mr. Hyde. An imperfect analogy, she mused. Mr. Hyde was a murderer and Basil Devonshire was only a minor thief.

At least she hoped that was his most disagreeable quality.

CHAPTER 8

Monday Noon:

B asil left the museum precisely at twelve noon. The two sisters sat behind the counter, greeted visitors, answered questions, and, during slack periods, chatted with each other. When no visitors were present, they discussed the town of Saltaire and the museum itself.

Procne brought up the subject of the volunteer who organizes volunteers. "What do you think of Basil?" she asked.

"He seems to be a control freak. And he switches easily from rudeness to gallantry." Philomela expounded about his behavior when the grandmother put a ten dollar bill in the donation box. "His smile made me nervous," she concluded. "It seemed to depict self-satisfaction and shiftiness."

"Self-satisfaction and shiftiness." Procne laughed. "That describes Basil pretty well."

Philomela grinned, acknowledging both her description of the man and her less than perfect word habit of alliteration.

Hearing someone walk down the outside stairs, she looked toward the main entrance.

An attractive lady with curly black hair walked through the open doorway.

"Hi, Grace," Procne said. "Haven't seen you in a while."

"Yes, it's been a few weeks." She unbuttoned the top buttons of her smart gray coat. "Has Basil gone?"

"He left twenty minutes ago," Procne said.

"Oh, I was going to ask him to take me for lunch."

"Too bad you missed him." Procne flamboyantly extended her right arm. "Grace. I'd like you to meet my sister, Philomela Nightingale. Philomela, this is Grace Devonshire, Basil's wife."

The two women exchanged pleasantries then Grace turned back to Procne. "I'm going to look at the wood-turning display. I understand some of the items are for sale." She disappeared around the corner and was gone for a several minutes. On her return she stopped at the counter and leaned her elbows on it. "Procne, you're Selene Hamilton's neighbor, aren't you?"

"Yeah, I am."

"Have you ever attended any of her healing circles?"

"No, I haven't. But she once asked me to attend. She stressed how every participant must visualize the sick person as being healed. Concentrating for a long time on one subject is not my strong point. My mind wanders too easily. I was afraid I'd start squirming and ruin it for everyone else, so I declined."

"You did the right thing. I attended my first one a week ago, and it'll be my last. Like you, I had trouble concentrating for more than a minute or two."

The subject of healing piqued Philomela's interest. "How many were in the group?"

"Four of us. Three meditated and I thought about

roasting a leg of lamb spiced with rosemary for dinner. Selene picked up on it."

Procne leaned forward with apparent interest. "Did she really?"

"Yes. She asked who was thinking about putting a leg of lamb in the oven."

"See, Philomela," Procne said. "Selene really is amazing. She's a true mind reader."

"I didn't like it." Grace frowned. "In fact, I found it downright scary. Our thoughts should be private, not open to someone else."

"Mental telepathy is a recognized form of communication," Philomela murmured. "Many of us, however, seem unable to make use of it."

Grace stared at Philomela. "I should hope not."

"How many ill people did you try to help?" Philomela asked.

"Five. Two seniors with the flu, one suffering from dementia, one recovering from quadruple by-pass heart surgery, and a young man with colon cancer."

Philomela nodded her head. Recalling that Procne had told her Selene held two healing sessions a week, she asked Grace for confirmation.

"Yes, the healers meet Tuesday and Thursday evenings," Grace replied. "Between meetings they try at specific hours to send positive vibrations to sick or troubled people. It's stupid, a complete waste of time."

"I wonder if it really helps." Procne spoke more to herself than to the other two women.

Grace vigorously moved her head from right to left and back again. "Not very likely."

"I bet it sometimes helps," Philomela said. "The more healers involved the more intense the positive vibrations, and the more chance a person will be helped."

Grace shuddered. "The whole thing is spooky. It

smacks of the occult—witchcraft, voodoo, hypnotism."

"According to what I've read," Philomela said, "hypnotism is no longer considered occult. A few decades ago it existed in the realm of magic and supernatural, now it is accepted by science and is used to help people quit smoking, eliminate pain, and jog memories."

"It's just a bunch of power-hungry people trying to gain control of others." Grace raised her chin and sniffed as if that were the final word on the subject.

Philomela was not ready to let it go. "As in every group, a few power-hungry people may try to wiggle their way to the top and take control. However, most telepathic healers try to help others. They use their abilities for good, not for self-indulgence or evil."

"I think Selene should stick to sewing," Grace pronounced "A few weeks ago, she altered two new dresses for me, and she did a good job. Last week she shortened my new pants and a skirt and they're fine. That was when she asked me to attend the healing circle." Grace sniffed again, this time with obvious annoyance. "While I was leaving the circle, she spoke to me with great rudeness."

"Rude? Selene?" Procne shook her head in disbelief. "What did she say?"

"She said I should get a job to pay for all my purchases. Hmmph. The nerve. So much for healing." She buttoned her coat and turned toward the entrance door. "I must go. If Basil comes back, tell him I'll see him at home."

"Okay," Procne said.

Philomela watched Grace go out the museum door. As the gray coat disappeared up the stairs, she turned to her sister. "Was Grace supposed to meet Basil here?"

Procne shrugged her shoulders. "Not that I know of."

"Well, she definitely let us know what she thinks of healing circles." For a moment Philomela was pensive, thinking about the departed woman. Then she asked, "Why would Selene suggest that Grace get a job to pay for her purchases?"

Procne shrugged. "Maybe because Grace likes to shop. But don't we all? I honestly doubt that Selene was rude. Suggestive, maybe. Even startling. But not rude. Selene is never rude."

A man entered the museum and their conversation faded away. Philomela noted his neatly trimmed beard and how his right hand held a leash. On the other end of the leash was a dog of questionable ancestry.

"Good afterrnoon, ladies." His R rolled with a Scottish burrr.

"Philomela," Procne said. "This is Hamish MacDonald. And that small creature near his feet is Hamish's best friend, Haggis."

Hamish shook Philomela's hand and Haggis wagged his tail. Procne pushed the guest book toward Hamish. He glanced at it then nodded his head appreciatively.

"Forr a Monday morrning, you've had quite a few visitorrs." He went behind the counter and carefully placed a cushion on the floor beside the high stool. Haggis curled up on the cushion and happily closed his eyes.

"Museum visitors will never suspect Haggis even exists," Procne said.

"He causes no trrouble."Hamish smiled at Procne. "Did Simon come in this morrning?"

"No. I understand he's working on a new display at home."

"He gets things done." Hamish patted his substantial abdomen. "I just ate lunch at the Historry Cafe. The fish chowderr was delicious. Best I everr tasted."

"Maybe I'll take Philomela there," Procne said. "That way I won't have to prepare lunch."

"Jean will apprreciate your patrronage. She worrks

harrd and I suspect she doesn't make a huge prrofit."

The two sisters said goodbye to Hamish, but not to Haggis who was sound asleep on his cushion. They climbed the outside stairs, reached the interlocking brick sidewalk, and paused to admire the window display of Jewelry for You. Procne waved her hand at a tall, mostly white-haired man coming out of the History Cafe. He returned her wave and disappeared next door into the law office of Poke and Swindell.

"That was Melvin Springer," Procne said. "Maxine's husband."

Philomela nodded. She recalled seeing him last night at the Fireside Pizza restaurant. He was indeed a handsome man, and his shock of thick white hair made his appearance even more striking. All he needed was a white beard and moustache to make him a thin Santa Claus.

But, if Shaun was correct, appearances could be deceiving.

CHAPTER 9

Monday, Early Afternoon:

Philomela followed Procne into the History Café and looked around. A plumpish woman about five feet two inches tall greeted them with welcoming words. "Happy days, Procne. How are things down below?"

"Excellent, Jean. We had fifteen visitors. Pretty good for a Monday morning. Hope we're not too late for lunch." She introduced Philomela and explained that her sister would be in town until Sunday evening. Then she said to Philomela, "Jean Greenfield is our local foodologist. She owns this café. She's an excellent cook and knows all about good taste and healthy nourishment."

Jean waved the compliment away. "Are you enjoying our miserable weather?" she asked Philomela.

"Yes, I'm enjoying your miserable weather. I left a temperature of twenty-five degrees below freezing. Even my eyelashes were frozen together."

Jean laughed. "That makes our eight above freezing bearable. What can I get you? The menu's on the board."

"Hamish said your fish chowder is the best he ever tasted," Procne said.

"He's my best advertiser. But the chowder is rather good, even if I do say so myself. Garlic toast comes with it."

Procne glanced at Philomela who grinned and nodded her head. "Two orders of fish chowder with garlic toast," Procne said.

"Was Basil at the museum this morning?" Jean asked.

"Yes, he unlocked the door. And he took Philomela on a quick tour."

"He's so kind, always helping others."

Procne coughed and cleared her throat. "Did Maxine Springer grace your premises this morning?"

"No, she didn't. That's rather surprising because she and Basil usually meet here on Monday mornings. Over coffee, they discuss fundraising methods for the museum. She always has such interesting ideas."

"She's creative as well as having good business sense," Procne said. "A rather unusual combination."

"Maxine's one in a million. Our town is lucky to have her. I'd like to ask her how I could perk up this place."

"It doesn't need perking up." Procne spoke with saleslady diplomacy. "But you never know, Maxine is such a genius, she might come up with a surprising idea or two."

Jean moved toward a group of six people attired in bright, new-age cycling outfits who were trying to drag two tables together. Jean helped shift the tables until they touched each other then helped place six chairs around them. Procne and Philomela strolled to the back of the room and claimed one of the many empty tables. A few minutes later, Jean's employee set fish chowder and garlic toast in front of them.

Philomela sipped two spoonfuls of soup. "Hamish was right. The chowder is delicious."

After emptying their bowls and eating their toast, they made their way to front door. With goodbye waves to Jean they went out to Main Avenue and walked on the interlocking brick sidewalk. Procne pointed out important landmarks: Upscale Garments and Whimsical Woman dress shops, Cut and Curl hair salon, Fireside Pizza restaurant, a hardware store, and a few coffee shops.

Meandering along the sea-walk toward Procne's townhouse, Philomela stopped to admire the freshly cut winter-pansies in the clasped hands of the bronze man sitting on his bench. A warm breeze brushed her face and messed her hair.

"It's getting warmer," she said.

"A Pineapple Express is coming in from Hawaii."

The breeze reminded Philomela of warm Chinook winds blowing over the Rockies and raising winter temperatures in Calgary. Lagging behind Procne, she unbuttoned her jacket, gazed out at the gray water, and in midstride bumped into her sister.

"Oops, sorry," Philomela said.

Procne, it turned out, had stopped to chat with Selene Hamilton. Philomela gazed at the psychic who even in midday looked like an ethereal moon-goddess. A bluish shawl flowed from her shoulders, her fair hair curled in gentle wisps around her face, and her benevolent smile reminded Philomela of other-worldly paintings of Mary, mother of Jesus. Looking more closely at Procne's neighbor, Philomela again wondered if her ethereal appearance was contrived by make-up, hair- style, clothing, and acting ability. Or was her appearance ethereal because she truly was ethereal?

The three women formed a loose triangle at the edge of the path and discussed Canadians' favorite subject—

weather. They agreed that, considering the month was January, today's warm temperature was remarkable, much too pleasant to stay indoors. Like a waning moon, the topic gradually faded and Selene started a new subject.

"Procne," she said, "are you involved with Saturday's fashion show at the Adept Adult Day Center?"

"Yeah, I am. I've been running around like a headless turkey for the last two weeks. As you know, Maxine's a bit of a slave driver. She's extremely capable, but she's also a ruthless delegator. She delegated me to be a gopher—I go for this and I go for that and then I wonder what I'll go for next. The clothes for the show will come from both Whimsical Woman and Upscale Garments."

"Who will model them?" Selene asked.

"Sheila, Maxine, three of the Center's volunteers, and yours truly. Six in all. I'm going to model some funky outfits from Whimsical. Maxine will model classy ones from Upscale. Sheila and the volunteers will wear a mix from both shops."

"Sounds lovely." Selene smiled, as if envisioning the array of clothing, "Being tall and willowy, you, Sheila, and Maxine will look stunning. All three of you could compete for having the best figures in town, probably on the island. I envy you."

"Thanks for the compliment. But being tall isn't always great. I've been known to bump my head on the upper part of a door frame. Let's forget height and figures. Why don't you come to my place for happy hour at five this afternoon? I'll give you herb tea, wine, or something else if you prefer. Just us three girls." She accentuated "girls" by making airy quotation marks with the second and third fingers of both hands.

"Sounds nice," Selene said. "I confess I like being called a 'girl.'"

"You look like a young girl." Philomela smiled at her sister's neighbor. She was pleased with Procne's invitation because it would give her another opportunity to study the slippery shaman. The more she saw of the unusual woman, the more she wanted to see her. Her curiosity about Selene was growing exponentially. Selene the aggressive email sender and Selene the gentle neighbor seemed at such odds with each other. If the website belonged to her, why did she deny being computer literate? Lying was a vice that true shamans avoided.

"Since we were at your place on Sunday evening," Selene said, "why don't the two of you come to my place this afternoon?"

"Sounds okay with me," Procne said.

"That would be lovely." Philomela smiled, thinking it would give her a chance to see where the ethereal charlatan lived and worked. It crossed her mind that she was becoming more and more obsessed with the psychic.

Selene resumed walking toward the town center and the sisters strolled in the other direction toward Procne's townhouse. They exchanged a few observations, but mostly they walked in friendly silence and mused upon private thoughts.

Philomela's thoughts dwelled on the two emails that had arrived late last night or early this morning. A much appreciated missive from Brent described the ski lodge—his bedroom, the dining room, the sitting room, and its large fireplace. He also told her about his skiing prowess on powdery snow. Selene's third violet missive was less appreciated, yet she remembered it clearly.

Rae:
The Celestial Beings wish to remove all negative influences in your life. You are under extreme stress and need help to overcome obstacles. This is an opportune

time for you to connect with the Celestial Beings and with your Guardian Angel. They will forecast future happenings then guide you through difficult times. To receive these wonderful and lasting benefits, just click on the blue link.
Selene

Last evening, Philomela reluctantly had clicked on the infamous blue link. It had brought up another request for $49.00 to be paid with credit card or PayPal. Having received no acknowledgment of the first $49.00 she had sent, Philomela refused to send any more money to the greedy charlatan.

Back at the townhouse, she forgot about Selene's drink's invitation and went to her niece's bedroom. She sat down on a chair, took out her iPad, and read another message from Brent.

Dear Philomela:
John and I lunched with interesting people today, two from Australia and two from Sweden. All four are excellent skiers. Give my regards to Procne. Wish you were here. I miss you."
Hugs, Brent

She missed Brent, too, but she was glad he was having a good time. In a different way, she also was having a good time. She enjoyed Procne's company and felt confident the museum volunteer's intriguing money problems would be solvable. She wondered if talking with Basil and encouraging him to return the stolen money to the museum donation box would be a good option. During such a conversation, she might learn more about why he borrowed money from the classy-looking Maxine Springer.

She leaned back in the chair and thought about Procne's retirement suggestion. Should she and Brent pack up their Calgary lives and move to the town of Saltaire? She was a bit young to retire and Brent, being healthy and still enjoying his work, would want to delay retirement for as long as possible. However, he was at an age when he should start thinking about it, at least start thinking about semi-retirement.

She loved winter, but every year coping with snow-shoveling and freezing temperatures became more difficult. The temperate climate of the Pacific Northwest would be easier to handle. Here, folks of all ages didn't worry about scraping frost from car windshields, freezing their ears, or walking on snowy sidewalks that might cause a fall, creating a broken hip, arm, or leg.

At that moment a new message arrived, so instead of closing her iPad, she read the fourth missive from Selene.

Dear Rae:
Thank you for the $49.00. The Celestial Beings are honored and pleased with your generosity. They and your Guardian Angel want to warn you about a few forthcoming disruptive events—problems with China, large earthquakes, erupting volcanoes, USA's gigantic debt, stock market crashes, and Muslim terrorist attacks. When the time is ripe, your Guardian Angel will tell you how to cope with these disruptive events.
Love, Selene

Philomela was pleased that Selene finally acknowledged her forty-nine dollar payment. The money seemed to have encouraged the psychic to use the salutations of *Dear* and *Love*. Abruptly a disconcerting idea came to mind. Had Procne's neighbor tuned into her skeptical thoughts? Had mental telepathy prompted Selene to acknowledge receipt of the money? As for the psychic's warning about disruptive forthcoming events, anyone who read newspapers and watched the news on television already knew about stock market crashes, ISIS terrorist attacks, US debt, earthquakes, and erupting volcanoes. Fortunately, this last missive had no blue link and no request for more money.

Things were looking up.

CHAPTER 10

Monday Afternoon:

A few taps on the bedroom door coincided with Procne's voice. "Philomela. It's almost five o'clock. Selene's expecting us."

Several minutes later, Philomela stood in the open air vestibule and watched her sister knock on Selene's door. The door opened immediately, almost as if their hostess had been waiting with one hand on the inside knob. Her fair hair was piled on top of her head with wavy wisps falling at each side of her face and down the back of her neck. Her hair and slim body reminded Philomela of a fairy, not that she had ever seen a real fairy, and Selene's round, serene face and smooth skin could have been those of a moon-goddess. Philomela's mythological musings were enhanced by Selene's shimmering blue-gray tunic and dangly silver earrings.

A cat with camouflage coloring—brown, black, beige, and cream—skittered from behind a chair, darted past them, and disappeared into another room. A second cat, the big black one, sauntered majestically up to Selene and brushed against a leg of her silky pants. The cat paused, his yellow eyes looked up at the newcomers and studied them for several seconds, and then he turned, raised his tail high in the air, and disdainfully walked away.

"Your cats don't like us," Philomela said.

"Hecate is slow to make friends. He'll get curious and come by later to check you out.Artemis is skittish. She may or may not make another appearance."

"I like your Greek trinity of mythological names," Philomela said.

"Not many people realize that Hecate, the goddess of dark, Artemis, the virgin huntress, and Selene, the moon goddess, are sometimes considered one and the same. My parents gave me the name, Selene, but I'm guilty of naming the cats."

Following their hostess past an open kitchen and a dining alcove, they entered a large sitting area. Philomela inhaled a pungent aroma. Incense. She felt her nose twitch and hoped the aroma wouldn't instigate a bout of coughing or sneezing. Trying to ignore the scent, she gazed at the pale blue carpet and off-white walls, and found the colors relaxing. She was sure the peaceful ambience would help the healing circles concentrate on healing and put troubled people seeking help at ease. Two paintings caught her attention, one of stars and a crescent moon shining on a calm sea, and the other of a gibbous moon beside dark clouds and beaming down on the white-caps of a stormy sea. The aroma of incense seemed to fade, probably because she was getting used to it.

Selene indicated two loveseats, both of which were upholstered in an off-white fabric complemented by flowers of myriad shades of blue. Cream-colored ceramic lamps sat on two pale oak end tables. A matching coffee table held a bouquet of white and pink flowers attractively arranged in a low blue bowl. Philomela remarked that

Selene's pastel color combinations were pale, perfect, and peaceful. No one replied, so she kept her next thought to herself. She used to think green, the middle of the color spectrum, was the most relaxing color, but Selene's combination of blues and off-whites did a good job, too.

When their hostess offered a choice of ginger tea or Pino Grigio, both sisters chose the latter. Selene served the white wine in two stemmed glasses then set a tray with Camembert cheese, sesame rice crackers, and olives on the coffee table. "Please, help yourselves," she said.

Philomela took a rice cracker, placed a dab of cheese on it, and took a bite. As it crunched between her teeth, she glanced out the window. Dark had descended but a gibbous moon, much like the one in the painting, ascended brightly above the eastern horizon. Unlike the painting, there were no dark clouds and no whitecap waves. Moonlight searched and shimmered on the water, and Philomela imagined Selene sitting here, guiding a distressed soul through a traumatic crisis to a port of optimistic hope. According to Selene's webpage, her help would be free, except, of course, for the forty-nine dollar donation to the other-worldly Celestial Beings.

It occurred to Philomela that perhaps she and Procne were in this home for a specific, unknown reason. A spooky thought. Could they be in need of some sort of guidance? Would advice for Philomela be the same as that already received by Rae? Did she and Procne really need Selene's spiritual help?

Perhaps it was the inverse. Perhaps Selene needed help from them.

Philomela sat up straight, studied her hostess, and listened to her converse with Procne. They were discussing fashions. Selene described how she created a complicated garment to fit a lady with unusual measurements. For a person supposedly steeped in spiritualism, she was very knowledgeable of the earthly problems of figure shapes and the delights of fine fabrics and intricate designs. Of course, as a seamstress she'd have to know such things. Philomela liked clothes, too, especially shoes, but not as passionately as Procne, and not as selectively as Selene.

As if feeling Philomela's eyes upon her, Selene turned to her.

"You're certainly aware of what's new in the fickle field of fashion," Philomela said.

"I have to be if I want to help customers."

Hecate glided toward Selene and leaped up on her lap. Philomela openly admired the feline's graceful movements and how the black hair contrasted with Selene's blue-gray tunic. Watching the cat nestle on Selene's lap, Philomela guided the conversation from the lightness of fashion toward the heavier one of theft.

"Selene, do you know Basil Devonshire?

"I've met him briefly at various functions. I know his wife better than I know Basil. Grace is a sweet person, almost childish. In some ways, she seems never to have grown up. She recently attended one of my healing circles."

Philomela waited, hoping the psychic would elaborate on her healing circles. When nothing more was forthcoming, she asked, "Did you know that Basil coordinates the volunteers at the Historical Museum?" Selene nodded and Philomela continued. "He also unlocks the door on the mornings when the curator is not there. Procne deals with Basil quite a bit."

"People who volunteer their talents and time are commendable," Selene said.

"Yes." Philomela suspected her voice lacked conviction because in that instant her thoughts shifted to Basil stuffing his pocket with money from the donation box.

She gave her head a tiny shake. "On the surface, Basil is fairly pleasant."

"He's kind to his wife," Selene said.

It seemed to Philomela they were talking in circles. Neither said anything false or disparaging nor did they say anything praiseworthy or important. Thinking of Procne's description of Basil's encounter with Maxine outside the History Cafe and Selene's remark about his being kind to his wife, she asked, "Do you think he's capable of having an adulterous affair?"

Selene picked up her glass and nonchalantly sipped her herbal tea. "Of course."

Philomela was surprised. She hadn't expected her hostess to be so nonchalant or so forthright. "Why do you say that with such ease?"

"Under the right circumstances, any of us might be capable of doing so."

Philomela couldn't imagine circumstances allowing her to have an intimate relationship with anyone but Brent. But who knew? She pushed her questioning further. "Do you know for sure if Basil is involved with a woman other than his wife?"

"There are rumors. But rumors are often false."

"Could you tell me who told you the rumors?"

"I'm afraid not. It's confidential."

"I understand." Philomela was silent a moment then specifically got to the point of theft. "Selene, I'm going to tell you something in confidence. Procne saw Basil steal money from the museum donation box. And, apparently, he owes money to her boss, Maxine Springer."

Selene nodded. "Yes, I'm not surprised. He's under a great deal of stress. Unfortunately, his coping methods are not the best."

"Theft is a coping method?" Procne was indignant. "I think theft is a grievous sin. It's also illegal."

Selene neither agreed nor disagreed with Procne. She simply remained silent.

Philomela realized Procne was passing judgment, whereas she and Selene were trying to be non-judgmental, at least until they knew all the facts. In a sense, she and Selene were following a couple of biblical statements. "Judge not and you will not be judged," and "Vengeance is mine sayeth the Lord." Not that she and Selene evaded judgment or sought vengeance. Nor, it seemed, did either of them dogmatically follow a specific religious creed.

Philomela knew her own sense of spirituality was vague, but when it came to action, she sincerely believed in "doing unto others as she would have them do unto her." Being a shaman, Selene's spiritual abilities and physical activities should be above and beyond the norm. But did she forego all that for a hidden agenda that took advantage of others? Were her relaxing home decor and her ethereal personal appearance designed to deceive clients? In other words, did her outward trappings bamboozle clients? Was she a so-called psychic who fooled people with superficial showmanship rather than true shaman-ship?

Selene seemed unaware of Philomela's mental questions, not in tune with her less-than flattering-thoughts. Instead, Selene remained focused on the puzzling museum volunteer. "Basil has never raised a hand or said a harsh word to Grace," she said.

Philomela wondered if her words implied that Basil should be reprimanding his wife. Or perhaps Selene mentioned the subject of raising a hand and speaking harsh words because she knew of Procne's mistreatment by the jerk she had married. Philomela intended to later ask Procne if she had ever mentioned her ex to her ethereal neighbor.

Suddenly, Selene sat up straight, closed her eyes, and shuddered. Then she opened her eyes and cleared her throat. "Sorry about that. I just saw that same dead woman again. She was lying on a tan colored couch."

"Who was it?" Procne asked.

"I don't know. I didn't see her closely enough, but it was the same person I envisioned on Sunday at your place. I think she's still alive."

Philomela remained silent, recalling Selene's agitation over the scene her mind-eye's had observed before they departed for Fireside Pizza.

"You can't prevent the death?" Procne asked.

"No. As I said last night, I don't know who it is, or where or when it will happen."

"Selene," Philomela said, "your innate talent as a seer helps people in times of emotional stress and poor health. But you said your psychic ability doesn't help you personally, especially with any form of gambling. Do you ever get a hint of help from a spirit guide or a guardian angel in your mundane, everyday life?"

With a wan smile, Selene shook her head. "As I said, I have to learn everything the hard way—by experience. That's one of the reasons I must always be open and honest with myself and with others."

"I see." But Philomela didn't really see much at all. It was as if she looked through a glass darkly.

Procne reverted to a previous topic of conversation. "Selene, do you have a suggestion regarding Basil's museum theft?"

Selene glanced at the ceiling then looked at Philomela. "As Procne's sister, you must have a theory about what course of action she should take."

"At this moment, I suggest she do nothing."

"That's what I suggest, too." Selene smiled at Philomela. "You and I are on the same wavelength."

Philomela wasn't sure about the two of them being on the same wavelength. But she was sure the psychic had asked for her theory on what Procne should do because she herself had no idea about how Basil's theft should be handled.

CHAPTER 11

Tuesday Morning:

Sunshine softened the blue sky and beamed down on the sisters as they almost skipped along the interlocking brick sidewalk. Like young schoolgirls, they made silly remarks that ended with bouts of laughter. Laughing at one of the remarks, they entered the History Café.

"Hello, you two." Jean's words were clear and her voice was perky. "Your joy is contagious. I feel happier already."

"You mean we spread joy like a virus spreads disease?" Philomela asked.

"Well, yes, though that's an odd comparison." Jean showed a row of white teeth. "I'm sure your joy goes hand in hand with healthy food. What can I get you?"

"Two mugs of healthy coffee, please." Philomela had recently learned that contrary to the previous view, coffee was an antioxidant and increased longevity.

"Two throwaway mugs of coffee," Procne corrected. "Provided those containers won't destroy the environment."

"They'll disintegrate," Jean said confidently.

Philomela paid the café owner, and the two sisters picked up their throwaway mugs. They waved farewell, went outside, and walked down the first two steps of the open-air stairway. Seeing Basil standing on the bottom landing, they stopped and watched him unlock the museum door and open it.

"Hi, Basil," Procne called.

He glanced up the stairs and nodded politely. "Good morning, ladies. How are you today?"

"Very well." Their reply in unison set off another bout of laughter, and they resumed walking down the stairs.

He responded to their mirthful outlook differently from Jean. Instead of showing a row of white teeth, he stared at them as if they were two strange insects. Then he stepped into the museum and efficiently turned the sign from *CLOSED* to *OPEN*. The sisters followed him inside.

Basil strode to the counter and walked behind it. Procne went up to the counter, leaned on it, and flipped the pages of the guestbook. Philomela made small talk by asking Basil how long he had lived in Saltaire.

"The bank transferred me here fourteen years ago. When it came time to retire I was already living in the town of my choice."

"How fortuitous," Philomela said.

"Yes, it was." He glanced at his watch and in a businesslike manner said, "I should go to the staffroom and switch on the background music before any visitors arrive."

"I'll do it, Basil," Procne offered.

"No. I'll go. I need the exercise." With an almost smile, he quickly walked around the counter and headed for the interior stairs.

Procne went behind the counter and perched on the high stool. Philomela followed her and sat down on a lower straight back chair. In the ensuing silence, Philomela watched her sister neatly print in block letters the day, the month, and the year at the top of the page of the guestbook.

Completing the task, Procne glanced at her sister. "I don't hear any background music. Basil must be having trouble turning it on." She leaned her elbows on the counter and grinned. "Oh well, let the visitors come. You and I are ready for anything."

But they weren't ready for anything. Certainly not a piercing, anguished yell.

Like a siren, the sound penetrated their ears and startled their minds. It made their bodies jump in the air then fall back onto the stool and chair.

"Good grief!" Philomela exclaimed. "What was that?"

"Basil?" Procne looked around as if expecting to see him. "No one else is here."

They gazed at each other in alarm then simultaneously leaped to their feet.

Philomela dashed past the model train and the temporary wood-turning display. She flew down the stairs, passed the closed door of the curator's office, and, at the open door of the staffroom, heard a distraught lament.

"This isn't true. It can't be true."

A shudder of fear trembled through her body. What was happening? She stepped into the staffroom and paused, expecting to see Basil fussing with the stereo. He wasn't near the shelf that held the audio equipment. She took a deep breath, expelled it, and saw him kneeling beside one of the tan colored sofas.

His position resembled a person in prayer. His knees rested on the floor, his body leaned forward, and his head almost touched the head of someone lying face up on the sofa.

Recalling Selene's vision of a dead woman on a tan colored sofa, Philomela shivered. "Is anything wrong?" she asked.

The question was idiotic because she knew full well that something was terribly wrong.

Basil turned to her. His face was pale. His expression was stricken. His eyes were glazed. He opened his mouth, but no words came out.

She hurried toward him. "What is it Basil?"

"M—Maxine." His voice trembled with emotion. "She won't wake up."

Philomela's eyes focused on the woman supine on the couch. Compared to the classy lady she had seen two nights ago at Fireside Pizza, this one was almost unrecognizable. No longer was Maxine a picture of perfect beauty. Her hair resembled a broken bird's nest, her clothes were in disarray, and the makeup on her face was streaked as if disturbed by a struggle. But it was the expression on her face that shocked Philomela. It registered either agony or terror. Or was it an expression of shock? Death had not come peacefully. Then she saw why. Blood oozed through the front of her white silk blouse, spread to her black suit jacket, and seeped onto the tan cushion of the sofa. She had been stabbed.

Philomela stupidly stated the obvious. "She's dead."

Basil gently stroked Maxine's hand as if trying to stimulate the flow of blood. "Here's the knife." His free hand reached toward the floor.

Philomela grabbed his arm and stopped his fingers from grasping the knife. "Don't touch anything, Basil. This is a crime scene. Fingerprints are important."

"Blimey." He looked up at her, aghast. "The knife was lying beside her when I came in the room. I automatically picked it up. Then I dropped it on the floor. I didn't believe what was actually in front of me. I thought it was a foolish prank." Moisture trickled over his lower eyelids.

"We'll have to inform the police that you touched both the knife and her hand."

He let go of Maxine's hand and it flopped on the middle seat of the sofa. He stared at it a few seconds then looked up at Philomela. "Police?"

She thought his eyes resembled two black blobs of oil. He seemed stunned and unaware of the severity of the situation. Her own awareness, however, was on high alert. Her eyes shifted from Basil's horror-stricken face down to Maxine's blood stained pantsuit and silk blouse. She saw a black clutch purse sitting at the other end of the sofa and one of Maxine's black suede pumps lying on its side on the floor. Though thoroughly dismayed, Philomela wanted to rifle through the purse in case it offered a clue to the perpetrator of this dastardly deed. She refrained from touching it—she knew about fingerprints.

"Did you touch anything else in this room?" she asked.

He cleared his throat twice, apparently trying to regain composure. "The doorknob." His right hand brushed his cheek then fell to his chest. "The door was closed so I opened it."

Philomela nodded her head, knowing this was something else to tell the police.

CHAPTER 12

Tuesday Morning continued:

Opening the door was a logical thing to do." Philomela tried to offer encouragement by gazing sympathetically at Basil's pale face. "And I'm sure the police will understand why you picked up the knife and held her hand."

Hearing footsteps, she looked up and watched Procne walk through the open doorway.

Her sister stopped and stared at the scene in front of her. Her lower jaw dropped and her head moved from side to side. In a state of total disbelief, she inched her way toward the sofa. Reaching it, she gazed down at her former boss, seeming unable to comprehend that this was someone she knew, someone she had worked for, someone she had admired. She opened her mouth as if to speak but no sound came forth.

Philomela thought Basil resembled an emotionless zombie as he looked up at Procne. A few seconds later, he spoke. "I came into the room to turn on the stereo and saw her leg near the edge of the sofa. I thought a street person had somehow gotten inside and was sleeping here.

When I realized who it was, I thought she must have come to attend an early meeting and fallen asleep. And then I saw the blood." He shook his head. "Who would do this? Why would anyone hurt Maxine?"

Philomela watched blood drain from her kid sister's face, making it dead white. Her eyes stared in an unfocused manner at the figure lying on the sofa and, like Basil, she looked traumatized, unable to comprehend that the woman had been murdered.

Philomela felt troubled and distraught, but she knew her feelings couldn't compare to that of her two cohorts. Unlike them, she hadn't known and worked with the victim. Besides, she had helped solve a couple of murders in the past, and this gave her the benefit of being able to understand the situation and think more clearly. It was up to her to provide the other two with any help she could. Knowing her sister's proclivity for action, Philomela figured a form of motion would be the best way for her to cope with the traumatizing circumstances.

"Procne," she said, "why don't you go upstairs and phone nine-one-one?"

Her sister failed to respond.

Philomela repeated the request in a louder tone of voice. After a few lengthy seconds, Procne nodded a reply. Like a robot, she turned and, with jerky steps, left the room.

Philomela tried to project a feeling of calmness toward Basil. She knelt beside him and gently touched his shoulder. "Basil, there's nothing we can do for Maxine until the police arrive. Why don't you come over to a chair and sit down?"

He gazed at her as if puzzled, as if he wondered who she was. Then her words seemed to penetrate the little gray cells of his brain. He nodded and rose unsteadily to his feet. For a minute, she feared he might lose his balance and topple over. She quickly straightened her own knees and placed her hand under his elbow. She guided him to an armchair. He plopped on it like a jellyfish falling onto a smooth rock.

"Basil, have you ever seen a dead body before?"

"My parents, at the funeral home."

"So this is your first mur—" She stopped mid-word.

With glazed eyes, he stared at her. "I've never been involved with murder. Not until now."

"Just sit and rest while Procne calls nine-one-one. The police will respond quickly." Philomela's effort to make mundane conversation was less than successful, but she tried again. "Did you know Maxine quite well?"

"Yes, very well." Slouching back in his chair, Basil moved his head from side to side, less in response to her question and more in disbelief of what he was seeing on the sofa. Finally he whispered, "She managed two good businesses and was active in the community. She was a good person."

A perfect eulogy, Philomela thought, made by someone dazed and in shock. Though anxious to see how Procne was faring, she deemed it unwise to leave Basil alone with the victim.

"Let's go upstairs, Basil," she suggested. "If visitors come to the museum, we'll help Procne explain that there's been an emergency. We'll ask them to come back another day."

He responded by giving Maxine's motionless body a lingering gaze. Then he rose from the chair and trudged wearily toward the entrance. Philomela followed him, occasionally tempted to help him along with a few pushes, but she kept her hands at her sides. His feet eventually dragged up to the main entrance and his eyes gazed blankly at Procne who sat on the stool behind the counter. Philomela noted how her arms crossed in front of her body, as if trying to provide warmth. For the second time that morning, Philomela suggested that Basil sit down, this time on the chair beside Procne behind the counter, the one she had vacated what now seemed like hours ago.

"No, my dear, you sit down." He behaved courteously like a pre-controlled robot.

"Basil," Philomela responded, "Maxine's death has shaken you more than it has me. You knew her, I didn't. Forget about being a gentleman for a few minutes. Please sit down before your knees collapse and you fall on the floor."

He slowly did as she suggested.

"I phoned the police," Procne murmured, her voice cracking with emotion. "And I phoned Sheila Trust. She was wondering why Maxine hadn't opened Upscale Garments. She said she'd keep the closed signs on both stores until further notice.*"*

Philomela nodded then turned to Basil. "Have you any inkling who would want Maxine dead?"

Basil lowered his upper eyelids and shook his head. "I have no idea." Then his moist eyes looked up at her. "She was energetic, clever, and kind—most of the time. There was no reason for her to be murdered."

"Do you know if she had any enemies?" Philomela asked.

Basil shook his head. "I don't know of anyone who would want to kill her."

Philomela glanced at her wristwatch then studied her sister who sat motionlessly on the stool. "What about you, Procne? Can you think of anyone who might want Maxine dead?"

"Owners of other dress shops." Procne's voice grew in intensity. "They hated her enthusiasm, her innovative ideas, and her marketing ability."

Her sister's response seemed emotional and

farfetched, so Philomela was inclined to discount it. "People may have been jealous of her success, but surely not jealous enough commit murder. Can you think of anyone else who might have wanted her gone?"

"No. No one."

"Did the person at nine-one-one say how long it would take the police to get here?"

Procne shook her head. She gazed into space and flung her arms from the front of her body out to each side. "Why here?" she asked. "Why would someone kill her in the museum? Why not in one of her dress shops or in her own home? Wouldn't that be more logical?" She looked over at the man sitting on the chair beside her and lowered her arms. "Basil, how did the murderer get into the museum?"

Basil shrugged his shoulders. "I don't know."

"Had anyone tampered with the locks on the door?" Philomela asked him.

He shook his head. "Not that I noticed."

"I understand not many people have a museum key," Philomela said. "Did Maxine have one?"

His face remained ashen. "No."

"Could Maxine or the murderer have stolen a key?" Philomela asked.

Basil leaned back in the chair and shrugged.

"Who besides you and Simon Fraser have keys?"

"Hamish Macdonald and Melvin Springer. They're both on the Board of Directors. They have keys in case Simon and I are not available. Maxine is—um—was—a member of the museum board, but only directors have keys."

"So Maxine could have taken Melvin's key and made a copy."

"I suppose so."

"Four people have keys," Philomela mused. "Simon,

Basil, Melvin, and Hamish. Each of them will be considered suspects. And the police will try and figure out who could have obtained a key and made a copy of it."

Basil sighed and it sounded more like a groan. He stood up and grasped the telephone sitting under the counter. "I'm going to phone Simon Fraser and Melvin Springer."

"Yes," Philomela said, "the curator should know what's happening here. But don't phone the victim's husband. The police will officially inform Melvin of his wife's death. They know how to impart sad information, and they know how to cope with grieving relatives." She could hardly believe she was taking control of the situation. But it made sense because Basil and Procne really were still in shock. How could they accept that a woman they had admired and worked with had been murdered almost under their very noses?

She listened to Basil blurt on the phone that Maxine Springer had been killed in the staffroom of the museum. "Simon, it's not a joke. I found her body." He listened for a moment then shut off his phone and looked at the two sisters. "Simon's coming over."

CHAPTER 13

Tuesday Morning continued:

Footsteps thundered down the outside stairs. Philomela leaned on the counter for support and nervously gazed at the museum entrance. What if the murderer was returning to the crime scene? Her nervousness turned to relief as the blue uniforms of two police officers, one male and one female, appeared at the door. With no hesitation they strode inside, looked around, and walked up to the counter.

"I'm Corporal Stinson," the male officer said, "and this is Constable James. What's going on here?"

"Murder." Philomela spoke slowly and tried to appear cool and collected. She must have failed because the corporal frowned as if she were telling an inappropriate joke. She opened her mouth again and, this time, tried to impart knowledge in a logical and straightforward manner. "I'm Philomela Nightingale. This is Procne Ellis and Basil Devonshire. They're volunteers in the museum and I was helping them. Basil found the body. The victim is Maxine Springer, owner of two dress shops, Upscale Garments and Whimsical Woman."

Constable James gasped. "Maxine. I know her. I bought things at Whimsical Woman."

"I'll take you downstairs to the crime scene." Philomela cleared her throat, walked to the miniature train, then moved past the wood turning display. She glanced back and saw Corporal Stinson and Constable James following close behind her. Basil and Procne walked a short distance behind them.

Inside the staffroom, Philomela unnecessarily pointed at the motionless body and softly murmured, "Maxine Springer."

The police stared at the corpse for a few seconds then, side by side, moved close to the sofa.

Philomela could see from the shocked expressions on their faces that they were not immune to horror. "There's a knife lying on the floor," she said. "I'm afraid Basil touched it before he realized the circumstances were so serious."

"Sorry about that," Basil muttered. He stood beside Procne in the doorway and nervously twitched his fingers. "I was too upset to think."

Corporal Stinson stared at Basil and Procne. "Well, has anyone touched anything else?"

"I held her right hand," Basil replied.

The corporal studied him. "Anything else?"

"I gripped the doorknob when I opened the door and came in the room. For the last few years I've been in and out of this room untold times. I couldn't count all the things my fingers have touched."

The corporal nodded his head with apparent understanding. "Before finding the body, had any of you noticed anything suspicious? Anything even slightly unusual?"

Basil, Philomela, and Procne gazed at Corporal Stinson and slowly shook their heads.

Procne, having regained a semblance of composure, cleared her throat. "When we arrived this morning, everything seemed perfectly normal—at first. We simply followed our usual morning routine. Basil came down here to turn on the sound system. Then he shrieked. Philomela and I dashed downstairs."

Corporal Stinson nodded again. He looked down at the floor and studied the knife but didn't touch it.

"Have any of you seen this knife before?"

Procne shook her head. So did Philomela.

"It could have come from the kitchen," Basil said. "It looks like a butcher knife." He walked stiffly through the staffroom to the kitchen archway and the corporal followed him. Basil passed under the arch, moved to the cupboards, and stretched his hand toward a drawer. He was about to open it when Corporal Stinson grabbed his arm.

"Stop. Fingerprints."

"Right." Basil flapped his offending hand in confusion. "The cutlery in this top drawer is used for making snacks. I don't know if the weapon came from here. But it looks as if it could have."

Corporal Stinson asked a few other questions then zeroed in on their whereabouts during the last twenty-four hours. Basil said he locked up the museum yesterday at four p.m. then went home and was with his wife until nine-forty-five this morning.

Philomela said she and Procne had drinks at Selene Hamilton's townhouse then were at Procne's place until they walked to the museum this morning and met Basil at the main entrance.

Constable James wrote this information in her little black notebook. She asked for their names, addresses, phone numbers, and email addresses and wrote them in the little notebook.

"I phoned the curator, Simon Fraser," Basil muttered. "He should be here soon."

"What about visitors coming to the museum?" Philomela asked. "Should we turn the open sign to closed?"

"Definitely," Corporal Stinson replied. "The museum is out of bounds. It is now a crime scene."

Philomela walked to the main entrance, shut the door and locked it. She turned the sign so the closed side faced out to the landing at the bottom of the stairs. She walked back and stopped beside Corporal Stinson. "Will you let the victim's husband know about her death?" she asked.

"Yes. Constable James and I will visit him shortly. But before we leave, we'll need a museum key." He looked questioningly at all three.

"I have one." Basil dug in his pocket and handed a key to him.

"I'll return it when we're finished," the corporal said. "Who else has a key?"

Basil replied with three names—Simon Fraser, Melvin Springer, and Hamish MacDonald. Constable James wrote the information in her black notebook.

"There's nothing more you need do right now," Corporal Stinson said. "We have your phone numbers and addresses. We'll get your fingerprints later and probably ask a few more questions. Right now you're free to go."

Basil, Philomela, and Procne bid the police goodbye. As they made their way in single file up the outside staircase, Philomela had a horrible thought.

Did Basil purposely pick up the knife and drop it on the floor because his fingerprints were already on it?

CHAPTER 14

Tuesday Morning continued:

Stepping from the top step to the sidewalk on Main Avenue, Basil, Procne, and Philomela saw Simon Fraser running toward them. Simon stopped short and, like a rabbit caught in car headlights, stared at them.

"The police are still here," Basil said, and his voice cracked with emotion. Looking paler and more distraught by the second, he briefly described the scene in the staffroom.

Without saying a word, Simon dashed downstairs and pounded on the museum door. Someone opened it and he disappeared inside.

"Poor Simon," Procne said. "The museum is his baby."

At that precise moment, Jean Greenfield stepped outside the History Cafe. She stood on the interlocking brick sidewalk in front of the door and crossed her arms below her bosom. "I saw police go downstairs. What's going on?"

"The police are investigating a problem." Philomela knew her answer was a gross understatement of what was actually happening, but she thought the police should be the ones to announce that a murder had been committed.

Unconcerned with any type of protocol, Procne loudly blurted, "Maxine Springer was murdered!"

"What?" Jean's eyes widened in horror and her jaw dropped in disbelief. She stared at all three of them then found her voice. "Maxine Springer was murdered?" Like a robot, she repeated the words a second time. "Maxine Springer was murdered?"

Philomela nodded, glanced at Procne and Basil, then gazed questioningly at Jean. "Can you tell me why in the world someone would want her dead?"

Jean shuddered and shook her head. She pivoted toward the café and, visibly shaking, opened the door. As if clinging to each other for support, the other three automatically followed her inside. Philomela asked for coffee. Jean filled four mugs and, because the room was empty of other customers, sat with them at a small square table. All four wordlessly sipped their dark brews.

"We know the where of the murder," Philomela eventually murmured. "But we don't know the why, or the when, or who actually dunnit."

After much pointless speculation about who might be the perpetrator, they reached no conclusion. Finally, Jean gathered up the empty mugs and returned to the other side of the counter. The other three quietly said goodbye and walked outside. For a few seconds, they gazed silently at each other and at the stairway. Then Basil said his car was parked in a nearby parking lot. He bade them goodbye and walked away. The two sisters mutely made their way in the opposite direction toward Procne's townhouse.

Inside her home, Procne busied herself in the compact kitchen. Philomela climbed on a stool and leaned her elbows on the eating counter. She looked out the window and tried to focus on something other than murder.

"The view from your window is gorgeous." The view was the only positive thing that came to mind. "The scene has a patina of peace that sooths the soul."

Procne, who was plugging the coffee maker in a wall socket, turned and gave a weak smile. "Forever alliterate," she said.

"Ah, my usual word weakness." Philomela sighed then shifted her attention to the stainless steel refrigerator and dishwasher. The red canisters sitting on the counter above the dishwasher caught her eye. "The red accents make your kitchen incredibly cheery. I wish I felt as cheery as those canisters look." Her sister failed to respond so she tried her hand at humor. "You should name your kitchen the Scarlet Scullery."

Procne frowned, unamused. "My kitchen is not a scullery."

"You're right." Philomela felt properly reprimanded. "The kitchen is a cheery extension of the lovely living area."

Several minutes later, the two sisters sat side by side at the eating counter and gazed out the window. Though they had drunk coffee at the museum before Maxine's body was discovered and later at the History Cafe with Basil and Jean, they each held a red mug and sipped some more. Philomela was going to make a humorous remark about coffee being a healthy drink, but instead she turned from the window and gazed at her sister.

"How many people will be affected by Maxine's death?" she bluntly asked.

Procne was pensive for only a few seconds. "Melvin, Basil, Simon, Jean, Sheila, Selene, me. And, of course, regular customers at the dress shops."

"Are there a lot of regular customers?"

"Yeah, lots. Grace Devonshire is one of them."

"Could any of Maxine's customers have a reason for wanting her dead?"

"I doubt it. Certainly not Grace. Most customers love coming into the shops."

"What about Maxine's husband?"

"Melvin is tall, handsome, and has a good sense of humor. He is kind and considerate. He's everywoman's dream man."

"Shaun didn't think so," Philomela said.

"Well, maybe Melvin's youthful testosterone once ran rampant. Maybe Shaun was exaggerating. Maybe Melvin was too young and innocent to understand the consequences of a fling."

"Even the dullest of young men knows how babies are conceived," Philomela said. "How did Melvin treat Maxine?"

"Romantically. At least whenever I saw them together. He used to look at her as if she was the most beautiful woman in the world. And maybe she was, she certainly was in his eyes. They did lots of things together—out for dinner, attending live theatre and other community events." Procne took a sip of coffee and looked thoughtfully at her red mug. "Philomela, you know a bit about police procedure. What steps will the police take now?"

"They've already asked us questions and, right now, they're probably getting fingerprints at the crime scene and taking photographs. They'll try to figure out where the knife came from. They'll seek out people who were near the museum Monday evening and Tuesday morning. They'll ask us more questions, and they'll take our fingerprints."

Procne glanced at her wristwatch. "I suppose that by now Corporal Stinson and Dickless Tracy will have told Melvin about Maxine's death."

"Dicklesss Tracy?" Philomela stared at her sister. She

didn't know whether to laugh or to reprimand her. "Are you referring to Dick Tracy, the detective in that old comic strip?"

Procne nodded. "Dickless Tracy is what some of us call a policewoman. We don't mean it in a derogatory sense. After all, it's a mere fact."

"Feminists might find the term disparaging. So might some men."

"Well, it isn't meant that way." Procne shrugged. "Because of Maxine's death, we'll have to cancel Saturday's fashion show. Too bad. Adverts are out and everything's almost ready to go."

Philomela gazed thoughtfully at her sister, closed her eyes for a second, then opened them wide. "Could you and Sheila put on the show without Maxine?"

"In the past, Maxine was a wonderful front person, and Sheila and I did all the grunt work. Right now, as I said, everything's almost ready to go." Procne hesitated, obviously deep in thought. "All that's left to do are outfitting the models, writing descriptions of the clothes for Rebecca Steyn—she's the pianist and commentator—to read, and moving the actual clothes from the shops to the fashion-show venue. At the show itself, we'd have to help dress the models so they can strut their stuff while Rebecca describes each outfit."

"So you and Sheila, with Rebecca's help, could easily put on the show."

Procne nodded her head.

"Would you consider doing it?"

"I don't know."

"What about Sheila?"

"She probably would, mainly because she's interested in owning both businesses. She'd have snatched them up ages ago if Maxine had agreed to sell."

"And what about you?" Philomela asked. "Would you

be willing to help put on the show without Maxine?"

Procne hesitated a few seconds. "Maybe. But I'm not sure about Rebecca. She's more emotional than Sheila and me. She might have trouble carrying on."

Philomela noted that the discussion was bringing color back to her sister's face. "Was Rebecca a close friend of Maxine's?" she asked.

"They were friends, but not close. Rebecca volunteers her musical talents at Adept Adult Day Center one afternoon a month. She often participates as master of ceremonies at various functions."

"If you had been the one to die," Philomela said, "what would Maxine do?"

"Oh, she'd carry on. She'd have Rebecca announce that the show was a memorial to me."

"Maybe you should do the same for Maxine."

Procne stared at Philomela and the whites of her eyes increased in size. "What a brilliant idea. How did I warrant having such a clever sister? I'll phone Sheila and Rebecca right now and see what they think."

Procne leaped to her feet and made the calls. Her face beamed when she came back to the eating counter and plopped down on the stool. "They both think it's a wonderful idea, a real tribute to the deceased owner. All we need is another model to replace Maxine. Maxine was fantastic—tall, graceful, willowy. At this late date, she won't be easy to replace." She hesitated and studied her sister. "Philomela, maybe you could do it."

"No. Not me."

"Why not?"

"Well, for one reason, I'm short. But mainly because I'm not local. People attending the show will want to see models that live in the area." Philomela studied her sister a moment. Then she asked, "How about Selene? She's not tall, but she's of medium height and has a slim build.

She looks delightfully fragile. She'd be a nice contrast to the willowy height and classiness of you and Sheila Trust."

"That might work. In fact, I think it would work. Rebecca could explain how Selene sewed alterations for customers at both of Maxine's shops." Procne nodded thoughtfully. "This is getting better all the time." Then she stopped speaking and put her hand over her mouth. "I'd almost forgotten why we're considering such plans."

"Putting on the fashion show will be good medicine for everyone. It'll reduce morbid thoughts. It'll keep you focused on the bright side instead of on the dark side. You'll turn the sad happening into a successful memorial to a respected citizen."

Procne almost smiled. "And you'll help me."

"I'll do what I can in the background."

"You could help write the fashion commentary. You're better with words than I am."

Philomela smiled at her sister. "You're pretty good when you want to be, especially when it involves clothes."

But her smile faded as thoughts of the fashion commentary morphed into thoughts of the crime scene. Envisioning Maxine's bloody silk blouse and black suit jacket, she wondered if stabbing with a knife was something a woman would do. Most murders committed by women involved poison, cars, or guns. What about Sheila? Would she kill with a knife in order to obtain ownership of the dress shops?

CHAPTER 15

Later Tuesday Morning:

A loud pounding startled Philomela out of her brief reverie. Thoughts of Sheila having a motive to kill Maxine faded. She sat up straight and leaned away from the eating counter.

"Who can that be?"

"I don't know." Procne jumped from her stool and quickly moved toward the door.

Philomela heard the door open and listened to her sister greet the newcomer: "Hello, Shaun. This is a surprise."

"Procne," Shaun said. "Thank god, you're here. I was at the barber shop and heard a rumor that someone had been murdered in the Historical Museum. I'm glad it wasn't you."

"Me too. Come on in."

"So the rumor's false?"

"No, Shaun, the rumor's true. Maxine Springer was killed—in the museum staffroom."

"Come on now, you're joking."

"No, I'm not joking."

"That's awful. Murder, in Saltaire. Maxine—I—I can't get my ahead around it."

"I know. I feel the same way." She led Shaun into the kitchen. "Poor Melvin. You once said you knew him at university. Did you know Maxine, too?"

"I'd seen her around, but I didn't know her very well." He gazed from Procne to Philomela. "This is terrible news."

Philomela nodded agreement. "Procne and I were at the museum when Basil found her."

He frowned as if not understanding her words. "Basil found her? And you two were there?"

"That's right," Philomela said. "The victim was lying on the couch."

Shaun shook his head and turned to Procne. "I thought you volunteered at the museum on Monday mornings, not on Tuesdays."

Philomela was surprised that he knew Procne's schedule. She wondered if he always kept track of her sister's daily activities. If so, did he do so because he liked her? Or was he a busybody who stuck his nose into everyone's business? Hopefully, he was just a considerate neighbor.

"This morning, Philomela and I substituted for a sick volunteer," Procne said. "Would you like a cup of coffee, Shaun?"

"Something stronger would be better."

"Circumstances sort of warrant booze." Procne walked around the eating counter toward the coffee pot. "But it's too early in the day for strong drink."

"You're right." He sat on a third stool and looked from Procne to Philomela. "So it was Basil who actually found the body."

Procne set a mug of coffee in front of him. "It was dreadful for Basil because they were quite chummy."

"What do you mean, chummy?"

"Well, they both volunteered on the museum board. And the two of them often discussed innovative ideas for the museum."

"I see." He was silent for several seconds. "Exactly how was Maxine killed?"

Procne described the murder site in detail, including the knife, the blood on Maxine's shirt and jacket, and the arrival of the police.

"Now the museum is a crime scene," Philomela said. "Yellow police tape blocks the stair and elevator entrances."

Shaun looked questioningly from one sister to the other. "Do the police have a suspect?"

Procne moved her head from side to side. "Not that we know of. Personally, I can't think why anyone would want to kill Maxine. Oh, maybe a jealous clothier or maybe Basil. Basil owed her money."

"Did he?" Shaun seemed surprised.

"We don't know that for sure," Philomela interjected. "Even if he did owe her money, surely that's no reason to murder her."

"You wouldn't think so." Shaun gazed steadily at his red coffee mug. Then he glanced sideways at Procne. "Do you think Melvin might have done it?"

"I doubt it. I know you dislike him, Shaun, but he was devoted to Maxine. He couldn't do enough for her. He even sent flowers to her for silly anniversaries like when they first met and when she bought her first shop. Not many husbands do things like that. Most don't even remember the date of their wedding let alone when they first met."

"Maybe Melvin improved with age," Shaun admitted. "But does a leopard really change its spots?"

Philomela studied Shaun and contemplated his words.

If, as he implied, Melvin had been a thoughtless, self-serving youth, were the considerate actions that Procne witnessed a result of love and a well-developed maturity? Were Melvin's actions designed to give Maxine joy? Or were they intended to distract observers while he pursued a personal selfish agenda? Could he have murdered his wife? At the moment, Melvin, the new widower, was a conundrum.

"According to you, Procne," Philomela said, "he was a perfect husband. Did he and Maxine disagree on anything? Did they ever get angry with one another?"

"I suppose so," Procne replied. "They're human. Though, I never heard them exchange a harsh word or even argue in public."

Shaun gazed at Procne. "Did the police take your fingerprints?"

The phone rang. Without answering Shaun's question, Procne jumped to her feet and took the phone from its charger. She carried it to the sitting area and left Philomela and Shaun to quietly rehash the day's events. On her return to the kitchen, she set the phone on its charger. "That was Sheila. She had closed both shops this morning because of Maxine's death and now she thinks we should open them again tomorrow. That way we can spread the word about the fashion show and tell everyone it will be a memorial to the deceased owner. She's going to phone Selene and ask her to model."

"Good." Philomela nodded approval. "I wonder if anyone thought of a funeral."

"Sheila said it won't be for a week, mainly because of the police investigation. That will give Maxine's relatives lots of time to get here. She has a brother in Calgary, a sister in Toronto, and one in Florida."

"I wonder how her husband is taking it," Philomela mused. "Has anyone heard?"

"Sheila said he's devastated. He's not going outside, just burying himself alone at home."

"Did she talk on the phone with him?" Philomela asked.

"She did better than that. She took him a chicken casserole. Sheila doesn't cook very much so I suspect she bought it." Procne smiled. "Working girls have ways to produce good meals."

The corners of Philomela's mouth curved upwards. "Well, there's nothing wrong with that. Packaged frozen foods have come to my rescue on more than one occasion. Sheila's a busy lady."

"Right," Procne said. "Besides, it's the thought that counts."

Shaun gave a half-hearted grin. "I'd be pleased to receive a casserole from anyone on any occasion."

"I suppose that's a hint." Procne gently shook her head then returned to the topic of the new widower. "I can't imagine Melvin becoming a hermit. He's incredibly social. He thrives on companionship. If he's holing up alone, he must be utterly devastated by Maxine's death."

"Or," Shaun slowly said. "He might be putting on a good show."

CHAPTER 16

Wednesday Morning:

Procne sat beside her sister at the eating-counter, nibbled on a piece of toast, and gazed through a large pane of glass at sky, water, islands, and two sailboats. The scenic picture instilled her with feelings of airy peace and earthly wisdom. She didn't know if the airy peace connected her with Buddha and the earthly wisdom rose from Einstein, nor did she care. She simply knew the picturesque scene helped to distance her from recent events—horrid events of which, at the moment, she had no desire to discuss.

"Philomela," she said, "did you know that boats without sails are called stinkpots? And boats with sails are called rag-fliers?" With purposeful nonchalance she raised a forkful of scrambled eggs and put it in her mouth.

"Living on the seashore has filled your little gray cells with a lot of nautical nonsense."

"You could be right. But didn't you always want to know about stinkpots and rag-fliers?"

"Indeed."

Procne grinned at her sister. She suspected that Philomela, like herself, was doing her best to suppress thoughts of Maxine. Continuing their breezy and rather silly conversation, Procne fell back on her favorite subject—fashion. "I've been thinking about what will be in style next year. Leggings and high boots have been popular for a while. I wonder how long it'll be before pant legs become wide again."

"I have no idea," Philomela said. "Perhaps the Greek muses could answer that question. Let's see…Calliope is the muse of poetry, Thalia is the muse of comedy, but I don't know a muse of fashion." She shook her head with mock seriousness. "Speaking of fashion, I have three pairs of straight leg pants and, as far as I'm concerned, they'll never go out of style."

"Boring, boring."

"I suppose classic styles aren't as much fun as funky fashions." More or less proving her remark, Philomela stared pointedly at Procne's five strings of beads and matching bracelets.

"Alliteration—again."

Philomela ignored the reference to her verbal weakness. "Your dress and jewelry are fun to wear and smashing to look at. But, Procne, aren't you overdressed for work?"

"Not for my work. Wearing the merchandise helps to sell it."

"Only if the wearer has a fantastic figure and a flamboyant flare that shows garments and accessories to advantage. You, of course, have both. Your work is so different from mine. When writing and editing I'm a perfect slob."

"That's because only your darling husband and your one employee see you." Procne finished eating her eggs and toast and glanced up at the wall clock, the one with haphazard numbers and letters that spelled, *Who Cares?* She considered giving the clock to Philomela because it was a reminder of her ex-husband. They had bought the clock on a visit to Mexico. It had been a good holiday— only once had his fist connected with her ribs.

"I emailed Brent last night and told him about the murder. Now he'll start to worry about me."

"I know. He doesn't like you getting involved with bad things." Procne stood up and carried her plate and cutlery to the dishwasher. "Time's flitting and we have work to do."

Philomela got up and followed her example. When the dishwasher was loaded, she verbally went over Procne's schedule. "Normally, you work at Whimsical Woman on Thursday, Friday and Saturday. Because of yesterday's circumstances, who knows where you'll be next week?"

"Correct. Today I'll be at Whimsical Woman and Sheila will be at Upscale Garments. We'll both advertise the Saturday fashion show as a memorial to Maxine. The one good thing about January and February is that we open the dress shops half an hour later—ten a.m. instead of nine-thirty. If we hurry right now, we'll have time to pop into the History Cafe and grab a coffee. Jean's always a fountain of the latest gossip. She'll know what's happening at the museum."

They donned rain jackets and went outside. Hurrying toward the business section, Procne breathed in the salty air and felt its moistness brush her skin. The temperature was warm so she knew the Pineapple Express was still in effect. On Main Avenue, she peered over the yellow crime-scene tape down the stairway to the shadowy landing of the museum. It crossed her mind that Maxine Springer would never again make use of those stairs. She took a long, deep breath, trying to overcome a heavy feeling of sadness. The salty air seemed to work—she suddenly felt lucky to be healthy and alive.

Inside the History Café, Procne noted that most of the tables were taken up with customers. She exchanged pleasantries with Jean, ordered two mugs of coffee, and asked if there was any news about the murder.

"Yesterday, activity in the museum was non-stop. People came and went, carrying all sorts of equipment. The body was carried upstairs on a stretcher and taken away by ambulance." The corners of her mouth drooped sorrowfully and she moved her head from side to side. "Not much activity down there today. I wonder if the medical examiner will do an autopsy." She handed coffee to the sisters.

Four new customers entered the cafe and the corners of Jean's mouth quickly turned upward. Two of the newcomers sat down at a table near the door and the other two formed a line behind the two sisters. Procne moved to a side counter and added cream and honey and cinnamon to her coffee while Philomela, who liked hers black, carried her mug to the front window counter. Procne eased onto the stool next to her and looked out the window at people passing by on the sidewalk. She reluctantly shifted her eyes to the right and stared at the yellow tape at the top of the open stairway. Trying to think of happy things, she looked away and thought of how much she enjoyed volunteering at the history museum. She liked chatting with visitors, especially local residents who came in for the first time—they were always surprised to discover that such an interesting facility existed in their home town. Tourists from away usually asked pertinent questions and made observations that widened her horizons. For the umpteenth time she thanked her lucky stars that she had moved to Saltaire.

And, of course, there was the curator, Simon Fraser.

He would be a true asset to any business, or project, or community. He continually amazed her with his clever ideas and talented abilities to construct things. Topping everything else, he was smart yet had a pleasant manner when interacting with people. He maintained the museum as a living and welcoming place.

A vaguely familiar voice interrupted her rumination. Holding her coffee mug in midair, Procne leaned backward, listened, and tried to determine who belonged to the voice. "I hear you borrowed money. That was fucking stupid of you." Procne cringed. The only person who talked like that was her ex-husband.

"Your accusation is pedestrian and inane." Procne recognized the articulated response as coming from Basil Devonshire.

"Fancy words do not a genius make." The first voice was still unrecognizable.

"My fancy words are superior to your mundane ones. If you had done what I asked, I would not have had to borrow." Ah, Procne thought, Basil again.

"I couldn't find a fucking buyer."

Procne identified the first speaker. "Do you recognize those two voices?" she whispered to Philomela.

Philomela nodded her head. "Shaun proved Basil's point by mundanely using a common swear word as an adverb to modify the adjective, stupid. Then he used it as an adjective to modify the noun, buyer."

"How am I going to pay her back?" Basil sounded desperate.

"Fuck. I don't know?"

"Good grief. Shaun just used that common word as an expletive."

Procne giggled. "I've never heard Shaun speak like that. He always behaves so gentlemanly when he's with us." She twisted around on her stool, stretched her neck, and saw the two men sitting several tables away. She had not noticed them earlier, and she suspected their intense conversation had prevented them from seeing her.

"It takes time to sell stock," Shaun said.

Philomela smiled at her sister. "That common word may have originated from an acronym—For Unlawful Carnal Knowledge—you know, putting the first letter of each word together to form a new word."

Procne raised her eyebrows. "Yeah."

"Another explanation is that the four-letter word originated from an old German word, fucken, meaning to penetrate."

Procne giggled. "Only my sister would know so much about a common swear word."

"Were you aware those two fellows knew each other well enough to have coffee together?"

"No, I didn't."

Philomela gazed steadily at her sister. "Yesterday when we told Shaun about Basil finding the victim's body, he gave no indication that he knew Basil very well—not even after you mentioned his debt to Maxine."

"I shouldn't have said that." Procne bit her lower lip. "That's probably why he knows about Basil's debt." She glanced at her wristwatch. "Darn. I'd like to stay and listen to them some more. But I have to open the shop." She drained her coffee mug and stood up.

"My coffee's still hot," Philomela said. "I'll linger a little longer."

"In other words, you'll be your normal self—a curious snoop."

"Sweet sister, how can you say such a thing? I only want to finish drinking this delicious, healthy brew."

Procne snorted. "Come over to the shop after you finish detecting. Then you can tell me all about your observations." Picking up her purse, she glanced over at the two men who were still intent on their discussion. She deposited her empty coffee mug, waved farewell to Jean, and walked to the door. Outside the cafe, she looked through the window, flipped her fingers at her sister, and strode along Main Avenue toward Whimsical Woman.

She thought of Maxine and the terrible manner in which she died. Thank goodness working in the dress shop and preparing for the fashion show was helping to push those dark thoughts to the back of her mind.

CHAPTER 17

Wednesday Morning continued:

Philomela slowly sipped her coffee, gazed through the café window at passersby and tried to hear the conversation between Shaun O'Reilly and Basil Devonshire. Unfortunately, just as it started to get interesting, they lowered their voices, perhaps realizing other patrons were listening to words they shouldn't hear. As a result, she missed the gist of the rest of their discussion. She finally leaned forward, picked up a local coffee house newssheet from the counter, and read a couple of jokes.

Then she heard Jean Greenfield clearly ask, "Did you get enough to eat, Basil?"

Lowering the newssheet, Philomela twisted around and saw Jean lean close to Basil's head. The scene reminded her that Procne had once said Jean was fond of Basil and would do almost anything he asked. There was no doubt that she currently attended to his caffeine needs. Philomela heard the cafe owner and the customer make a few verbal exchanges, but because of nearby laughter she failed to distinguish their words. She wished she could read lips.

The two men stood up, and she quickly turned to the window and raised the newssheet to partially hide her face. Pretending to read, she peripherally watched Basil and Shaun walk to the main door. She could have reached out and touched them, but they didn't even glance in her direction.

"You should find out if she had a written record of it," Shaun said.

"How would I do that?" Basil asked.

"Did she keep her files at home or in one of her shops?"

"I don't know."

Shaun opened the door. "You can't check her house. I understand her bereaved husband is home putting on a show of lonely grief. You'll have to scout around and study other things."

Philomela heard no more because the two men stepped outside and the door closed behind them. Through the window she surreptitiously watched them briefly chat then stride off in opposite directions. She drained her coffee mug, stood up, and carried her empty mug to the main counter. Jean was busy with other customers so Philomela left the busy History Café without saying goodbye.

Walking briskly on the interlocking brick sidewalk of Main Avenue, she responded to the smiles and greetings of everyone she met. Even people using walkers or scooters seemed pleased to see her, probably due more to the warm air and the pleasant atmosphere than to her glorious self. They may not have heard of the recent tragedy. Or perhaps they had heard the bad news and were using a positive attitude to get on with personal tasks. The town was so pretty and its residents so friendly that Procne's suggestion jumped to mind—yes, Saltaire would be a lovely place in which to retire. Of course, it would take time and persuasiveness to convince Brent to think of cutting back on his work load.

There was a downer to living here, and the recent murder crawled like a worm into her thoughts. How many of the friendly people she was meeting had any connection with Maxine's death? She stopped walking. What if one of the smiling people she passed had committed or helped commit the dastardly deed? The dismaying thought became pertinent as a woman invaded her space and glared into her face. The woman's width almost matched her height so Philomela nervously shifted sideways. Brushing against Philomela's side, the woman slowly moved on. Philomela wondered if she suffered from a variety of health problems.

Thoughts of the unhappy woman faded, only to be replaced by visions of Maxine lying on the tan sofa. Was her murderer still in Saltaire? Or had the culprit already flitted faraway? Philomela assumed the perpetrator was male, but that could be a misnomer. The stabbing could have been done by someone of any sexual persuasion.

She thought of all the females she had recently met— Selene, Grace, Sheila. Surely none of them was emotionally capable of stabbing anyone. Then again, if a female's adrenalin was raised by anger, her increased strength could easily enable her to jab a knife into the person who had triggered the bad emotion.

Good grief. If only her thoughts could solve the crime and lock up the perpetrator. But it would take more than thoughts to find the culprit.

Philomela pushed the idea aside and strode quickly toward Whimsical Woman.

CHAPTER 18

Late Wednesday Morning:

Coming abreast of Upscale Garments, Philomela slowed her pace and stopped to look at a rack of clothes sitting outside the door. She flicked through elegant white blouses, black and white sweaters, and black skirts and pants with matching jackets. The sale prices, she noted, were well beyond her financial reach. She peered through the glass door and caught a glimpse of the stylish saleslady.

Sheila Trust, attired in a classy black dress, stood by a garment rack organizing pants—doubtless designer ones. She looked smart and efficient, the perfect saleslady. Philomela smiled as she considered the woman's sur-name. Trust. The name should instill confidence in all her customers. Then again, perhaps not. A nervous, insecure person might find Sheila intimidating, simply because her appearance was so perfect and her manner so queenly. Though these qualities were admirable, Philomela knew they could easily become over-bearing and pushy. She recognized a few of these traits because, on certain occasions, she herself was guilty of them.

At that precise moment, Sheila raised her head and glanced out the door. She saw Philomela and gave a friendly wave. Philomela returned the wave then strolled to the adjacent shop.

She opened the door of Whimsical Woman and a little bell tingled, announcing her entrance. Seeing a white-haired lady chatting with Procne, Philomela noted her sister's rusty-orange dress and elaborately beaded jewelry. Her outfit really did enhance the funky ambience of the store. Even Procne's foxy half-glasses added a dash of pizzazz, and her pleasant attitude mirrored Sheila's, yet the two women and their places of employment were complete opposites—one an epitome of fashionable perfection and the other a model of zany casualness. She heard the white-haired lady ask Procne if the jewelry she was wearing was for sale.

Procne nodded and pointed to a stand displaying an assortment of necklaces, bracelets, and earrings. "Here are lots of similar items," she said.

Philomela realized her sister's double duty performance of model and saleslady was a good selling ploy. Her body showed off the pretty merchandise and, at the same time, her pleasant personality helped sell it. The lady studied the jewelry then moved to a rack of dresses. Philomela walked over to her sister.

"Did you finish your sleuthing?" Procne whispered.

"Yes. And my coffee, too. In case you're interested, those two chatty fellows walked out the door of the cafe without seeing me. I heard them make a couple of interesting remarks." She saw Procne's eyebrows rise quizzically. With a touch of drama, Philomela added, "They were discussing files."

Procne's eyebrows knit together, but before she could question her sister, the white-haired lady turned to her. "Do you have this dress in a size six?"

"I'm afraid not," Procne replied. "But Joseph Rib-coff's clothes fit small. If you like the dress, this size eight is worth trying on." The lady took the dress into a fitting room, and Procne looked questioningly at her sister. "They were discussing files?"

Philomela moved close to her. "They hope to find a special document amongst the owner's files—a document referring to a mysterious loan."

Procne's eyes widened and her head bobbed up and down.

"They wondered if her files were kept in one of the shops or in her home," Philomela continued.

Procne silently grabbed Philomela's hand and led her between racks of clothing to the back of the shop. She pulled her through a door into a small room. Philomela gazed first at a computer sitting on a desk then off to the left at three filing cabinets. At the right side of the desk she saw two racks of hanging clothes plus a wall of shelves holding boxes and packages.

"The document might be here." Procne pointed to the three filing cabinets. "But somehow I doubt it. Every-thing here pertains to the business. That loan was person-al." The bell on the front door tingled and she muttered, "Someone just came in. I have to go." She hurried toward the front of the shop.

Philomela started to follow her, but when her sister loudly said, "Hello, Basil," Philomela twisted her feet and turned around. She heard Procne ask, "Are you going to buy a fashionable outfit for your wife?"

"She needs no help from me. Except to pay the bills. I'm here because my sister's birthday is approaching. Usually I buy her a book, but this year I decided to give her something more decorous."

"You've come to the right place, Basil. How about a scarf? A shawl? Some jewelry?"

"She doesn't wear much jewelry, but a scarf might be nice."

Philomela glanced over her shoulder and surreptitiously watched Procne lead him to a display of scarves hanging in front of a clothes rack. Procne pointed out their distinctive features—fabrics made of silk, polyester, cotton, and designs that were subdued or garish. Then the doorbell tingled again.

Procne greeted the newcomer by name. "Good morning, Sarah. How are you?"

"Not good. My back's bothering me and the chiropractor isn't any help. Neither is the physiotherapist or the doctor."

"That's too bad." Procne turned back to Basil, rather abruptly Philomela thought.

"I heard the news about Maxine," Sarah said. "I decided to come and see how you're doing. Ooh, my aching back. I have to sit down on this chair and rest a bit."

The newcomer plopped on the straight-back chair near the cash counter, Basil continued to study the scarves, and Philomela edged into the doorway of the office.

The white-haired lady came out of the dressing room, glanced around, and asked everyone what they thought of the dress she was wearing. Basil said the color enhanced her skin and hair.

"Awesome," Procne said. "The dress hits you in all the right places."

The lady called Sarah said nothing.

The white-haired lady turned to Procne. "You were right. The size eight is perfect. I think I'll buy it." She disappeared into the dressing room.

Philomela watched Procne show Basil a few more scarves and listened to her answer his questions. Then Sarah captured Procne's attention by asking about the jewelry display on the cash counter. Footsteps approached. Philomela stepped into the office and slipped over to the rack of clothes. She ducked behind one, tying to make herself invisible. If anyone saw her, she could pretend to be studying the colorful garments. The sound of throat clearing made her stop breathing. A file-cabinet drawer slid open and she breathed again, as softly as possible. A few papers were shuffled then the drawer closed. Another drawer opened.

"Basil." Procne stood at the door of the small office and stared at him. "What are you doing? Those filing cabinets hold nothing but boring order-forms, invoices, and receipts. That rack of clothes over there still has to be priced. Would you like the job of ticketing them?"

"I don't think so." He chuckled. "Ticketing is not my strong suit."

"Then you won't find anything of interest in here. Let's go out front. Maybe you'd like to look at jewelry for your sister."

Philomela heard the file-drawer close then their voices faded to the main part of the shop. She peeked around the clothing rack and, seeing no one, tiptoed to the doorway. She listened to Procne light-heartedly tell Basil that his sister would love a pale yellow scarf because it would go with anything. Peering around the door frame, Philomela saw Basil take a money clip from his pocket and hand cash to Procne. When the transaction was completed, he carried a rusty-orange bag out of the shop.

Philomela strolled nonchalantly out of the office and watched the white-haired lady leave the dressing room and walk over to the cash counter.

"I really like this dress." She placed the garment on the counter, took her credit card from her purse, and handed it to Procne.

Procne started to process the card when Sarah, still

sitting on the straight back chair, loudly pronounced, "You shouldn't buy that dress."

Procne, Philomela, and the white-haired lady turned and stared at Sarah. With an oversized shirt barely covering her body and an expression of superiority on her face, she sat like a well-fed queen on a tiny throne. Philomela had a flash of recognition—she had almost bumped into Sarah on Main Avenue.

"Why shouldn't I buy it?" the white hair-haired lady asked.

Philomela expected Sarah to say the dress had a sewing flaw or a rip in the fabric. Instead, she said, "That dress doesn't look good on you."

"Doesn't it?" The customer seemed surprised. She stared at Sarah with real concern.

"No, it bunches up at the back."

"Oh…yes." The white-haired lady chuckled, held up the dress and pointed to a slight bustle effect at the back. "It has a small gathering. It's supposed to slim my waistline and accentuate my buttocks."

"It looks terrible on you."

Seeing the appalled expression on Procne's face, Philomela could barely stifle a laugh. Was the frumpy fashion expert going to kill the sale?

The white-haired lady looked Sarah up and down. "Well, I think I'll buy the dress anyway," she finally said,

When the transaction was completed, Sarah got up and, without a word, walked to the door and went outside.

The white-haired lady watched her disappear. "I certainly hope that woman's opinion is wrong."

"It is," Procne assured her. "That dress looks smashing on you."

"Be like the weather," Philomela suggested. "Don't pay any attention to criticism."

The lady chuckled. "I'll keep that in mind."

Procne inserted both the dress and a fashion show announcement into a rusty-orange bag. "The fashion show is on Saturday," she said. "It will be a memorial to Maxine."

"What a lovely gesture. I'll try and get there." The customer picked up the bag, thanked Procne, and, with a happy lilt, walked to the door. She went outside and disappeared.

Procne rearranged the scarf display and Philomela watched her. "You made two unusual sales today," she said. "The first was a pale yellow scarf to a reluctant buyer. The second was a dress to a buyer who was almost jinxed by an unlikely fashion expert."

Procne groaned. "Sarah comes into both dress shops almost every day. She used to drive Maxine crazy because she always found fault with something and never bought anything. I think she's the most negative person in Saltaire."

"Is she okay?" Philomela asked. "I mean mentally and physically?"

Procne shrugged. "I don't know. But I do know she needs more exercise and less junk food. She always has a complaint. The latest is her back. If there's such a thing as a negativity gene, she has it. As for Basil's purchase of the scarf...well, you're right, I'm not sure he really wanted it."

"It gave him a good excuse to come and check out the office. He probably thinks his *I-Owe-You* is in one of the filing cabinets."

Procne looked pensively at her sister. "If he found the document, what would he do with it?"

"Destroy it. Eradicating the evidence of a loan is the best way to avoid repaying it."

"I suppose so. Do you think Basil and Shaun are in cahoots?"

Philomela opened her mouth to answer but the tingling doorbell stopped her. Her mouth closed and her eyes rested on an attractive lady with curly dark hair walking toward them. The door automatically clicked shut, and a chilling draft crept through the shop. Philomela shivered.

"Hello, Grace," Procne said. "You remember meeting Philomela at the museum?"

"Yes, indeed. Nice to see you again." She smiled at Philomela, fingered a couple of scarves, then held one up in the air. "This is very attractive. It would go with a few of my clothes."

Philomela noted the newcomer's curvy figure and admired her success at accentuating her good points and camouflaging her not so good ones. At the same time, Philomela glimpsed a person she recognized come up to the door and peer through the window. Basil Devonshire stared at her, and she stared back at him. Philomela doubted he could see his wife who stood behind the scarf display, but there was no question about him seeing Philomela.

She saw his lips form a thin line, his forehead furrow into two vertical lines, and his eyes grow cold. She thought his expression registered both annoyance and puzzlement. Was he wondering how she suddenly got inside the shop? Did he suspect she had been hiding in the small office during his hurried search through the drawers of the filing cabinet? She watched him abruptly turn and walk away.

Oblivious to her husband's brief appearance at the door, Grace nodded her head, gently held a scarf against her neck, and looked in a mirror. "I think I'll buy it," she said. Then, as if recalling the deceased owner of the dress

shop, she asked Procne, "How are you surviving the trag-
ic circumstances?"

"I'm muddling along," Procne replied. "Basil was
here earlier, and he seems to be coping, too."

Grace seemed surprised. "What was he doing here?"

"Buying a scarf for his sister's birthday."

"Her birthday? It's not until June." Grace sighed.
"He's still sad and upset about finding Maxine's body. It
was terribly traumatic for him. He can't believe anyone
would want to kill her."

"I can't believe it either." Procne emphasized the
point by pursing her lips and moving her head from side
to side.

Grace looked over at Philomela and changed the subject. "I hope you're enjoying your stay in Saltaire."

"I am. The weather here is much warmer than in Calgary. Yesterday wasn't very enjoyable though—when
your husband found the dead victim in the museum. That
was dreadful." Philomela looked at Grace's face and felt
a need to elaborate. "It was especially bad for Basil and
Procne because they knew the victim."

Grace lowered her eyes. "Basil was distraught. He
didn't sleep well. He wasn't much better this morning—
until Shaun phoned. They planned to have coffee together, probably the best thing Basil could do. Talking with
other people might help him realize that life goes on."

"Possibly," Procne said. "But Maxine's death is a
shock for everyone. She was such a good boss and such
an asset to the community."

"Do you know when the funeral will take place?"
Grace asked.

Procne shrugged her shoulders. "Sometime after the
police give their okay. And, of course, after the relatives
arrive."

"This may sound callous, but I want to buy a black

outfit for the funeral. I've avoided wearing black the last few years because it accentuates my wrinkles. Wrinkles are so depressing. But I've discovered that as long as I have color around my neck, black is okay." She glanced down at her red raincoat.

Philomela recalled that, on Monday, Grace had worn a smart gray coat. This one was brighter and cheerier. "Your coat looks lovely on you, Grace. Red supposedly provides energy. It's just what we all need. You cheer us up."

Grace smiled graciously. "Maxine was one of those people who could wear black and look elegant in it. It didn't drain color from her face. Of course, her makeup might have helped. She always looked wonderful, and she always wore clothes that were appropriate for each occasion. I want to look good for her final send-off."

"Upscale Garments has a lot of black outfits," Procne said. "The clothes there are classier than the ones here. Of course it's a matter of personal taste."

"Is Sheila at work today?" Grace asked.

"Yes, she is. You'll be interested to know that she and I have decided to carry on with the fashion-show on Saturday. It will be a memorial to Maxine."

"Nice. No doubt, you'll show funeral outfits. With all the elderly people here, we go to a lot of memorials and celebrations of life."

Procne gulped. "I hadn't thought about that. The tradition of black for funerals is no longer carved in stone, but your idea of having a good assortment of black outfits is a good one. I'll mention it to Sheila." From the counter, Procne picked up a sheet of colorfully printed paper. "Maxine had these notices printed. Lunch will be in the lower level of the old church and the show will be upstairs. As you know, the Adult Day Center is a worthwhile charity. And the price includes both lunch and the show. A real deal."

"I hadn't planned on going." Grace's eyes skimmed the notice. "But since it's a charitable event honoring Maxine, I might change my mind. Do we pay there?"

"Yeah, at the door." Procne grinned. "You'll know most of the models. Selene Hamilton is one of them."

The corners of Grace's lips turned down. Her eyes shifted slightly to the right, and Philomela wondered if she was in pain.

"We'll show several new spring fashions." Procne's words rang with true excitement as she added, "They're lovely. Other outfits will remind us that a few months of winter remain. I know you'll enjoy the show."

"I hope so." Grace wandered over to the display of costume jewelry and fingered a necklace with matching earrings and bracelet. "These would look nice on my purple sweater." She held the necklace under her chin and looked in a mirror. Without hesitation, she opened her purse and brought out her credit card. She bought the scarf and the three-piece jewelry set. After Procne put the purchases in a rusty-orange bag, Grace carried them to the door then stopped and turned around. "I'll go and see if Sheila has any black items that fit me."

Watching Grace go out the door, Philomela felt uneasy. Grace had shown a curious lack of emotion regarding Maxine's death. And she had been overtly displeased with Selene's participation in the fashion show. Knowing her two observations might be triggered by an overactive imagination, Philomela hesitated to mention them to Procne. A minute later curiosity got the better of her.

"Procne, was Grace being stiff-upper-lipped about Maxine's death?"

"Grace isn't the stiff-upper-lip type. To be honest, not many people in Saltaire considered Maxine a close friend. But they respected and admired her. That certainly includes Grace."

"I see." Philomela didn't really see, because Grace Devonshire still puzzled her.

Recalling the woman's less than pleased reaction when Procne mentioned Selene's participation in the fashion show, Philomela wondered if her annoyance originated from Selene's suggestion that she get a job. Or perhaps it had something to do with Grace's husband. Did Grace think the psychic knew details about Basil's and Maxine's relationship other than volunteering at the museum? Was it possible that Grace reacted with anger toward her suspected competitor?

Procne's voice jarred Philomela back to the present. "...normally, I bring a sandwich and eat it in the office during a slack period. But this morning my mind was so full of Maxine I forgot all about making lunch."

"I'll go to your place and make sandwiches then bring them here."

"Great. My stomach's growling like an attack dog.

Philomela left the dress shop. Walking spiritedly along Main Avenue, she thought not of lunch, but of murder.

CHAPTER 19

Wednesday Noon:

Contemplating different motives for murder, Philomela turned off Main Avenue. As she neared Procne's townhouse, her thoughts flitted from females like Grace to males like Basil. When Basil peered through the shop window, his face indicated puzzlement, surprise, annoyance. He seemed to wonder how and when she got into the shop and how much she had seen of his activity in the back office. Did he worry that both she and Procne had witnessed him rifle through the filing cabinet drawers? Did he debate with himself about how far he should go to retrieve the I-Owe-You? Did he think theft and destruction of the note would be an excellent way to avoid repayment?

She stopped midstride. Could he already have killed Maxine in order to terminate the debt?

Philomela shuddered. Surely the always proper Basil was incapable of committing such a horrendous crime. Then again, if he had a dual personality like Dr. Jekyll and Mr. Hyde he would be capable of doing anything.

Inside Procne's townhouse, she pushed Basil to the

back of her mind and concentrated on mixing tuna, mayonnaise, sliced onion, chopped celery, salt, and pepper in a small bowl. She put the mixture between slices of multi-grain bread, added lettuce and kale, then placed the sandwiches in a plastic bag. After taking two pork chops from the freezer to thaw for dinner, she readied herself to return to the dress shop. She walked into the open-air vestibule and met Selene coming out her door.

"Hi, Philomela." Selene glanced at the plastic bag Philomela was carrying. "Are you by any chance going to Whimsical Woman?"

"Yes, I'm taking lunch for Procne and me."

"May I walk with you?"

"Of course." Philomela opened the grilled door and held it open for Selene. The door clanged shut and they strolled side by side on the interlocking brick sidewalk.

"Procne asked me to come to the shop," Selene said. "We have to decide what garments I'll wear at the fashion show."

"That'll be fun."

"I guess so. I don't know about being a model, though. It makes me nervous. I've always been the seamstress—behind the scenes—never a person in the spotlight."

"You'll do well, Selene. Your natural walk is graceful and you have a nice figure."

"You're very reassuring, Philomela."

"I'm serious. And I'm glad Sheila and Procne decided to continue with the show. It gives everyone something positive to think about."

"That's true. Dedicating the show to Maxine was a brilliant idea. Attendees will be reminded of the vibrancy of her life rather than the morbidity of her death."

Was Selene praising the idea because she telepathically knew Philomela had originally made the suggestion to Procne? Or did she really believe the idea was brilliant?

"I wonder if the killer will ever be found," Selene mused.

"Do you have any inkling of his or her identity?"

"No. Nor does anyone else. Including the police."

They walked a short distance then Philomela broke their silence. "While I was at the dress shop this morning, Grace Devonshire came in."

"Was she upset about Maxine's death?"

"She didn't appear to be. Finding a black outfit for the funeral was uppermost in her mind."

"Oh, dear. I hope she doesn't buy an expensive one."

Selene's remark increased Philomela's opinion that Grace and Basil were unusual, a very odd couple. "Basil also came into the shop," she said. "He went into the back office and opened filing cabinet drawers as if searching for something. Can you think of any reason why he'd behave so brazenly?"

Selene slowly shook her head.

"I think he was looking for his *I-Owe-You.*"

"Oh, the debt he owed Maxine? The one you mentioned the other evening?"

"Yes. What do you think?"

Selene stopped walking and gazed up at the sky. Philomela wondered if she were seeking heavenly answers to an earthly question. Starting to move forward, Selene murmured, "Basil is complicated. His confident attitude hides multi problems."

"Such as?"

"His expenditures are larger than his income."

"Surely that's not a motive for killing Maxine."

"It shouldn't be," Selene said.

Gazing at her, Philomela wished the fey woman's intuitive abilities would come to the fore, allowing her to identify the perpetrator. If she knew anything about the crime, she certainly wasn't verbalizing it.

Philomela's doubts about Selene's psychic abilities resurfaced so she turned and looked straight ahead. Granted, twice Selene had foreseen a dead woman on a tan sofa, a woman who could have been Maxine, but she still didn't seem to realize that Philomela and Rae comprised one and the same person.

If Selene knew that Rae, her new email client, was in fact Philomela, why didn't she mention it? For that matter, why didn't Philomela mention it to Selene? Because she wanted to gain more knowledge about Procne's money-grubbing neighbor.

Too many questions. Too few answers.

Suspecting the woman's psychic talents were inconsistent, working only occasionally, Philomela turned the conversation to mundane trivia. She chatted about the weather and what it would be like to live in Saltaire's temperate climate.

Selene responded by pointing out a few benefits of living here. "We don't need heavy warm coats or snowboots. We don't worry about cars starting in winter or having to scrape ice and snow off windshields. Nor do we trudge through slippery ice and deep snow. The town has everything, yet is small enough so we can walk everywhere. And of course we live beside the Pacific Ocean."

"That's all good, especially for older people." Enjoying the conversation, Philomela briefly forgot about the murder.

Inside Whimsical Woman, the two sisters immediately focused on outfitting Selene for the fashion show. With a practiced eye, Procne chose three garments and hung them in the dressing room. Selene put on the first one while the sisters sat in the office eating tuna-fish sandwiches.

When Selene announced she was ready to show off the dress, the sisters left their half-eaten sandwiches on the desk and walked out to the main part of the shop. Watching Selene flounce in front of a full-length three way mirror, Philomela raved about how well the dress fit and how nice it looked on her. Procne suggested Selene practice walking like a model by putting one foot directly in front of the other. Selene mastered the walk quickly then returned to the dressing room. The sisters went back to the office, finished eating their sandwiches, then again came out and watched Selene walk back and forth wearing a pink lounging outfit. The pale color accentuated her etherealness and the outfit drew attention to the best parts of her slim figure.

Several minutes later, Selene came out of the dressing room attired in the third outfit and Philomela burst into gales of laughter. "You look like a little girl playing dress-up in her mother's clothes. Those pants and jacket are way too big for you."

At that moment, a customer entered the shop and Procne leaped to attention. "Work calls," she whispered. Strolling to the front of the shop, she cheerily said, "Good afternoon." The newcomer asked about Maxine Springer and Procne sadly answered her questions.

Meanwhile, Selene selected two outfits off a rack and went into the dressing room. Philomela slipped into the office, cleaned up the lunch remnants, then returned to the main part of the shop. She saw Procne put a bulky red cardigan into a rusty-orange bag and heard her making pleasant small talk.

"I'm sure you'll get a lot of wear out of this sweater," she said.

The customer nodded agreement, clutched the rusty-orange bag in her hand, and, with a wide smile on her face, left the shop.

Procne turned and sauntered toward her sister. "Another happy customer," she said.

Selene exited the dressing room and gazed at her reflection in front of the three-way mirror. "Procne, if I were as tall as you I'd be a better model. What are you? Five feet nine inches?"

"Five feet nine and one half inches," Procne replied.

"The half inch is what makes Procne a good fashion model," Philomela said. She grinned then studied Selene. "You must be five foot five," she said.

"You're dead on. Sorry, dead is a bad choice of words."

Philomela ignored Selene's remark. "I'm the vertically challenged one here. I almost reach five foot three if I really stretch. Good grief, listen to us—like many older Canadians we still use inches instead of centimeters."

"We're the generation who suffered the changeover," Selene said.

"As long as the United States uses feet and inches," Philomela said, "the changeover in Canada will never be complete. Personally, I think changing to metric was one of our prime minister's less-than-brilliant laws."

Selene returned to the dressing room and quickly came out wearing the second outfit she had chosen, a violet top with matching pants.

"Speaking of brilliant," Philomela said, "that describes you, Selene. Violet makes you look so gentle and so spiritual."

Selene gave an enigmatic smile. "The top and pants fit and the color suits me. I might buy it after the fashion show is over. She donned a few more outfits and all three finally agreed on the five garments she should model at the show. Philomela jotted notes about each outfit in her notepad.

"You'll have to wear your own shoes," Procne said.

"Do you have a couple of pairs that will look good with those outfits?"

"I do," Selene said.

"Good. I'll hang these glad rags on the show rack in the office. One volunteer from the Adult Day Center has been here, but two have yet to come." The bell on the door tingled. "Maybe this is one of them now." Procne moved quickly forward then stopped. Her shoulders slumped as if heavily burdened. "Oh no. Sarah Winston. Again" She moved in slow motion toward the newcomer.

"Procne," Sarah said, walking toward her. "A serious rumor is going around town. People don't believe Maxine's murder was committed by a local resident. They think it was done by a visitor, probably someone from Calgary." She glanced over at Philomela.

Philomela stifled a gasp. The woman was accusing her of murder.

"Ridiculous," Procne said. "Unless the visitor was insane, why would he or she kill Maxine?"

"I don't know. But I thought you should know about the rumor because the police have already heard it." She glared at Philomela then turned and marched outside.

"She's a...feces...disturber and a troublemaker." Procne grinned then shook her head. "I bet she started the rumor and told the police about it."

Selene sighed and her facial expression was pensive. "She's a young soul, searching for identity."

"Do you really think so?" Philomela asked.

"Yes, I do. Unfortunately, Sarah's traveling on a disruptive path and doesn't want to get off."

Philomela wasn't sure about the young soul implication, but she certainly agreed that Sarah was on a disruptive path. "What does she do beside start rumors and cause trouble? Does she work as a housewife? Does she have a job outside the home?"

"She's a divorcee," Procne said, "and she wanders around town bothering people and criticizing everybody and everything. I think she collects alimony and I think she expects everyone to treat her like a queen. By now, most Saltaire residents will have heard the rumor that a visiting Calgarian, possibly my sister, murdered Maxine."

"Not many people will believe her." Selene picked up her purse and moved toward the door. "Thanks for helping me choose outfits for the show. It was fun. I promised to visit a lady in the hospital who is dying of cancer. She wants me to affirm that she's starting off on a new adventure. So I have to go."

Philomela was tempted to ask if she could go with her, mainly so she could see Selene in full spiritual mode. She wanted to know and understand the extent of the psychic's abilities. But before Philomela broached the question Selene was gone.

Two customers straggled into the shop and started to browse. Philomela busily arranged pants in order of size, and Procne rearranged the jewelry display. One customer searched for a more-than-perfect garment for a less-than-perfect price, and the other customer checked out a coat sale that Maxine had promoted last Friday. A few people came in to get information about the murder, and most ended up buying something and promising to attend the fashion show. All in all, Procne sold three coats, two jackets, one pair of leggings, and three sweaters.

The two volunteers from Adept Adult Day Center came in and provided many giggles as they tried on a variety of outfits. With help from Procne and Philomela, they chose the handsomest and best fitting ones for the fashion show. Philomela jotted notes in her note pad.

When the small hand of the clock rested on five and the large hand sat on twelve, the sisters readied the shop for the night. Philomela re-hung a few sloppily placed garments, and Procne hid the float—the money kept for making change—under the carpet in the smallest dressing room. They put on their coats and gloves and Procne turned the Open sign to Closed.

Outside, she locked the door and turned to Philomela. "The end of another day. All's well that ends well. Unfortunately, I think our Pineapple Express is being forced out by a cold front."

They leaned into a strong wind and headed for home.

Procne prepared rice and vegetables, and Philomela cooked the pork chops she had taken from the freezer earlier. After eating dinner, they talked about how best to describe the outfits at the fashion show. The master of ceremonies would need a clear description of each garment so Philomela studied her jottings in her notebook. Then she shivered.

"Listen to the wind whistle and whine around the windows. I feel as if a recently departed soul walked beside me." She set her notebook on the coffee table beside her iPad, turned on the outside light, and opened the gliding door. Stepping out onto the deck, she peered at the thermometer hanging on the outside wall. She quickly returned inside and shut the door firmly. "The wind almost blew me away. The temperature has dropped. It's only two degrees above freezing."

"Oh, the cold front has arrived." Procne's words came forth like a lament. "I hope we get snow instead of freezing rain."

"Imagine. Snow in January." Philomela smirked, not bothering to remark that Calgary also got snow in September, October, November, December, February, March, and April.

She sat down on a sofa, picked up her iPad, and opened it. There were three new messages.

Aloud she read one from her dependable employee.

Hi, Philomela,
Calgary is thirty degrees below freezing, but the cold temperature didn't upset the photo session with the new advertiser. I inserted the photo with the text into the February draft. The advert looks good. Hope you're having a grand time with your sister.
Cheers, Janice.

The second email was from Brent. She also read it aloud.

Dear Philomela:
Please keep your nose out of that murder case. Let the police search for clues. Murderers are dangerous people, and the police understand how to handle them. You know how I worry about you.
Today heliskiing was great, but a blizzard threatens to curtail activities tomorrow. Time will tell. Only three more days—I can't believe how fast the time has gone. Next time you must come with me. You'll love heliskiing.
Give Procne a hug from me and take three hugs for yourself
Love, Brent

"Is Brent being optimistic?" Procne asked. "Would you love heliskiing?"

Philomela chuckled. "Yes to your first question and no to your second."

"The weather sounds dreadful in both Calgary and on the mountain top. I guess we're the lucky ones. Right now we have wind and rain, but the temperature's still above freezing."

Philomela looked at her sister and ran her tongue over her lips. In mock seriousness, she said, "I once heard a Canadian climatologist say, 'The British have the Monarchy, the Americans have Hollywood, the French have Romance, and the Canadians? Well, they have Weather.'"

Procne giggled. "That's too true to be funny."

Later that evening, Philomela lay in bed in her niece's room and closed her eyes. Instead of sleeping, she listened to the wind howl outside. A Cedar branch scraped against the window as if asking to come inside for warmth. She hoped the gale wouldn't blow the tree through the window onto her bed. Finally, she turned on the bedside lamp, climbed out of bed, and opened the window. Cold air roared into the room. She shivered and quickly closed the window. Though not freezing outside, it really was a dark and stormy night.

She scrambled back in bed and thought of the three electronic messages that had arrived earlier in the evening. Brent had survived another day of heliskiing and had commented on Maxine's murder:

…please keep your nose out of that murder case. Let the police search for clues…You know how I worry about you.

Yes, he did worry. He disliked her getting involved with the seedy side of life. He even worried about her rubbing shoulders with the homeless and the druggies when researching an article. Thoughts of her trying to solve a murder would dampen his fun heliskiing. Perhaps she shouldn't have mentioned it.

Janice had managed the photo session very well and had brought the February e-draft up to date. "She's a wonderful employee," Philomela murmured to herself. "Not only can she pronounce and spell February and Wednesday, but she's almost efficient enough to produce the magazine by herself." Philomela mentally patted herself on the back for being such a good teacher and mentor. Then she murmured, "Good grief, I may be putting myself out of a job."

Thoughts of her successful magazine faded to oblivion, replaced by the third electronic message she had received that evening. She purposely had not read it aloud to her sister. Though unimportant, the message was worrying and annoying. She picked up her iPad and re-read it.

Dear Rae:

You haven't replied and I am truly dismayed. The Spiritual Beings are distressed because they know you need help and time is running short. I read the Tarot cards for you this morning and discovered you are not achieving your potential. The Spiritual Beings are gathering in preparation for the Cerulean Moon when all things will become available to you. In order to be prepared, you must start working on it now. I'm here to help you. Please click the blue link and reply quickly.

With love, Selene

Philomela knew that cerulean meant blue, azure blue. She didn't know if Cerulean Moon meant two full moons in one month—commonly known as "blue moon." She didn't think either January or February was a blue moon month, but she'd check a calendar tomorrow and perhaps the message would become clear. She clicked the blue link. Up came two lines of print.

In order to receive advice from the Spiritual Beings and take advantage of the Cerulean Moon you need only send $49.00.

She shut off the iPad, turned off the lamp, and pulled up the covers. Outside, the wind screamed and howled against the window. At least the wind didn't have a blue link requesting money.

CHAPTER 20

Thursday Morning:

Philomela woke up and listened to the wind whistle and whine. It reminded her of a winter blizzard in Calgary, but when she climbed out of bed and looked out the window, no snow met her eyes. Instead, she saw a brightly dawning sky, cedar branches waving in the air, green grass covering the ground, and white-capped waves crashing against the shore.

Her bare feet padded to the windowless bathroom where she performed her morning ablutions. Mentally, she wondered what the day would bring to her sister and her sister's friends. Once again, Procne's life was in flux. No longer would she work on Thursday, Friday, and Saturday at Whimsical Woman while Sheila worked at Upscale Garments. She would be at Whimsical six days a week until Maxine's last will and testament was read. Normalcy was gone. Maxine's death changed everything.

Feeling clean and fresh, Philomela put on a new pair of black tights and a long green sweater that matched her eyes. At her sister's insistence she had purchased the youthful clothes yesterday at the funky shop.

"It looks less summery than the black skirt and mid-drift white top," Procne had said.

Finding the outfit surprisingly comfortable, she walked free and easy to the kitchen, where Procne stood in front of the microwave doing something with its keypad.

"Good morning, Procne."

"Oh, hi, Sis. The power went out during the night. Thank goodness the Hydro magicians restored it before I got up. I've already reset the clocks on my bedside table and on the oven. Now I'm doing the microwave." She completed the task, moved to the cook-top, and stirred a pot. "I'm making oatmeal porridge," she said.

"I love porridge in winter. It provides warmth and sustenance." Philomela took the juice carton from the fridge and half filled two glasses. "Porridge sticks to the ribs and insulates the body from freezing cold. This juice, on the other hand, has had a lot of fiber removed, leaving mostly sugar and water. But what the heck—everything in moderation." She set the two glasses near the spoons on the eating-counter.

Procne brought two steaming bowls to the eating counter and sat down beside her sister. They doctored their porridge with brown sugar, bananas, yogurt, and milk then ate while chatting about the local weather forecast. Discussing scattered showers and wind helped Philomela avoid the subject uppermost in her mind.

When the phone rang, Procne nonchalantly picked it up and said hello. She listened to the person on the other end and, Philomela saw her eyebrows slowly knit together.

"So the murderer's still at large." Procne listened for several seconds before speaking again. "Yes, I'm sure you're doing all you can." She listened for another minute then asked, "Do you think the murder was random or was it planned?" She nodded her head. "Okay, we'll be there shortly. Toodles." She put the phone on its charger.

"The police?" Philomela asked.

"Yeah. Dickless Tracy wants us to go to the police station this morning to have our fingerprints taken. We won't have time to go for coffee at the History Cafe. Too bad. We'll miss the morning gossip."

At nine-twenty they stepped onto the interlocking brick sidewalk and were almost blown away. The wind's strength surprised Philomela. Though the temperature was above freezing, the chilled wind and high humidity penetrated her clothes and settled in her bones.

Entering the warm police station, she experienced a sense of relief. Her relief, however, was short lived.

Instead of walking into a place of organized law and order, she found herself surrounded by chaos and confusion. People ran back and forth and round and round in circles. Behind a counter one person picked up phones, another person called out questions, and a young girl looking frenzied typed at a computer. No one paid any attention to the two sisters. Philomela stood at the counter, coughed, and then loudly cleared her throat.

The young girl looked up from her computer. She clicked a few more keys, stood up, moved to the counter and, blinked at them. "Sorry, we're behaving like idiots here. There's been an accident on Main Avenue." She shook her head. "A murder and a hit-and-run accident in two days. Things like this don't happen in Saltaire."

Apparently, Philomela thought, they do. Aloud she agreed with the young girl. "Saltaire is usually quiet and peaceful. Not a town in turmoil."

She nodded agreement. "May I help you?"

"We're here to have our fingerprints taken," Philomela replied. "We were at the museum when the murder victim was found."

The young girl placed her right hand on her cheek and stared at them. "Oh!"

Philomela wondered if she suspected them of being perpetrators rather than innocent discoverers of the body. A sudden gust of cold air swirled around her legs and she jerked around to see what caused it. A tall man walked through the open doorway. The door closed behind him and he strode directly to the counter.

Below thick white hair his eyes glared at the receptionist. "As a member of the Historical Museum board, I need to have my fingerprints taken."

"These two ladies were here first," the young girl replied. "I'm afraid you'll have to wait."

He pushed back his shoulders and stared hypnotically down at the receptionist. "I am Melvin Springer."

Philomela was reminded of an insect-hater staring at a small, innocent ladybug. She saw the girl blink at him as if not knowing what to do.

The man's name obviously meant nothing to her. Seeing a flush of angst, or perhaps anger, spread across Melvin's face, Philomela leaned over the counter.

"This man's wife is the murder victim. Out of respect for his loss, I think Mr. Springer should be looked after first."

The girl's face paled. "Oh, I—I'm sorry. This way please." She led the annoyed man into the adjacent room. A moment later she returned, looking as if she had been stepped on and squashed.

"Don't be sad," Procne said. "He didn't even thank us for giving up our place in line."

"I didn't know the name of the murdered lady," the girl murmured. "He told the officer that I was a negligent fool and should be fired."

Appalled, Philomela looked at her sister. "I thought you said Melvin was always polite and pleasant. That fellow doesn't fit my idea of pleasant, let alone polite."

Procne was obviously dumbfounded. "You have to admit the dreadful situation could make any husband distraught and unthinking."

"Unthinking enough to make an innocent young girl lose her job?"

Procne shook her head in puzzlement. "I've never seen him behave like this, not ever."

A few minutes later, the object of their conversation re-entered the room and, without so much as a nod, marched past them to the front door. He stepped outside and another gust of cold air blew into the room. The door banged shut and the young receptionist sighed with what seemed like relief. She led the sisters to the room Melvin had just vacated.

With black smudged fingers, they re-entered the reception area, thanked the young girl, and headed for the front door. Again it opened and this time the cold wind blew Constable James into the room. She struggled against the wind and closed the door. Then she saw Procne and Philomela.

"Fingerprints all done?" she asked.

They replied affirmatively.

She nodded then walked over to the young girl. "The ambulance has taken Ms. Hamilton to the hospital."

"Hamilton?" Procne's voice squeaked in alarm. "Selene Hamilton?"

Constable James turned from the receptionist and looked at Procne. "Yes. Do you know her?"

"She's my neighbor. Was she struck by a car?"

"It was a case of hit and run."

"Is she seriously hurt?"

"They'll determine her injuries at emergency."

Visibly upset, Procne placed both hands over her cheeks.

Philomela feared this could be too much for her sister—first her boss and now her neighbor. Maxine dead and Selene in emergency, possibly at death's door. Trying to appear calm, Philomela took her distraught sister's arm and suggested that perhaps her neighbor sustained only minor injuries. She bade goodbye to the young receptionist.

Constable James stepped forward and opened the door for them. "If you think of anything regarding the murder," she said, "even if it seems unimportant, please phone me." She gave them her card then closed the door behind them.

The wind still blew fiercely from the northeast and pushed them forward along Main Avenue. At the doorway of the dress shop, Procne took the key from her purse. With her other hand she grasped the doorknob and was about to insert the key in the keyhole when she looked through the window.

"Yikes," she exclaimed. "The office light's on. I'm sure I turned it off last night." Without inserting the key, she turned the doorknob and the door opened. Her eyes widened in alarm as she turned and stared at Philomela. "I know I locked this door last night."

Philomela felt her heartbeat increase in speed, but she tried to speak calmly. "Maxine had a key to this door as did Sheila and you. Whoever unlocked it is probably long gone. Perhaps Sheila was here and forgot to lock it." She moved with pseudo confidence in front of her sister and stepped into the shop.

CHAPTER 21

Thursday Morning continued:

Suppressing a twinge of fear, Philomela switched on lights and walked up to the first rack of clothing. She circled it, did the same with other racks, and concluded nobody was hiding behind or amongst the garments. She moved to the cash counter, paused, and took a deep breath. She walked behind the counter. Nobody was there and nothing seemed amiss. Glancing at Procne who stood frozen near the front door, Philomela felt a twinge of alarm. She took another deep breath and made her way to the well-lit office. With each step, the beat of her heart increased in sound and speed—lub-dub, lub-dub, lub-dub. She paused near the door. Expecting someone to jump out at her, she nervously peeked around the doorframe of the office.

"Good grief!!" she yelled.

Procne thawed and came to life. "What? What is it?"

"It's a disaster. Papers are scattered like snowflakes all over the floor." Philomela stepped into the small room. Trying to avoid stepping on papers, she walked past the filing cabinet's partially open drawers and checked behind the racks of clothing. "No one is here," she called.

Procne scampered to the doorway, stopped, and stared at the paper littered floor. "What in—Who would do this?" White faced, she turned to her sister. Then she spat out one word, "Basil."

"We don't know that for sure," Philomela replied. "But I do know we must call the police."

Procne responded by snatching her cellphone from her purse. For the second time in two days she punched nine-one-one.

Watching her, Philomela felt another twinge of alarm—would the police label the shop a crime scene? If it became off-limits, how in the world could she and Procne remove items for the fashion show? How could they organize a show with no clothes to model? She refrained from voicing her concern because right now her sister had more than enough worries. Philomela didn't want to add hypothetical complications to Procne's real ones.

"Why don't the police come?" Procne wrung her hands and paced up and down the shop. "What's taking them so long?"

"Procne." Philomela then tried to lighten the situation. "I think your middle name is 'Impatience.'"

Procne stopped pacing and stared at her sister. Her lips were pursed together, but they slowly relaxed into a near grin. "That's because our parents' couldn't name me, 'Brilliant,' since my older sister already had it."

Philomela chuckled at Procne's attempt at humor. The humor worked and the tension lessened as Procne gazed at her sister with moist eyes and the corners of her mouth turning up. But the attempts at mirth were short lived.

"I must tell Sheila what happened." Without another

word Procne dashed through the shop and out the door. Two minutes later she returned with the clerk from Upscale Garments in tow.

"Good gracious." Sheila stared agape at the papers covering the floor. "What a mess. Why would anyone do this? Why would anyone steal dress-shop invoices and order forms?"

Philomela's mouth formed a silent "O" as a new reason for searching the filing cabinet came to mind. "Perhaps someone thought the float was hidden in here," she said.

"You could be right." Sheila turned to Procne. "At night Maxine sometimes took the money home and sometimes hid it in different places in the shops. Procne, what did you do with it last night?"

"I left $110 in small bills and change in an envelope under a carpet." In a business-like manner she strode from the office and Sheila and Philomela followed her. Inside the smallest dressing room, they watched her bend down, lift a corner of the carpet, then stand up straight. In her hand, she waved a white envelope. "Here it is." She walked to the cash counter, dumped the money from the envelope on the counter, and counted it. "The float's all here."

"Strange," Philomela murmured. "You'd think someone searching for cash would break into the cash drawer. But it seems undisturbed."

"If I were a thief wanting money," Sheila said, "that's the first place I'd look."

"I guess we can eliminate a money thief." Philomela remained silent for a few seconds as she thought of Procne's first accusation. Had Basil tried to find his I-Owe-You to Maxine?

She kept her thoughts to herself, not wanting to falsely accuse an allegedly innocent man. Being a rumor monger like Sarah Winston was not one of her ambitions.

As if this were a normal working day, Procne careful-ly placed coins and bills in their designated slots in the cash drawer. She completed the task just as the bell above the door tingled and the police marched into the room.

Philomela recognized them and nervously walked to-ward them. "Good morning Corporal Stinson and Con-stable James."

"You had a break-in?" Constable James asked.

Philomela's previous experience with police came to her rescue. She calmly explained the situation in detail and guided them to the rear of the shop. Procne and Shei-la listened and silently followed close behind.

Constable James stopped at the door to the office and gazed at the papers strewn all over the floor. "Oh dear," she said. "This really is a mess. Did the vandals take any-thing?"

"I don't know." Procne stepped forward, bent down, and studied a pile of papers. Then she looked up at Con-stable James. "It looks as if they just tossed the contents of the filing cabinets on the floor. We haven't touched anything. But Sheila and I can't understand why anyone would want order forms, invoices, and receipts. Cash is never kept in these cabinets."

"Who would know that?" Corporal Stinson asked.

"Probably only those who work here," Procne replied.

"Was anything mindlessly vandalized? Equipment? Furniture?" He gazed at the walls, the computer, the desk, and then turned back to Procne.

She shrugged helplessly with palms up then moved to the computer to see if it was damaged. "I don't think so."

Before she could touch anything Corporal Stinson stopped her. "We'll check for problems after the finger-printing is finished.

Still worried about access to merchandise for the

fashion show, Philomela reluctantly asked, "Will the shop be taped off as a crime scene?" Hearing Procne loudly suck air into her lungs, she knew her sister previously had not thought of such a scenario.

"I don't think that'll be necessary," Corporal Stinson said.

With relief Procne audibly expelled air from her lungs.

"Taking photographs and fingerprints shouldn't take too long," he said. His cellphone rang and he opened it.

"Fingerprinting you two ladies is unnecessary," Constable James said, looking directly at the two sisters. "Your prints are already on file. But you, Mrs. Trust, will have to be fingerprinted." She looked at Sheila then glanced over at Corporal Stinson who was talking on his cellphone. Waiting for him to finish his call, she wandered around the shop, surreptitiously admiring the clothing.

Philomela came up to her. "Was this morning's hit and run victim badly injured?"

"I haven't heard," Constable James replied. "I hope not."

Procne overheard their brief conversation and joined them. "I think I'll phone emergency and find out how Selene is doing." She made the call on her cellphone. Apparently satisfied with the answers to her questions, she said thank you and snapped the phone shut. "Selene was treated for minor bruises and scrapes and will soon be released. The nurse asked if I could pick her up. Selene needs clean clothes because hers are torn and muddy. I have a key to her place so that won't be a problem."

Constable James smiled, obviously pleased with Procne's announcement. She then greeted two newcomers laden with equipment and took them to the back office. They were technicians who photographed the messy office and took Sheila's fingerprints. Corporal Stinson, who had shut his cellphone, asked the three women a few more questions about various items in the office and then gave Sheila permission to return to the shop next door. He explained to Philomela and Procne that the perpetrator probably wore gloves, but in case he hadn't, the finger-printing procedure would be followed. The bulk of the police work was quickly finished, and Corporal Stinson told the sisters they could check the computer and start to clean up the mess in the office.

Left alone, they proceeded to do exactly that.

"The police didn't take as long with this break-in as they did with Maxine's murder," Philomela said.

Procne nodded and left the office to attend to three customers who had entered the shop. She answered questions about the fashion-show then left the customers on their own to browse. Purchasing a few items, they commiserated about Maxine's death, and Procne did not enlighten them about last night's break-in. After the customers left, she returned to help Philomela tidy up the office.

They worked efficiently, found dates on invoices and receipts, then filed them in proper order. The job took less time than they expected. In what seemed no time at all, Procne left Philomela in charge of the shop and went to pick up Selene.

CHAPTER 22

Thursday Afternoon:

Procne stepped inside Selene's townhouse and made her way to the bedroom. She dropped a pair of stretchy pants, a long sweater, two undergarments, a jacket, and a pair of shoes into a canvas bag then took the bag downstairs to her white Mazda. She drove from the underground parkade and, fifteen minutes later, parked at the local hospital's open-air parking lot. She put money in a machine and miraculously it worked—a ticket popped out. She placed the ticket on the car's dashboard.

Carrying the bag filled with Selene's clothes into the emergency waiting room, she nervously glanced around.

Several people were doing exactly what the room was designed for—waiting. Some sat and gazed into space, two read magazines, one read a paperback book, a few paced aimlessly back and forth, a couple sat nervously tapping their hands on their knees, and a young girl texted on an iPhone. One person slumped down in a chair as if asleep. Or dead.

Procne braced herself and took a deep breath. She hated hospitals. They were full of sick and injured people. How the staff managed to be sympathetic yet cheery was beyond her understanding. She forced her feet to step across the floor and stop in front of a lady sitting at a desk.

"I'm here to pick up Selene Hamilton. I have some clean clothes for her."

The lady smiled. "Oh, excellent. I'll check to see if she's ready to leave." She stood up and disappeared behind a door.

Procne wondered if the lady was a nurse, a receptionist, or a cleaning lady. Long gone were the days when nurses could be distinguished by white uniforms, starched caps, and distinctive pins.

Procne eased onto a nearby chair, expecting a long wait. Her expectation proved wrong—in a matter of minutes the lady-of-unknown-identity returned.

"You may bring the clothes to Ms. Hamilton right now," she said.

Nervously following the mystery lady into the inner-sanctum, Procne glanced from side to side, almost expecting the hands of a skeleton to reach out and grab her. The mystery lady stopped at a wall of white curtains and pulled one aside. There, adorned in an unglamorous hospital nightshirt and lying peacefully on a bed was the hit-and-run victim.

Procne stared at her. "Selene, are you okay?"

"I'm fine, Procne. No broken bones and only a slight concussion." She smiled, sat up, and watched her neighbor set the clothes on the bed. "My clothes are a mess. Thanks for bringing me something decent to wear."

"You're welcome," Procne said.

"The clothes I was wearing will end up in the garbage."

The mystery lady pulled the curtains shut. While Selene changed from the loose hospital gown to her ordinary clothes, Procne waited outside the curtained area. She watched nurses go from one bed to another, checking intravenous tubes, counting pulse beats, taking blood pressures and temperatures. She hoped no one would go into cardiac arrest or die while she stood quietly waiting for her neighbor. It was with extreme relief that she saw the curtain shift and Selene emerge.

They walked in single file through the waiting area to the front door. Leaving emergency behind, Procne glanced over at the hospital's main entrance and caught a glimpse of Simon Fraser—or his double. Startled, she stopped walking and watched him disappear inside the hospital. Why, she wondered, was he here?

Was Simon ill? Was he visiting a sick friend? Or maybe he needed to have a diagnostic test of some kind. She pushed all these ideas aside, led Selene to the white Mazda, and helped her get into the passenger seat. Then she drove slowly from the hospital parking lot.

"Selene," she said. "Did you experience a premonition of your hit and run accident?"

"Not really. Yesterday I had a brief inkling of an accident, but where it was located, when it would happen, and who was involved were unclear. No impish voice gave any warning of my own involvement."

"Well, I'm glad you're okay. I'd hate to lose you as a neighbor. I'd also hate to lose you as a model on Saturday afternoon. Will you be up to strutting in front of a bunch of people?"

"I think so." Selene raised her bandaged left arm. "My arm was scraped and bruised, but nothing serious. Will this bandage mar the outfits?"

Procne chuckled. "It'll add drama. Have you any idea who hit you? A man? A woman? A young kid?"

"It happened so fast I couldn't focus on any details. I was crossing the street toward the museum when a car appeared from nowhere. It knocked me down then screeched around the corner. All I knew was the car was dark in color. It could have been black, gray, dark green or navy blue."

"Helpful—but not very. Would meditation help you envision the car?"

"I could try, but things don't work that way for me, especially when my personal life is involved. I foresee things for others but never for myself."

"Mmm." Procne silently tried to understand her neighbor's mystical world, but it was just too eerie to grasp. Instead, she thought of the driver of the car. "Maybe the driver was drunk or a kid hopped up on drugs."

"It doesn't really matter. Whether drunk, on drugs, or sober, the driver could have killed me. But here I am— alive and well." She looked out the window as Procne eased the vehicle down the ramp to the parking area below their living quarters. When the car was parked and the ignition turned off, Selene turned to Procne. "Thanks for bringing me home from the hospital. I appreciate it."

"You're welcome, Selene. You were smart to suggest we exchange house keys in case of an emergency. This was an emergency, and you could say your suggestion proved to be prophetic." Procne got out of the car, picked up the bag of damaged clothes, then walked beside Selene to the elevator. On the main floor, inside Selene's townhouse, Procne helped her lie down on one of the loveseats then made her a pot of chamomile tea.

Selene sat up, held her teacup in the air, and closed her eyes. She opened them and said, "I hate to ask this, but would you and Philomela have time after work to stop by and help me with a Ouija Board?"

"Ouija Board?" Procne giggled with surprise. "Why in the world do you want to use one of those stupid things?"

"Well, I thought with Philomela's hint of second-sight we might find the hit-and-run driver. I think he or she should be made aware of what he did and be reprimanded."

"Okay, I'll ask her."

"You see, Procne." Selene hesitated before continuing. "I have a nagging feeling I was targeted."

"Targeted?" The idea stunned Procne. "You think someone purposely hit you then left you lying injured on the road?" Selene nodded and Procne said, "And you have no idea who did it."

Selene lowered her eyes and shook her head.

CHAPTER 23

Thursday Mid-Afternoon:

Philomela watched Sarah sit on the chair beside the cash counter and listened to her criticize two young women trying on coats. The doorbell tingled and Philomela turned. Procne entered the shop and hurried over to her sister.

"Selene's okay. She suffered only a slight concussion and minor cuts and bruises."

"That's good to know." Philomela was relieved to know Selene had suffered no serious injuries.

"What's wrong with Selene?" Sarah's voice squeaked from the chair near the cash counter.

Procne rolled her eyes at her sister but said nothing.

Pleased that Sarah's critical attention had shifted from the two customers trying on coats, Philomela watched her stand up and make her way to Procne.

"I asked you a question, Procne. Why don't you answer me?"

"Selene was knocked down by a hit-and-run driver," Procne politely said. "She was in emergency at the hospital, but I picked her up and drove her home."

Sarah and the other customers in the shop had not heard about the accident. Curious, they gathered around Procne and pumped her with questions. She gave them a superficial account, describing the car as dark and the cuts and scrapes on the victim's arm as needing a small bandage. She did not mention Selene's suspicion of being targeted. She concluded by saying, "Thank goodness, Selene will be able to model at the fashion show on Saturday afternoon."

Almost as if trying to help Procne for her good deed, everyone purchased something and left carrying a rusty-orange bag. Everyone except Sarah. She hung around and, like a snake waiting to strike, watched Philomela. Finally, apparently finding the object of her attention boring, she wandered to the door and, without making any purchases, went outside.

"I thought she'd never go," Philomela said. "She watched me like a hawk ready to pounce on my every movement. I could have murdered her."

"Not a bad idea." Procne giggled then collected herself. "I really didn't mean that. She's an awful pain in the neck but I don't wish her any harm. She never buys anything, but who knows? Maybe she can't afford to." Procne's head moved from side to side. "I must tell you something that could be important. Selene doesn't think she was in the wrong place at the wrong time. She thinks she was targeted."

"Targeted?" Philomela stared at her sister. "Good grief. Why would anyone purposely want to hurt her?" Then she remembered the website and the emails. Could the money grubbing tactics have angered a client into trying to put the psychic out of commission?

"Why indeed?" Procne asked. "She's not mean, abrasive, or money hungry. All she does is help people."

Philomela silently grappled with the disturbing news.

An accident was one thing, but being targeted was another. It was puzzling. "Hurting Selene makes no sense. Breaking into the dress shop and messing up the office makes no sense. For that matter, murdering Maxine Springer also makes no sense. This whole thing is becoming more and more illogical"

"What's happening to my beautiful town?" Procne threw up her hands and flopped on Sarah's recently vacated chair. "Saltaire is being overrun by crazies. Speaking of crazy—Selene requested that after work you do the Ouija Board thing with her. She says she can't envision anything for herself, but you, with your hint of second sight, might make the Ouija Board answer questions correctly. She hopes to find a clue about the driver of the hit-and-run car."

"Ouija Boards make me nervous. I don't understand how they work. I've read that they might attract malevolent spirits."

"Will you do it for Selene?"

"Yes, of course I will."

CHAPTER 24

Thursday Mid-Afternoon:

The bell above the door tingled and, to Philomela's surprise, a tall man entered the shop. He hesitated a few seconds and looked around, as if uncomfortable in a place selling ladies wear. The tinge of white at his temples suggested age-related wisdom but, as he moved forward, his stride registered youthful exuberance. Philomela peripherally saw her sister stand tall and tightly tuck in her tummy. Looking more closely at Procne, she saw her face flush and her right hand fly to her chest and rest over her heart.

The man walked toward them and stopped. He smiled pleasantly. "Good afternoon, ladies. I hope all is well with you."

Procne mutely nodded her head.

Her sister's silence prompted Philomela to take the initiative to respond. "We're fine, thanks. How about you?"

"The same. I had coffee in the History Cafe this morning, and Jean Greenfield told me that Procne's neighbor had been injured in a hit-and-run accident."

"Selene Hamilton," Procne said, finding her voice. "She was taken to emergency. She had a slight concussion and a few bruises and scratches, but otherwise she's okay. I picked her up at the hospital and brought her home a short while ago."

"That was good of you." He nodded at Procne then looked at her with apparent sympathy. "You've coped with more than your fair share of trouble this week."

The flush on her face deepened and she glanced at Philomela as if seeking refuge. "Thank goodness my sister's here. She's a big help."

"I'm Simon Fraser." He extended his right hand to Philomela. "We haven't formally met."

"I'm Philomela Nightingale. I saw you briefly Tuesday morning on the museum stairs." She accepted his hand and was pleased to feel its pleasant firmness. "As curator of the museum, you've coped with a lot, too. You must be distraught about what happened there. Is the museum still closed?"

"Yes. But we plan to reopen on Friday. Tomorrow morning."

"Do you know if the police have any suspects?" Philomela asked.

"Not that I've been told." He shook his head, his jaw clenched, and his eyebrows knit together. His lips spit out, "It was a vile thing to do."

Philomela felt empathy for his passion, but she tried to mellow it by shifting the conversation back to when Maxine was still alive. "Procne tells me that Maxine was a helpful member of the museum board, but not one of the directors."

"She was a valuable member, always coming up with creative yet practical ideas. She was a positive force, and we'll miss her greatly." He gave a soft, reflective sigh that contrasted sharply with the intent of his next words.

"I hope her killer is caught and gets his just rewards." His voice echoed eerily around the room.

Procne studied him, apparently surprised at his words. Then she said, "Simon, with Maxine gone, her dress shops are up in the air. I might have to take a leave of absence as a Monday museum volunteer and work here full time—until things are sorted out. Sheila and I are continuing with the fashion show on Saturday, and we intend to dedicate it to Maxine. Right now, I can't make any long term plans. It'll depend on Maxine's estate and what Melvin decides to do with the shops. Who knows if he'll keep or sell them?"

Simon nodded as if pondering her words. "Melvin and I had a drink together late yesterday afternoon. He said Ken Swindell will read the will after Maxine's relatives arrive. The two dress shops, as we all know, were Maxine's passion, not his. She did the everyday accounting but he did the income tax for her. Nothing will be decided until after the reading of the will."

"Sheila wanted to buy Maxine's shops," Procne said. "I heard her ask Maxine about it on more than one occasion. I assume she'd still like to purchase them, though I'm not sure if her finances would warrant buying both."

"Melvin told me most of Maxine's relatives should be here tonight. That means the will might be read in a day or two. Then everyone will know where they stand."

Listening to Simon, Philomela warmed to him. He seemed smart, practical, yet sincere and sympathetic. She could see why Procne held him in high regard. But did her regard for him go beyond admiration? Was she physically attracted to him? That possibility allowed Philomela to brave a question. "Simon," she said, "did you know that Selene suspects the hit-and-run was not an accident? That she was targeted?"

Simon's brow furrowed. "Is she serious?"

"Yeah, very serious." Procne, not Philomela, replied.

"I hope she's wrong. An accidental hit and run is bad enough. A premeditated hit and run is a murder attempt." His face paled. "Do you think Selene's car accident could be related to Maxine's murder?"

The sisters each responded with a head shake and a shoulder shrug.

"I hope one of our museum volunteers isn't involved with all this." As if suddenly feeling weak, he sat down on the chair by the cash counter.

Philomela felt a sudden concern for him. "Simon, are you feeling all right?"

"I'm fine. It's been a bad week, that's all. Murder, museum closing, now hit and run. Topping everything else—today, I had to admit my wife to hospital."

Seeing an expression of what seemed despair cross his face, Philomela felt at a loss for words. Then, trying to be optimistic, she said, "I hope your wife will soon be better."

He shook his head. "I doubt she'll ever live at home again."

Philomela was surprised because she had never heard anyone mention anything about Simon's wife. She knew it was none of her business, but she could not leave the conversation hanging. "Is it cancer?" she asked.

"No, it's early onset Alzheimer's. Angelina is very young to develop it, but the disease runs in her family. We had hoped she'd escape it." The palm of his left hand cupped his chin and his fingers smoothed the lower part of his face. His hand dropped to his side and he rose to his feet. "I didn't intend to burden you two ladies with my problems. I just wanted to make sure you're okay."

"We're okay," Procne said. "And we appreciate your concern. If I can do anything to help with Angelina, please ask."

He smiled at her, and Philomela thought his expression registered more than appreciation. Affection perhaps? Or was her imagination running rampant again?

"Thanks for the offer, Procne. If something comes up and I need help, you'll hear from me. Let me know about your volunteering." He stood up and gave them a wan smile. Then, with a goodbye wave, he turned and walked out of the shop.

Procne flopped into the chair he had just vacated. "What a bummer," she said. "On top of everything else, he's worried that a volunteer might be guilty of murder. I feel sick for him. During the past year, ill health prevented his wife from helping at the museum and made it difficult for her to attended social functions involving board members and volunteers. I haven't seen her for at least six months. Her health problems must have accelerated quickly. Poor Simon. Poor Angelina. I don't know how long she's actually had Alzheimer's."

"Probably for quite a while. How old is Simon?"

"I honestly don't know."

"I'd guess him to be in his early fifties," Philomela said. "His wife is probably close to the same age."

"When Selene and I were leaving emergency, I saw Simon go into the main entrance of the hospital. But I didn't see Angelina. She must have already gone inside."

"That illness is dreadful for both family and patient. It's worse when the afflicted one is relatively young." It flitted through Philomela's mind that not too many years ago she had considered the fifties as being old. Now she figured anyone in their fifties as being young.

Maxine was in that age bracket. So was Angelina. And so, heaven forbid, was she.

CHAPTER 25

Late Thursday Afternoon:

It was five-thirty-five when the sisters entered the open-air vestibule. Philomela watched Procne knock on Selene's door, insert the key, and open it.

"Anyone home?" Procne called.

"Hello." Selene's voice floated down the hall to the front entrance. "I'm in the living room."

Philomela followed her sister and saw Selene reclining on a loveseat. Other than a bandaged arm she looked quite perky.

"How are you feeling?" Philomela asked.

"Quite refreshed. I slept most of the afternoon."

"Good. Sleep helps the healing process."

"Did Procne ask if you'd be willing to use the Ouija Board with me?"

"She did. And I am."

"Some people think Ouija Boards are dangerous. They think they open the subconscious to playful or hostile spirits."

"Yes, I've read that," Philomela said.

"Knowing the risk, are you still willing?"

Philomela knew that a few Christian societies placed Ouija Boards on their forbidden list, due to the risk of attracting evil spirits. But she didn't know if other religions followed similar policies. It had crossed her mind that some religious leaders might discourage their followers from trying to communicate directly with a higher source because it would eliminate the leader's important position as an intermediary. If Selene was an honest shaman, there should be no problems and no risks with the Ouija Board. If she was a money grubbing charlatan, well, who knew what might happen?

"I'm willing to take the risk," Philomela said.

"While you two muck around with the Ouija Board, I'll make herb tea," Procne said.

Selene rose from the loveseat and both her guests followed her to the spare bedroom. Entering the room, Philomela looked around and noticed a laptop computer sitting on a small table. It was not turned on. She watched Selene open the door of a closet, reach up to a high shelf, and bring out a box. She set the box on the bed, opened it, and took out a wooden board and a heart-shaped piece of wood with a hole near the bottom.

"The name Ouija is based on 'yes' in French and German—Oui and Ja." Selene set the board on a low bench at the foot of the bed and held up the heart-shaped piece of wood. "This is the planchette." She set it on the bench beside the board and looked at Philomela. "Do you mind if we sit on the floor?"

"That's fine with me."

Procne, who stood near the door, cleared her throat. "While you two play with Oui and Ja, I'll go and make some tea. Have fun." She left the bedroom and walked toward the kitchen.

Selene and Philomela each sat in a semi-lotus position on the carpet at opposite sides of the bench. Like two meditating Buddhas, they lowered their eyes then looked up at each other and nodded. Gently, they placed their fingertips on top of the planchette.

A set of twenty-four letters, from A to Z, and a set of ten numbers, from 0 to 9, curved along the middle of the board. At the left top of the board was a large "Yes." On the top right was a large "No."

Selene said a short prayer requesting help and guidance. Then she asked, "Is anyone there?"

The planchette immediately responded by moving toward the top of the board and angling left. It's pointy end stopped on "Yes."

Selene cleared her throat. "Did someone try to kill me this morning?"

The planchette moved around the perimeter of the board, angled left and again stopped on "Yes."

"Do I know the person who tried to kill me?"

The planchette did another walkabout and made another stop on "Yes."

"Could you pin-point the person?"

The planchette moved to the middle of the board and sat there.

"My question was too vague," Selene said. "I'll try another. What color is the driver's car?"

The planchette moved so the hole in its base circled B then R then I then T then I then S then H then R then A then C then I then N then G. It circled around the board then sat briefly on G then R then E. And there it stopped.

"That's not a color," Selene said. "What is the name of the person who murdered Maxine?"

The planchette moved to S then suddenly started racing around the board like a whirling dervish. It continued its crazy dance until Selene lifted her fingers high in the air. She leaned away from the planchette as if fearing it might rise up and strike her.

"Either you and I aren't concentrating or an unwanted presence has taken over," she said. "We have to quit. Too bad we didn't receive a car color or the murderer's name."

"It gave us a color," Philomela said.

Selene looked at her and raised her eyebrows. "It did?"

"It spelled British Racing Gre. Because of Brent's interest in Jaguar cars, I know about British Racing Green. The color is a rich shade of dark green."

"Oh." Selene's mouth and eyes formed three circles. "That's helpful. All we have to do now is find someone who has a green car."

"A dark green car," Philomela corrected. She gazed pensively down at the letters on the board. "I wish more letters had been shown before whatever took over the planchette. It indicated only one letter of the murderer's name. The name starts with S."

"S." Selene's tongue lingered between her teeth. Then she asked, "Is S the first letter of a first name, a second name, or a surname?"

At that moment, Procne, carrying a tray with three cups of tea, entered the room. She stopped inside the door and gazed at the two women sitting on the floor with hands on their laps and the planchette sitting motionless on the Ouija Board.

She giggled. "Did Ouija tell you a bunch of nonsense?"

"Not really." Philomela rose to her feet and stretched. "The Ouija Board gave us a couple of clues. The hit-and-run car is a rich shade of dark green. The name of Maxine's murderer starts with the letter S."

"Whose name, besides mine, starts with S?" Selene asked.

"Simon Fraser," Procne replied. "Shaun O'Reilly.

Sheila Trust. Sarah Winston. Springers—Maxine and Melvin. Lots of people."

Selene's mouth formed a reverse crescent and her head slowly moved from side to side. "I can't believe any of those people would commit murder. Procne, do you know anyone who drives a green car?"

Procne shrugged. "There are a jillion green cars in Saltaire."

"Do any of the people you mentioned drive one?' Philomela asked.

"Umm…Shaun drives a red sports car. Simon drives a dark blue SUV, Maxine Springer's car was a white BMW, Melvin's is a black Range Rover, and Sarah drove a bright green Chevrolet before she lost her license five months ago. Sheila often drives the dress shops' white van, and Tom Trust—yikes, Tom drives a green Cadillac."

"Dark green?" Philomela asked.

"Not really," Procne replied. "It's a medium shade of green."

Selene got up from the floor and put the Ouija Board and planchette inside the box. She carefully closed the lid, placed the box on the top shelf in the closet, and closed the closet door. "Out of sight, out of mind." She walked to the bed and slumped down on it.

"You're still recuperating from your accident," Philomela said. "Drink your tea. You need nourishment and more rest."

"You may be right." Selene smiled at her and took a teacup from the tray. "Thanks, Procne. And, Philomela, thanks for the Ouija help, even though we didn't get the driver's actual identity."

"You're welcome. It was worth a try." Philomela took one of the cups from Procne's tray and sipped the warm liquid.

"How about some comfort food?" Procne asked. "A bowl of Mr. Campbell's tomato soup?"

"Sounds good," Philomela said. And Selene agreed.

Several minutes later all three sat at Selene's round table and enjoyed soup, celery sticks, cheese, and crackers. When the bowls were empty, Procne and Philomela cleaned up the dishes. Just as they finished, the doorbell rang.

"Who can that be?" Procne hurried to the door and opened it.

"Procne. What are you doing here?" Philomela recognized Shaun's voice.

"I'm looking after Selene."

"I was at the History Cafe. Jean said Selene was struck by a car. Is it true?"

"Yeah, it's true. A hit-and-run driver. But she's fine. Just tired."

"May I see her?"

"She's sitting at her dining room table."

Philomela stood up from the table. "Hello, Shaun. Please make your visit short. Selene needs rest."

Shaun ignored her and hurried over to Selene. He pulled a chair close to her and sat down. "Selene, are you okay?"

"I'm fine, Shaun. A bit shaken, that's all."

"Should you be in hospital?"

"I was there. They discharged me."

Listening to them, Philomela soliloquized mutely. *Selene doesn't need him pestering her. He means well, but he doesn't understand that people who have suffered shock need rest, quiet, and sleep, not stimulating conversation.* She moved over to Procne who was closing the dishwasher door. "If you have things to do," she whispered, "go ahead. I'll stay until he leaves."

Procne nodded, told Selene to phone if she needed

anything, and left. Philomela wiped down the kitchen counter and listened to Shaun question Selene about the accident. Finally, he kissed her on the mouth, offered to do anything he could to help her, and headed for the door. Philomela walked beside him.

"Does anyone know who hit Selene?" he asked.

Philomela shook her head. "Not so far."

As soon as the door closed behind him, Philomela returned to Selene, who admitted to feeling tired. They went to her bedroom, and Philomela put the phone on her bedside table. "Call Procne's number if any problem arises. We'll be here in five seconds."

In the outdoor vestibule Philomela walked past the door to Sheila and Tom Trust's townhouse. She wondered if Sheila should be informed about Selene's recovery from the accident. She decided that tomorrow would be soon enough.

Suddenly, two weird thoughts came to mind. Had Selene purposely hijacked the planchette because the answers were not the ones she wanted revealed? If the murderer's name started with S, Selene was a definite suspect. She may have graduated from money grubbing to murder. Or had the Ouija Board's effort been a partial failure because Selene, feeling unwell, had been unable to concentrate for a long enough period of time?

Inside her sister's townhouse, Philomela tried to be uplifting. "Procne, Simon Fraser's name starts with S, but I doubt he killed Maxine. He seems like a very nice man."

"He is." Procne, already in her pajamas, pointed to a blinking red light on the landline. "Look, someone phoned while we were out. I better check for messages."

"It might be the police." Philomela gave a quirky smile. "They probably want you to remember something unimportant."

Procne shook her head and smiled weakly. She picked up the phone and listened to the message. Furrows deepened between her eyebrows and her nose crinkled in puzzlement. Placing the phone back on its charger she stared at her sister. "That message was from Poke and Swindell law firm. At ten tomorrow morning they want me to attend the reading of Maxine's will."

Philomela frowned. "What a strange request."

"Why do they want me there?" Procne asked

Philomela raised her eyebrows then grinned. "Perhaps Maxine left you a new dress because you were such a good employee."

Procne looked sideways at her sister and shook her head. "I suppose that's as good a reason as any."

"Maxine was a clever lady. Doubtless her 'will' will be short and to the point. It will say—'Being of sound mind, I spent all my money.'" Philomela grinned again.

Procne rolled her eyes.

"What we should do now," Philomela said, "is work on the commentary for the fashion show. I have copious notes."

"Okay. With several references to the person being memorialized."

Later that evening, before climbing into bed, Philomela checked her iPad for messages. Brent's message was clear and to the point—the mountain weather was good and tomorrow would be his last day of heliskiing. Saturday he and John would drive home. He looked forward to picking her up at the airport on Sunday evening.

The second message with its violet print was not so clear.

Dear Rae:
I just returned from Greece after meeting with a dozen brilliant mediums, clairvoyants, and shamans. Your

name came up in one of our group visions, and I was told to inform you that the Cerulean Full Moon on Saturday night will be an important event in your life.

If you ask for our help, you will experience a rebirth that will allow you to fulfill your destiny. Come on now, Rae, do the right thing and attain everything you ever dreamed of having.

Much love, Selene.

Following the message was a line in blue print: *Click here to benefit from the Cerulean Full Moon on Saturday.*

She clicked the link. Up came a new message: *Receive a three month electronic course in Tarot reading, Numerology, and Astrology plus three discs of relaxing, meditational music for the bargain price of only $299.00.*

Philomela shook her head. She could buy books on those subjects for less money than that.

There was no question—Selene was an out and out liar. She had been here in Saltaire all week, even in hospital, yet she claimed to have just returned from Greece. Philomela re-read the message and felt her abdominal muscles contract.

Was she missing something?

CHAPTER 26

Friday Morning:

At breakfast, Philomela made no mention to her sister of the weird correspondence she was having with her email pal. Instead, she sat on the stool at the breakfast counter and listened to Procne chatter like a magpie about the commentary they had written for the upcoming fashion-show.

A short time later, while putting dirty dishes in the dishwasher, Procne voiced her concerns about the reading of Maxine's will—why had she been asked to attend and what could she possibly contribute to the reading? She then swished a mop over the kitchen floor and stated in detail the sundry tasks Philomela should perform while being in control of Whimsical Woman.

At nine-twenty, Procne led the way to the open-air vestibule. Philomela glanced at Selene's door, almost expecting the woman to magically appear, but her door remained closed. However, the door between Procne's and Selene's opened. A man exited and smiled at them. Philomela knew he looked familiar but couldn't remember why.

"G'morning, ladies," he said. "How are you today?"

"Very well," they replied in unison. Grinning at each other, they acknowledged being on the same wave length.

The man locked his door then looked questioningly at them. "Is it raining out there?"

"No," Procne replied. "It's just a Scotch mist."

"The type of Scotch that comes from a bottle?"

Procne gazed at him with mock innocence. "Tom, do you think single malt whiskey pours down from the sky?"

His smile extended from ear to ear. "That's my greatest wish. What a way to obtain my favorite libation!"

At this point, Philomela recalled why he looked familiar. She had seen him at the Fireside Pizza restaurant on Sunday evening. He and his wife had been with Maxine and Melvin Springer.

"Is Sheila still here?" Procne asked.

"She's long gone. Her boss's death plus the fashion-show have turned her into more of a workaholic than she was before." He gazed sympathetically at Procne. "That was a terrible thing—what happened to Maxine. Are you managing okay?"

"As well as can be expected. I'm lucky my sister is here. She's very supportive."

Tom stepped toward Philomela and extended his right hand. "I'm Tom Trust."

"Hi, Tom. I'm Philomela Nightingale." She shook his hand.

"Oh I'm sorry," Procne lamented. "I forgot you two hadn't met."

With a wave of his hand, Tom brushed Procne's apology aside. "I saw Basil yesterday. He's badly shaken."

"You know that he found Maxine's body." Procne shuddered and closed her eyes.

"Yes." Tom seemed momentarily to drift off in another world. Then he said matter-of-factly, "The murder and the hit-and-run won't do Saltaire's real estate market any good. Prospective buyers will think the town is a haven for criminals."

"Surely not." Philomela studied him, wondering if his assessment of the real estate situation was correct. Deciding it might be, she put a positive spin on it by ignoring the hit-and-run accident. "There was only one murder," she said. "And it seems to have been premeditated. There likely won't be any more."

"Yeah. It would be much worse if a serial killer was on the loose. Well, I better shake a leg. I have to meet a client and give him a price estimate on his house." He moved to the top of the stairway. "Nice meeting you, Philomela.

Philomela said goodbye and watched him descend the steps toward the parkade. She then followed Procne out of the open-air vestibule. Walking on the interlocking brick sidewalk, Philomela saw a green car ease up the driveway from the underground parking area. As it reached the street she turned to her sister.

"Is that Tom," she asked.

"Yeah. He impresses clients with his fancy Cadillac."

"A green car. Not dark enough to be British Racing Green. I wonder if Tom's middle name starts with the letter, S."

"I don't know," Procne said. "But I do know he's very knowledgeable about real estate. We're lucky to have him as president of our strata council."

"He's also very personable. And that's an asset for any salesman. In a lot of ways he's similar to Shaun."

"He and Sheila are completely different," Procne said. "She's energetic and high strung. He's laid back and relaxed."

"An example of opposites attracting?"

"I suppose so. But both are hard workers, and they get on well together."

As they approached the History Café, Procne stopped walking and gazed at her sister. "I wonder if Sheila will offer to buy both dress shops from Melvin Springer."

"Could she afford to buy both of them?" Philomela asked.

"It would depend on the price. She and Tom have no children to support, so their pockets probably jingle with more loose change than those who have kids. If she does buy the shops, I wonder if she would keep me on as a saleslady."

"She probably would."

Opening the door of the History Café, Philomela was surprised at how busy it was. Every chair and stool was occupied. Jean Greenfield gave them a hearty welcome, making Philomela feel like a favorite, long-lost cousin. The aromas of freshly ground coffee and steaming soups assailed her nostrils and made her mouth salivate. Jean's culinary expertise and her genial personality were on full display.

Leaning over the counter, Jean gazed with a serious expression at Procne. "Have you heard anything new from the police?"

"Nothing," Procne replied. "How about you?"

"Same," she said in a low voice. "But I have to confess—all this distressing news has been good for me. The cafe is constantly filled with curiosity seekers. They drink lots of tea and coffee and eat soup and sandwiches until they come out their ears. I've never been so busy."

"Your customers are the silver lining of murder's dark cloud," Philomela said.

Jean smiled, nodded, and then in a loud, cheery voice asked, "What can I get you two girls?"

"Girls?" Philomela laughed merrily. "Thank you for that."

"Two small coffees, please," Procne said. "For here."

Holding her full coffee mug, Philomela looked around the room and saw two people get up from a small table. She hurried over and claimed occupancy before anyone else could do so. She sat down on one of the empty chairs, watched her sister add cream and honey to her coffee then carry the doctored brew to the table. Procne eased onto the empty chair and looked around the room.

"I don't see anyone I know," she said. She took a sip of hot liquid then, gazing at her sister, reiterated details about caring for the dress shop. "You remember where the float is?" she asked. Philomela nodded. "Don't worry about the vacuuming—it can wait." Philomela nodded again. Then Procne smiled at her older sister and confessed, "I sure appreciate having you look after the shop while I attend the reading of the will. If Maxine leaves me a new dress, I promise to let you wear it."

"What a fit that would be—your miniskirt hitting my calves and your waistline drooping around my hips."

Procne chuckled and glanced at a couple of nearby customers. "I still don't understand why I have to attend the reading."

"Perhaps you'll only receive a small scarf instead of a new dress." Philomela glanced at her wristwatch. "If I want to open the shop on time, I'd better get moving." She drained her coffee mug, got up from her chair, and smiled at her sister. "Good luck."

With a goodbye wave to Jean, Philomela opened the door and went outside. She hurried along the interlocking brick sidewalk and paused at the shop called Shoe Steps. The window display had been changed, and she saw a pair of boots that caught her fancy. *Later*, she thought, *I might come and try them on.*

At Whimsical Woman she unlocked the door, went inside, and relocked the door. She wandered to the small office at the back of the shop and hung her coat on the same clothes rack she had hidden behind while Basil opened drawers of the filing cabinet. She walked over to the smallest dressing room, lifted a corner of the carpet, and retrieved the envelope containing the float. At the cash counter, she opened the envelope, counted the money, and neatly placed coins and bills in the appropriate compartments. Next she returned to the office, dragged out the vacuum cleaner, and took it to the front of the shop. Though Procne had said vacuuming wasn't necessary, Philomela wanted to help in any way she could. A flick of the switch brought forth a whirring sound, and the machine proceeded to suck up a few odds and sods from the all-purpose carpet.

A loud banging startled her. She fumbled with the switch and managed to turn off the noisy machine. The banging continued and she hurried toward the door. Through the window she saw a man wearing a raincoat and fedora. He continued to bang on the door and, for a couple of seconds, she hesitated. His violence worried her. Was it safe to let him in? Then, with a feeling of apprehension, she bravely unlocked and opened the door.

"Where's Procne?"

Annoyed first with his noisy banging and now with his impolite greeting, she forgot her initial apprehension. "At a meeting," she snapped.

He glanced down at the vacuum cleaner then up at her face. "Are you the cleaning lady?"

"No." She started to close the door and then recognized the features under the fedora. With a sudden flash of sympathy she said in a softer tone of voice, "I'm Philomela Nightingale, Procne's sister. She should be back in an hour or so."

"Oh."

"I'm sorry for your loss, Mr. Springer. I was at the museum when Maxine was found."

Appearing less angry, he studied her. "Maxine didn't deserve such a death. She was a good person. It shouldn't have happened."

"I agree. It shouldn't have happened. I'll tell Procne you came to see her." She watched him turn and walk in the direction of the History Cafe. A wave of sympathy for him passed through her.

Understandably, he was distraught and depressed. Losing a life partner so suddenly and in such a horrid manner could send any loved one over the edge. Now, on top of everything else, he'd have to contend with the reading of Maxine's will. No wonder he had spoken abruptly and banged the door so rudely.

"Good grief," she murmured aloud. "I didn't tell Melvin that Procne was at Poke and Swindell's law office." She wondered if he knew Procne had been invited to attend the reading of Maxine's will. Perhaps he had intended to walk with Procne to the lawyer's office.

With the will foremost in her mind, Philomela once again wondered why her sister should attend its reading. Could the reason really be that Maxine's bequests included a dress or a scarf for Procne?

CHAPTER 27

Friday Morning continued:

Procne strolled from the chatter and warmth of the History Cafe into the quiet and cool of the outdoors. She noted the yellow crime tape had been removed from the stairway to the museum, and then she entered the peaceful dignity of Poke and Swindell law office. A young receptionist greeted her. Procne explained her reason for being in the office and the receptionist indicated a stately armchair. Seeing no one else in the reception area, Procne sat down, picked up a business magazine, and perused its glossy pages. A few minutes later, the front door opened. She looked up and watched Melvin Springer stride into the room.

He glanced around, stopped in his tracks, and stared at her. "What are you doing here?"

She shrugged. "I haven't a clue. I was told to come to the reading of Maxine's will."

"Whatever for?" Not waiting for an answer, he stepped closer and glared at her. "I went to the dress shop to see you."

"Really? What for?"

"Not important." He marched directly to an inside door.

"You can't go in there," the receptionist cried. She leaped to her feet and ran behind him. Ignoring her effort to stop him, he opened the door and disappeared. "Oh no," the receptionist wailed. She threw up her arms in a futile gesture, bit her lower lip, and returned to her desk. She slumped into the chair behind it.

Surprised at Melvin's rudeness, Procne sympathized with the young girl. She hoped her boss, the lawyer, would not vent his anger on the poor girl for being unable to announce that Melvin was entering his private domain. The front door again opened and Procne saw Sheila Trust enter the room. Her eyes almost jumped out of their sockets as she looked at Procne.

"What are you doing here?" Sheila hissed.

"I don't know," Procne replied. "Why are you here?"

"You tell me and we'll both know." Sheila plunked her slim buttocks on a chair beside Procne and muttered, "This is all very strange."

Before Procne could reply, the main door again opened and a threesome, consisting of two women and one man, walked inside. The man strode up to the reception, and Procne heard him say they were Maxine's brother and sisters. The receptionist nodded, sadly expressed sympathy, and explained that Mr. Swindell would be with them in a moment. She suggested they take a seat. Before they could do so, the door to the inner sanctum opened and the lawyer himself stepped into the reception area. His body was rotund, his eyes sparkled, and when he spoke his voice was deep. "Good morning, everyone."

"Good morning," Procne said.

She gazed at the portly gentleman and wondered if Melvin was still inside the private office. Though she had not officially met the lawyer, she had often seen him about town.

"I'm Ken Swindell," he said, accentuating the last syllable of his name. He walked to each client in turn, shook their hands, and asked their names. "Please come into the boardroom," he said.

All five followed him to another door. Melvin Springer appeared and lagged behind them. Inside the boardroom, the lawyer waved his right hand toward a long, rectangular table and invited them to sit down.

Maxine's husband sat down at the foot of the table, her brother sat at one side of him, her two sisters sat at his other side. Sheila sat beside the brother and Procne sat beside Sheila. Mr. Swindell stood at the head of the table. He nodded at the empty chair beside Maxine's two sisters and stated the obvious. "We're missing one person."

Wondering who was supposed to fill the vacant chair across from her, Procne looked straight ahead. She admired red, black, and white paintings on the wall. The paintings had been done by First Nation artists and the scenes consisted of mountains, water, trees, birds, fish, and moons. In the misty backgrounds, shady spirits floated and their other-worldliness reminded her of Maxine. Glancing beside and behind her chair, Procne saw more paintings strategically hanging on the other three walls. Though colorful and pretty, the pictures fell to the back of her mind as the missing person entered the room. She breathed in deeply and wondered why he was here.

Mr. Swindell greeted the newcomer warmly then introduced him to the others. The newcomer settled in the vacant chair beside Maxine's sisters and gazed across the table at Procne. Mr. Swindell sat down and, facing Melvin Springer, picked up a glass pitcher from the table and offered water to the assembled group. There were no takers, so he poured water into a glass and took a sip himself. After setting down the glass, he opened a gray folder and studied it for a moment. Then he looked up and cleared his throat.

"Saddened though we are by Maxine Springer's untimely death, I thank all of you for coming on such short notice. I will now read Mrs. Springer's Last Will and Testament." He picked up his glass, took another sip, and cleared his throat. His deep voice rose and fell with the rhythm of a funeral dirge as he read the will.

"I, Maxine Springer, residing in the town of Saltaire in the province of British Columbia, being of sound mind, do hereby make, publish, and declare this to be my Last Will and Testament and do revoke any and all other wills and codicils made by me.

"Article 1.

"I direct payment of debts and funeral expenses to the administration of my estate.

"Article 2.

'I give six thousand dollars to the Historical Museum to be used as the curator sees fit.

"Article 3.

"All merchandise and shop equipment of Upscale Garments to be sold for three thousand dollars to Sheila Trust. If she declines this offer the shop's contents should be put for sale on the open market and the monies returned to the estate.

"Article 4.

"All merchandise and shop equipment of Whimsical Woman to be sold to Procne Ellis for the sum of three thousand dollars. If she declines this..."

A giant boulder seemed to clobber Procne's head. The assault confused her thoughts, un-focused her vision, and impaired her hearing. She vaguely heard Mr. Swindell say that each of Maxine's three siblings would receive eight thousand dollars—more than enough to cover their travel expenses to Saltaire. Melvin Springer, Maxine's husband, would receive all her stock-market investments, her white BMW, and her portion of the house.

Procne's thinking cleared a bit, and she thought the gifts to the museum, siblings, and husband made sense. But the bequests to Sheila and herself? Unbelievable. The opportunity to own a dress shop with all its contents for three thousand dollars seemed too good to be true.

Hearing Mr. Swindell say they could finalize the legal contracts today or tomorrow, she looked across the table at the latecomer. Their eyes met and her stomach fluttered. His face expressed as much surprise as she felt—Simon Fraser obviously had not expected a generous gift to the museum, just as she had not expected an offer to buy the dress shop.

Everyone else rose from their chairs and she and Simon slowly followed suit. Was the reading of the will completed? Feeling amazed and confused about Maxine's bequest, she followed Simon to the reception area. He turned and looked at her.

"Well, Procne. It seems you and Sheila will finance Maxine's gift to the Historical Museum."

She failed at first to catch his meaning, then her little gray cells clicked in, and she smiled. "Yes, three thousand from Sheila and three thousand from me would cover the six thousand dollar donation."

"It's a wonderful gift for the museum. And probably not too shabby a deal for you and Sheila. Do you think you'll take advantage of it and buy Whimsical Woman?"

"I'm too stunned to know. I thought Maxine might leave me a silk scarf. But an opportunity to buy the shop? That's too much—it had never entered my mind." She shook her head, still trying to comprehend the startling revelation.

"No matter how good the deal is," Simon said, "owning a dress shop is a big commitment."

"Yes, it is."

Mr. Swindell approached them and asked Procne if she had made a decision regarding the purchase of the shop.

"I'm too stunned to make a decision. I'll have to discuss it with my sister."

"No rush." Mr. Swindell smiled. "After you decide, let me know."

A minute later, she hurried toward the main door, caught up with Sheila and grabbed her arm. "Sheila, what do you think? Will you buy Upscale Garments?"

"Probably. It seems a good deal. The merchandise alone is worth more than three thousand dollars. Wholesale. But I'll have to put a pencil to it."

Procne silently nodded. Though still feeling stunned by Maxine's will, she realized she, too, would have to study the deal with logical business sense. "Besides the merchandise," she said to Sheila, "there are clothing racks, cash counter, shelves, desk, filing cabinets, computer, cash—"

"I know," Sheila interrupted. "And last week Maxine made a few large down-payments on the spring orders for my shop."

Procne lowered her eyes and stopped breathing—already Sheila was referring to Upscale Garments as "my shop." She looked up at her fellow, potential shop owner. "I'll check the recent order forms for Whimsical Woman—if the idiots who broke into the shop didn't take them. When Philomela and I were putting things back to normal, I spotted a few new order forms and some receipts. So I know exactly where they're filed."

"Sounds good," Sheila said. "Let's get together and compare notes—after the fashion show."

They left the law office together then parted company—Sheila to her prospective dress shop and Procne to the stairs leading down to the Historical Museum.

Procne ran quickly down the stairs, curious to know what was happening at the murder scene. It suddenly struck her that she was starting to get as snoopy as her sister.

CHAPTER 28

Later Friday Morning:

Procne cheerily greeted Hamish who sat with official dignity on a stool behind the counter. His dog was nowhere in sight. "Where's Haggis?" she asked.

Hamish smiled and glanced down at the floor. "Haggis is sleeping peacefully on his soft cushion."

"Is everything back to normal?" Procne asked.

"No. We'rre much busierr than norrmal."

"Ironic, isn't it. Curiosity seekers are increasing business in the History Cafe, too. The cliché is dead on— every dark cloud has a silver lining." Aware of having used the expression *dead on*, she grimaced. "Have you seen Basil today?"

"Aye, he opened the place then hurrried to a meeting with a rrealtorr."

"Oh, is he thinking of buying a new house?"

"He didn't say. He's very deprressed. Somehow he blames himself forr Maxine's murrderr. Howeverr, I don't think he plunged the knife into herr."

Procne shuddered. That was a dreadful thought. Obviously, Hamish didn't think Basil was the killer, but it seemed to have crossed his mind. She wondered if Basil really could have done the nasty deed. Could he have left Maxine lying on the sofa and then returned at ten a.m. as if starting a normal day? Was he capable of doing such a terrible thing? And was he a good enough actor to later behave so innocently and so distraughtly? She doubted all three counts. Besides, if he had killed Maxine, surely he would try to put the blame on someone else.

"Does Basil have a suspect?" she asked Hamish.

"Not that he mentioned. The police seem to lack suspects, too."

She felt relieved that Basil wasn't accusing anyone. Maybe that meant he really was innocent.

"The morrning of the murrderr I was walking Haggis and I saw Sarah Winston. We both saw someone running—" He stopped speaking and stood up. Three visitors had entered the museum and were approaching the counter.

Procne stepped aside to let them talk with Hamish. When they moved on and began studying various artifacts, she inched closer to the counter. "Hamish, I have a favor to ask. I have to work at Whimsical Woman on Monday. Could you take my morning shift here as well as your afternoon one? Or should I contact Basil to find a replacement for me?"

"Basil will be here this afterrnoon to lock up. I'll ask him to find someone. If no one is available, I'll do it."

"That's great, Hamish. Thanks ever so much."

She didn't explain her new reason for needing a replacement. Doubtless, he realized that with Maxine gone, Whimsical Woman would have to be tended by someone or else be shut down. She knew Maxine's bequests would become public knowledge soon enough, but at the moment Hamish was in the dark about them. She didn't enlighten him because she had no desire to discuss the dress shop with him or with anyone else until she talked with Philomela.

"Thanks again, Hamish. Toodles." She gave him an airy wave and went out the door. As she started to walk up the stairs a shadow fell ominously on her from above. Nervously, she looked up and saw a gigantic figure moving toward her. Her nervousness turned to pleasure.

"Simon, we meet again," she said.

"Are you still in shock over Maxine's bequest?"

"I am. How about you?"

"The same. I must say the museum will miss her expertise, but her financial gift will be appreciated and put to good use."

"I'll be working at Whimsical Woman on Monday morning. Hamish is going to ask Basil to find a substitute volunteer for me."

"Ah, yes. Looks like your days of helping out in the museum may be over. Too many new responsibilities. Are you still pondering a decision regarding the dress shop?"

"Yes." Suddenly she remembered Simon's personal problems. "How's your wife doing?"

"I visited Angelina early this morning. She told me she wanted to go home, but a minute later she had a cup of tea and forgot all about it. That's the way short term memory loss works."

Procne didn't know what to say. The situation was sad and totally beyond her understanding. "Are there drugs that could help her?" she asked.

"She's been on drugs for a couple of years. They helped at first, but not anymore. The doctor says she now has full-blown Alzheimer's."

"How do they know for sure?"

"The symptoms are memory loss, confusion, hallucination, unable to do simple chores, and failing the clock test."

"Clock test?" Procne had no idea what he was talking about.

"She's unable to draw a circle and put clock numbers in their logical places."

"Oh, Simon, that sounds awful. I'm so sorry."

"There's one good thing. She usually recognizes me."

Usually—that didn't sound good to Procne. But under the circumstances, recognition of him occasionally was better than no recognition at all.

What could be worse? Maxine's complete death or Angelina's partial one?

CHAPTER 29

Friday Noon:

Back at Whimsical Woman, Procne told Philomela about Simon's wife. Then she told her about Maxine's six thousand dollar posthumous gift to the museum. Lastly, she explained the bequests to Sheila and herself.

"Good grief, Procne. Are they good deals for you and Sheila? Or not?"

"I think they're good. But to be sure, I'll have to check invoices and receipts. I'll check the book value of the merchandise on the computer and then do a physical check."

"Buying a shop is completely different from a bequest of a scarf or a dress. It's a real life-changing bombshell. Do you think you'll buy it?"

The doorbell tingled and, instead of replying to Philomela, Procne turned and greeted two potential customers. Within twenty minutes, the potential customers became actual customers then left the shop carrying rusty-orange bags.

Procne edged close to Philomela and resumed their

conversation by answering Philomela's question. "I don't know if I'll buy Whimsical or not. I could do it by cashing in a couple of my guaranteed investment certificates. But before I decide to do that, I want to count all the existing merchandise. I also want to check the pre-payments of spring orders, outstanding bills, etc. How about helping me search the files for all that financial stuff?"

Philomela agreed to help, and they got right to work. Much to their surprise, they discovered receipts for large down-payments to the suppliers of spring orders, making outstanding debts almost negligible. Because of a pre-payment bargain, the rent had been pre-paid until the end of the year. These discoveries made Maxine's bequest even sweeter.

"Imagine working here rent free for a whole year," Procne said. "The more I look into things the more appealing the offer becomes."

"You could do a lot worse."

Procne's reply was cut short by the entrance of three women. Wearing her pleasant saleslady hat, Procne happily attended to their questions and requests. Hearing and feeling her stomach growl, she tried to cover up the sound by clearing her throat and animatedly chatting. The women seemed unaware of her hunger spasms and eventually departed carrying rusty-orange bags.

"Hunger pains are making my stomach grumble," she said to Philomela. At that moment, the bell tingled and she looked over at the door. "Oh no. Look who's here." She groaned softly.

"There are no customers," Philomela whispered, "so she won't be able to criticize or badmouth anyone."

"The police have a suspect for Maxine's murder," Sarah announced.

"Good," Procne said.

"The suspect came to town a few days ago." With a

superior smirk Sarah looked sideways at Philomela.

"My sister?" Procne shook her head. "She has no motive."

"I saw someone run from the museum early Tuesday morning."

Procne nodded. "Yeah, Hamish Macdonald said he also saw a person running away—"

"The person was your sister's size and height. She was wearing a black toque to hide her red hair. I've already told the police." She looked smugly at Philomela. "You're the chief murder suspect."

Philomela's mouth dropped open. A murder suspect? Could she really be the prime suspect? Logic surfaced. "All of us are suspects. Even you, Sarah."

"How dare you accuse me of murder. I haven't murdered anyone."

"Neither have I," Philomela said.

Sarah glared at her for several seconds then turned to Procne. "Unless you get rid of this rude person, I'll not come into this shop again."

"She's my sister. There's no way I'll get rid of her."

Sarah responded by turning around, walking to the door, and slamming it behind her.

"Well," Philomela said, "I was wrong. She found someone to badmouth. Me."

"Philomela, don't ever say you never did me a favor." Procne could hardly speak for laughing. "Let's celebrate."

"May the dear departed never return." Philomela smiled. "I don't wish anyone bad luck, but I suppose Sarah will find someone else to dump on."

"I'm sure she will. To celebrate her departure, I'll give you money to buy sandwiches at Quizno's."

Philomela walked to the nearby eatery and returned with two large sandwiches and two bottles of juice. They sat at the desk in the back office, eating, and were only interrupted twice—a lady who purchased a pair of leggings and a tunic top and another lady who bought a knitted dress. Both customers initially expressed sorrow about Maxine's demise, but when they left the shop carrying the distinctive rusty-orange bags, their goodbyes and demeanors were happy.

"The more I learn about this place the better I like it," Philomela murmured. "It really is a mood lifter. We all lament's Maxine's death, yet the atmosphere she created and the merchandise she purchased helps to cheer everyone."

"She'd like to have those words as a eulogy. There's no question, she did put her heart and soul into this place."

They finished eating lunch and started to check the actual merchandise. Between serving customers, Procne called the name and retail price of physical items, and Philomela, who sat at the computer in the office, typed them in a column. When every item in the shop had been listed, Philomela had the computer add up the column of retail figures. The total was short the book value of one scarf.

"Someone may have forgotten to put the sale in the computer," Procne said. "Or the scarf could have been a victim of shoplifting. The book retail merchandise is worth five thousand, nine-hundred and ninety-nine dollars. And that doesn't include shop equipment, large down-payments on spring merchandise, and the entire year's pre-paid rent."

Philomela subtracted forty percent off the physical total to get an approximate wholesale price for the existing merchandise. "Maxine's asking price is a bargain. Now—to purchase or not to purchase, that is the question."

"I'm tempted. What do you think, Philomela?"

"Maxine's bequest is very generous. If you accept the offer and then decide you don't want to own the dress shop, you can either sell everything intact or have a big blowout closing sale. The decision is entirely up to you, Procne."

"I'm tempted."

"Oh—" Philomela glanced down at her left arm and rubbed her wrist. "My wrist hurts. I didn't sprain it or bang it on anything. It must be arthritis. I guess age is catching up with me." She flicked her hand up and down and in the process noted her wristwatch. "Good grief! It's already three in the afternoon." She followed Procne from the office and once again rubbed her sore wrist.

The doorbell tingled and Philomela watched Grace Devonshire glide into the shop and glance around as if looking for other customers.

"Yesterday," Grace said to Procne, "I bought a black dress and matching coat from Sheila. The dress has a round neck and needs something to brighten it. I decided to check your scarves and jewelry." She held up a bag from Shoe Steps, opened it and brought out a pair of shoes. "I just bought these black pumps at Shoe Steps. They'll look nice with the dress."

"Very smart," Procne said. "They'll certainly enhance a black outfit."

Grace dropped the shoes back in the bag, walked to the jewelry display, and studied the assortment of sparkling accessories. She moved to the scarves and flicked through the soft fabrics, then she returned to the jewelry and tried on several items.

She decided on a brilliant necklace with matching earrings and bracelet and adeptly took her credit card from her purse. "If they don't look good with the dress, may I exchange them?"

"Of course," Procne replied. "But you'll have to present the bill, so hang onto it." When the transaction was completed, Procne nonchalantly handed Grace the rusty-orange bag containing her new jewelry. "How is Basil holding up?" she asked.

"He's a little better today. He thinks he knows who killed Maxine."

"Really?" Procne and Philomela spoke in unison.

"Yes, he suspects Melvin Springer. Melvin hasn't always been an upstanding citizen and Basil wonders if he has reverted to his earlier ways."

Philomela was pensive for a few seconds and then asked, "Did Basil know Melvin in their younger days?"

"No, but some of Melvin's past antics have become common knowledge."

"I recently heard about one from Shaun," Procne said. "And I must say that since Maxine's death, Melvin hasn't been his usual pleasant self."

"Did Basil mention what Melvin had done in his less-than-upstanding past?" Philomela asked.

"He stole text books from university classmates and pushed drugs. He took advantage of a couple of young girls and got them pregnant."

"Mm." Once again Philomela was pensive. Then she asked, "Does Basil have proof of these things?"

"Probably," Grace replied. "He seldom heeds gossip."

"The news about Melvin stealing and pushing drugs is new to me," Philomela said. "And I heard he got one girl pregnant, not two. Maybe all of it is gossip."

"I picked up Selene at the hospital yesterday," Procne said, changing the subject

Philomela saw Grace's knuckles whiten as she clutched her purse in one hand and the two shopping bags in the other.

"Fortunately," Procne blithely continued, "Selene wasn't seriously injured. Car accidents happen, but car drivers who hit pedestrians and purposely leave them are criminals."

Grace stared at her blankly and turned away. "Well, I must be off. I want to stop at the hardware store before going home. I need a new frying pan." She glided to the door and, without a word or a wave of farewell, walked outside and disappeared.

"Is Grace a spendthrift?" Philomela asked.

Procne looked questioningly at her sister. "I've never thought about it. Why do you ask?"

"Money doesn't seem to be a problem for her. She spends it liberally. Do you think she knows about Maxine's loan to Basil?"

"I don't think so."

"What about the Devonshire's financial status? Is Basil a secret gambler? Is Grace a compulsive shopper? I still wonder why Basil borrowed money from Maxine and tried to steal money from the museum's donation box. And why did Selene tell Grace she should get a job in order to pay for her purchases?"

Procne shook her head. "I can't answer any of your questions."

CHAPTER 30

Friday Afternoon:

At five-thirty-five, Procne closed the door of the shop and locked it. Walking beside her sister, she enjoyed the cool temperature and breathed in the fresh crisp air. On the sidewalk outside the townhouse, she saw Shaun and called out to him. He waited for them and shifted the bag he was holding in his right hand to his left hand.

"Hello, sisters. How're you doing?

"Pretty well," Procne replied. "How about you?"

"The same. I've been grocery shopping. Have you heard anything more about the murder?"

Procne shook her head. "Nothing."

"I suppose the police are doing the best they can. So far clues seem to be lacking. I wish I could help them."

"Me too," Procne said.

Shaun shifted his bag of groceries back from one hand to the other. "I suppose the police will keep mum until they have a definite suspect."

"Probably." Procne glanced at the bag he was carrying. "That bag looks heavy. Why don't you put your groceries away then come to my place for a pre-dinner drink?"

Shaun accepted with alacrity. Fifteen minutes later he was ensconced on a sofa, sipping the Scotch and water Procne had given him. He seemed his usual self—a gallant and light-hearted charmer.

"This is the life," he said. "A glass of Scotch and the company of two charming women." He smiled at the two sisters and sipped his drink. "I met with three investors in the city of Victoria this morning. They're well-heeled, sophisticated, and know what they're doing. I'm happy to say they were impressed with my investment strategies. All in all it was an excellent meeting."

"That's wonderful, Shaun." Procne sipped her red wine, and Philomela passed him a bowl of potato chips.

He picked up a few chips and continued his story. "I bought them lunch at the Union Club. I don't use that club as much as I should. It's elegant, quiet, a good place to discuss business deals." He popped a chip into his mouth.

"Do you work much at home?" Philomela asked. This was the first time she spoke since running into Shaun.

"I do. Computers make it easy."

"You must be a real computer nerd."

"Not at all." He smiled modestly. "But like most of my peers I'm certainly computer literate."

"I do emails." Procne grinned. "And I run the cash register. That's how nerdy I am. And I'm almost one of your peers."

Shaun laughed. "You're younger and you underestimate yourself. What about you, Philomela?"

"I use computers to compile my magazine. And I use google to obtain information—some of which occasionally is unreliable. It's amazing how encyclopedias have become a thing of the past. They're now such dinosaurs that even secondhand books stores don't want them."

"Do you still use paper dictionaries?" Shaun asked.

"I do." Philomela smiled. "But going back to the internet—I have a question for you. Is it possible that a person could put up a website using someone else's name?"

He studied her as if deep in thought. "It's unlikely," he finally said. "Did you have something specific in mind?"

"Not really," Philomela replied. "I just wondered."

Shaun watched her a minute and then turned to Procne. "How's the fashion-show coming along?"

"Things are under control." And she described the bequests Maxine left to the museum, to Sheila, and to herself.

"Wow." His eyes lit up with obvious interest. "Do you think the price for the shop is a good deal?"

"I'm sure it is. I just haven't decided if I'll follow through on it. It's a big commitment."

"Go for it, Procne. You'll do well." He grinned at her. "Soon you'll be able to invest with me and save for retirement."

"Retirement?" She laughed. "That's a long way off. I'm just starting to make enough money to buy frivolous things."

"Come on now, it's never too soon to start saving." Shaun drained his glass and set it on the coffee table. "To change the subject, when did you last see the police?"

"Yesterday. I think the murder has them stumped."

"I saw Basil the other day. He was upset."

Procne nodded and didn't mention having seen them together in the History Café. Nor did she mention his use of coarse language. "Grace Devonshire was in the shop today. She said Basil has a suspect."

"I suppose we all suspect someone. But that's a long way from a conviction."

"Who do you suspect?" she asked.

"No one in particular. Just a couple of possibilities."

"I wonder if Basil's sister will like the scarf he bought her," Philomela said.

Shaun sat up straighter as if her non-sequitur startled him. "Basil bought a scarf at Whimsical Woman?"

Philomela nodded. "For his sister's birthday."

"Nice. Very thoughtful." He finished his drink and rose to his feet. "Well, ladies, thanks for the Scotch and the conversation. I must go. I have an eight-o'clock meeting."

"You work long hours," Philomela said.

"And so do we," Procne interjected. "We have to meet Sheila at eight to deliver clothes for the fashion show. Are we workaholics?" No one answered so she followed Shaun to the door. Over her shoulder she called, "Philomela, I'll see Shaun out and pick up the mail."

When she returned, Philomela was surprised to see a stunned expression on her face. "Did Shaun hit you on the head? Or did you simply receive a pile of junk mail?"

"Neither," Procne replied. "I just saw a car drive past. As it went under the streetlamp I saw its color. A deep shade of green."

"Who was driving it?"

"I think it was a woman. But it could have been a man with longish hair."

Later that evening, alone in her bedroom, Philomela wondered about the hit and run. Had the driver unknowingly hit Selene? Or had the accident been intentional? Did the driver suspect that Selene knew details about Maxine's murder? Did he or she attempt to prevent her from ever revealing that knowledge? Philomela wished she knew the answers.

She also wished she could find a prime suspect for Maxine's murder. With the Ouija Board's "S" in mind, she thought of Melvin Springer, Shaun O'Reilly, Simon Fraser, Sheila Trust. And, of course, Selene Hamilton.

Basil and Grace Devonshire were out of the picture—unless their second names began with S.

What about motives for murder? Could Shaun have used the knife in anger because Maxine wouldn't invest with him? Could Simon have done the deed because he knew of Maxine's bequest to the museum and wanted to hurry it up? Perhaps Basil's vexation about Maxine's loan prompted him to act impulsively. Was it possible that Grace suspected Maxine of having an affair with her husband so tried to solve the problem with morbid finality?

Could Melvin have wanted to do away with his wife in order to inherit her estate? What about Sheila—could she have killed Maxine in hope of obtaining both dress shops? Would Tom have been her willing accomplice?

Philomela mentally went over the people and their possible motives again. All seemed logical and possible. But what about capability? Who of those suspects was capable of committing such a dastardly deed?

She wished her sleuthing skills included the cunning and brilliance of Odysseus, the Greek king who inspired the building of the Trojan horse. Unfortunately, her only similarity with the king of Ithaca was red hair.

With a sigh, she opened her iPad and read two messages. Brent had enjoyed his heliskiing week but was looking forward to getting home and seeing her again. Janice was enjoying the warmth of a Chinook wind and anticipating a weekend with her boyfriend at Lake Louise ski resort.

Their uplifting messages raised her spirits. Everything was fine with two of her favorite people.

Ready to shut down her iPad, she hesitated as a new message came in. Then she read.

Dear Rae:

Tomorrow night is the Cerulean Full Moon. With your permission the Celestial Beings will help your re-birth. All your dreams of love, wealth, and good health will come true. Don't miss out on this wonderful event. Please act quickly.

Much love, Selene

A blue link followed: *Click here to benefit from the Cerulean Full Moon.*

She stupidly thought not of love, wealth, and good health, but of a blue moon. A full moon seldom fell twice in one month. As far as she knew it was not happening this January. Was Cerulean Moon another name for the spectacle of two full moons in one month?

Curiosity overtook her and she clicked the blue link. Surprise! Surprise! *Send only $99.00 and all your dreams will come true.*

CHAPTER 31

Saturday Morning:

Saturday dawned sunny and crisp. Philomela thought it was a good omen for the fashion-show. The prospect of helping with the show filled her with a feeling of excitement. It lingered all morning as Sheila and Procne manned the two dress shops, and Philomela dashed around like a busy rodent—gophering for this and gophering for that. Her pleasantest gophering task consisted of walking under the clear blue sky to the History Cafe for three take-away coffees.

Inside the cafe, while waiting for Jean to fill take-away cups, Philomela noticed Basil Devonshire and Melvin Springer sitting at a nearby table. They were in deep conversation.

Jean noted her interest in the two men. "They've been here for half hour," she whispered. "The good news is that Melvin is getting out and about. Once again, he's behaving like a pleasant human being."

"Good news indeed," Philomela said. "Their discussion seems incredibly serious."

"Yes." Jean closed her eyes as if in deep concentration then quickly opened them and focused intently on Philomela. "It used to be Maxine and Basil who had serious discussions. This is quite a switch."

Oh, to be a fly on the wall, Philomela thought. Before picking up the three coffees, she sauntered over to the two men and greeted Basil. Then she said, "Mr. Springer, I'm Philomela Nightingale, Procne Ellis's sister. We chatted briefly yesterday morning on the doorstep of Whimsical Woman. I must say that was very generous of your wife to donate money to the Historical Museum and to give my sister and Sheila Trust opportunities to buy the dress shops."

With dry, but somewhat glazed eyes, Melvin gazed up at her. "Is Procne going to do the deal?" he asked.

"She hasn't decided yet.'"

"I think she should do it. Maxine admired her fashion sense and her down-to-earth approach with customers. In case Procne doesn't realize it, tell her that with Maxine gone I no longer have any interest in the shops."

"I'll give her your message." He nodded and she turned to Basil. "And you, Mr. Devonshire, are you feeling better now?"

"Better than I was. Thank you for asking."

"Do you know if the police have found any murder clues yet?" she asked.

"None that I'm aware of," Basil replied.

"You'll be glad to know Selene Hamilton is back to normal after her hit-and-run accident. In fact, she's feeling well enough to participate in the fashion-show this afternoon." She noticed Basil's eyes flicker. Did his knuckles holding his coffee mug whiten? *Alas*, Philomela thought, *my pesky imagination is running amuck—again.*

"I'm glad to hear it," Basil said. "She's an unusual woman."

Refraining from mentioning the British Racing Green

car or the letter S, Philomela smiled at the two men, went back to the counter, and picked up the coffee mugs. As she left the History Cafe, her thoughts lingered on Melvin. This morning he was a different man than when she had contact with him at the police station and on the doorstep of Whimsical Woman. Now he was less boorish and far more amicable. Perhaps he was relieved to have the reading of the will completed. Procne might be right—under normal circumstances, he was a thoughtful, generous person. She mentally chalked his boorish behavior up to shock and grief.

Carrying the three coffee mugs along Main Avenue, she recalled last evening when she, Procne, and Sheila had feverishly loaded the three clothing-racks into the white van. At the church, amid groans and giggles, they had lugged the three racks up the front stairs and put them in a small room off the front vestibule. In short order, they had converted the area into a dressing room. Two clothing racks held colorful, casual outfits, the other rack held dressier garments, several of which were black and white. As Grace had suggested—basic blacks could be used for mourning as well as for everyday events or for dressy occasions. While arranging the racks, Procne had asked Sheila if Basil had replaced his gray Chevrolet with a green car.

"I don't know." Sheila's reply was accompanied with a nonchalant shoulder shrug.

Still wondering who owned the dark green car that Procne had seen, Philomela put thoughts of last night behind her. She raised her head, glanced back at the morning sun, and smiled. The warm temperature was propitious for a fashion-show anytime of the year, and especially so for one near the end of January.

It was almost eleven-thirty when she and Procne prepared to leave the shop. Philomela felt fashionably up to

date, attired in the black and green outfit she had purchased at Whimsical Woman, but she wondered if it suit-
ed her age. Walking outside she asked Procne, "Do I look
like mutton dressed as lamb?"

"Not at all," Procne replied. "The outfit fits you perfectly and the green matches your eyes and looks good
with your red hair."

"I hope you're right." Watching Procne lock the door
of Whimsical Woman, Philomela admired her over-the-
knee boots, her black tights, and the multicolored top that
molded her slim body. Her kid sister resembled a tall
mythical Aphrodite, and Philomela imagined her standing
on embroidered flowers in Saltaire gazing at the storm
clouds of her ex-husband fading in the distance.

Sheila, on the other hand, looked like a wise Athena
adorned in a gray suit whose classic lines would stand the
test of time. She walked sedately from Upscale Garments
to the white van and glanced back at her two cohorts.
Philomela noted how her streaked hair was parted in the
middle and fell gently around her oval face, accentuating
her flashing eyes. Philomela wondered if she was excited
more about the fashion-show or about the prospect of
owning a dress shop.

Philomela sat on the passenger seat of the white Mazda while Procne drove the car to her townhouse. Selene,
who stood outside waiting for them, scrambled onto a
backseat. Several minutes later Procne parked her car in
the church parking lot.

Lunch was in full swing when they entered the lower
level of the church. Tables were draped with white table-
cloths on which sat three-tiered silver and crystal trays
laden with finger food consisting of dainty sandwiches
and sweets. Around each table sat four well-dressed ladies. Red and white flowers and red hearts adorned the
walls, and decorative streamers hung on windows, giving

the room a festive pre-Valentine theme. Philomela recalled Procne saying the theme had been decided by
Maxine because it would enhance lingering winter outfits
as well as new spring ones.

They paid cash to a volunteer sitting at a table near
the door then looked around for vacant seats. Procne
spotted Sheila and hurried over to her. Selene took Philomela's arm and led her to a table with two empty chairs.

"Good afternoon," Selene said. "May we join you?"
Both ladies answered affirmatively and Selene politely
introduced Philomela to Rebecca Stein and Sarah Winston.

"Sarah and I met at Whimsical Woman," Philomela
said. She smiled as sincerely as she could at Sarah and,
for her effort, received a frosty frown. Philomela sighed
and turned to Rebecca. "If I remember correctly, you're
the pianist and master of ceremonies for the fashion-
show."

"That's right. Procne told me you helped write the
commentary for each garment. They describe the items
very well. I hope to carry everything off without becoming a blubbering idiot."

Philomela nodded sympathetically and glanced
around the room. "This is a lovely tribute to Maxine
Springer. As a visitor to Saltaire, I'm unfamiliar with the
concept of an Adult Day Center. Perhaps you could enlighten me."

"It's similar to daycare for children," Rebecca said,
"except it's for adults, mainly those with health problems.
Each day clients are picked up by bus or brought here by
family members. They chat, eat lunch, and play games
such as bridge, dominoes, cribbage. They also have a
rousing singsong once a week."

"Do you play for the singsongs?" Philomela asked.

"I do, once a month. There are three other pianists so

there is a singsong once a week. One of the clients' pastimes is, 'trying to stump the pianist.' I know most of the old songs of their era so they seldom stump me. However, I must confess they occasionally succeed."

"Sounds like fun," Philomela said.

"It is." Rebecca nodded and smiled. "The Center provides other benefits too. Baths, foot-care, blood pressures, and other health needs. One of the most important features is its loan cupboard. For a small donation clients can borrow equipment such as wheelchairs, walkers, crutches, bedpans, bath-chairs, and hospital beds. It's a lot cheaper than buying equipment that will be used only for a short time."

"Makes sense," Philomela said.

"The Center provides a pleasant change of scenery for people who are normally housebound," Rebecca continued. "Another of its goals is to give respite to caregivers. A family member on duty fifty-two weeks a year needs a few short breaks."

Sarah reached across the table, took a dainty triangular sandwich from the tiered tray, and popped it in her mouth. She swallowed it then took another. "If we want to eat before the show," she said, "we'd better get busy." She reached for her third sandwich and her three companions followed by taking their first. With her mouth almost overflowing with bread, Sarah muttered, "This tray doesn't hold enough food for four people."

Philomela agreed—there wasn't enough food for four people with Sarah's appetite.

"If necessary," Rebecca said, "I'm sure we can get more."

"Well, these are the stupidest sandwiches I've ever seen." Sarah grabbed another one. With her mouth full, she said, "They're hardly one bite."

"It's an English High Tea," Philomela murmured.

"And the price here is far less than what you'd pay at a fancy hotel." She bit into a watercress and cucumber sandwich and glanced over at a neighboring table. Recognizing one of the occupants, she swallowed and leaned toward Selene. "Is that Grace Devonshire sitting behind you?"

Selene turned in her chair and looked at the four women seated at the adjacent table. In a pleasant tone of voice she said, "Hello, Grace. How are you today?"

"Oh." Grace's eyes widened and her left hand fluttered around her face and neck. "I'm fine." Her words were barely audible.

Seeing the teacup tremble in her right hand, Philomela wondered if Grace suffered from a chronic ailment. Alcoholism? Parkinson's disease? Fear? Nervousness?

Selene turned back to her companions, smiled beatifically, and reached for a second sandwich. Too late. Sarah grabbed it first. Theoretically, Philomela knew that each woman should have four tiny sandwiches. In reality, Sarah ate seven and the other three each ate three. Sarah then proceeded to eat lemon tarts, meringues, Nanaimo bars, scones with clotted cream and jam. The sweets disappeared from the lower shelves of the three-tiered tray as if being inhaled by a hungry street-person.

Philomela asked a few questions about the volunteers who helped at the Center and the fundraisers who raised money to pay expenses. Rebecca answered most of the questions and Philomela became more and more impressed with the goals and accomplishments of the dedicated people. However, she hoped she would never have to be a client of this or any other Adult Day Center.

Why? she wondered. Surely she wasn't hoping for immortality.

No, she just hoped for a quick passing from this earthly life to a spiritual one, a passing that would escape becoming incapacitated and depending on others for everyday needs.

"I work with the Tuesday Group," Sarah said. "We get together every Tuesday to knit and sew for the Center. We also eat lunch. We have no president or treasurer or secretary. We meet in each other's homes and sell our items at the Christmas bazaar. All the proceeds go to the Center."

"Very worthwhile." Philomela was surprised that Sarah did anything that might help someone else.

They were sipping tea and coffee when Procne came over to their table and gazed at Rebecca. "I hate to interrupt," she said, "but the show will start in ten minutes."

Rebecca drained her teacup, stood up, and, with a wave of her hand, hurriedly left the table. The other three finished their tea then went outside, hurried to the front of the church, and up the six steps to the front door.

CHAPTER 32

Saturday Afternoon:

Philomela entered the church vestibule and looked into the nave. Rebecca was already sitting at the piano checking audio equipment "Testing, testing," she said, and her voice echoed clearly from beside the stage to the entranceway. The piano was situated in such a way that she could see the stage, the audience, and the vestibule.

Sarah ignored her lunch companions, walked up the left aisle to the front row, and took possession of a prime seat. Selene and Philomela watched her then turned into the makeshift dressing room. It bustled with confusion. Procne directed one of the Center's volunteers to Sheila who glanced at the clipboard in her hand then directed the model to the classic rack. Sheila, already attired in her first modeling outfit, walked to the rack and pointed to a black suit and white shirt.

Procne guided another amateur model to one of the two casual racks and suggested she put her first outfit on right away. "Give your discarded clothes to Philomela," she said.

Procne then took off her own multi-colored top, boots, and tights and gave them to Philomela who hung them on a clothes rack at the back of the room. Procne slipped on a red dress, put on high-heeled red shoes, and carried a red coat that matched the dress. She walked over to her psychic neighbor and pointed to one of the casual garment racks.

"Selene, you can put on your first outfit—the pink loungewear." To all of the models, she loudly announced, "When each of you return from your performance, Philomela will take your cast-off clothes and hang them on a rack at the back of the room. You will then put on your next modeling outfit."

Sheila helped the third volunteer from the Center slip into a black pants-and-coat ensemble from Upscale Garments. Philomela hung the woman's personal clothes on the back rack. Piano music wafted throughout the building. The decibel rate increased as more and more ladies assembled in the pews.

"Are we ready?" Procne asked, surveying the other five models.

"As ready as we'll ever be," a volunteer from the Center replied.

"How about you, Selene?"

"I'm ready."

"Sheila?"

"I'm all set." Sheila glanced at her wristwatch. "It's time. I'll give the signal to Rebecca." She opened the door and stepped quietly into the vestibule. Standing at the entrance to the main aisle she raised her right arm and waved.

Philomela stood near the doorway and saw Rebecca, who was seated at the piano, nod her head at Sheila. She ended the melody she was playing, held her clipboard close to her bosom, and leaned toward the microphone.

She surveyed the crowd then she spoke slowly and clearly.

"Welcome to the Adept Adult Day Center's annual fashion-show. As you know, the Center provides a vital service for our community, mainly for people with health problems, their families, and their caregivers. On behalf of clients, volunteers, and staff at the Center, I wish to thank you for coming to support this worthwhile facility. All proceeds from the lunch and fashion show will help maintain the Center throughout the year. "Speaking of lunch, wasn't it delicious?"

Applause burst spontaneously and, when it died down, Rebecca continued. "The clothes shown today are from two of Saltaire's best dress shops: Upscale Garments and Whimsical Woman. As most of you know, the shops are on Main Avenue and the founder of both shops was Maxine Springer. Maxine was a pillar of the community, an astute business woman, and a reliable friend to all who knew her. Her unexpected death came as a shock to everyone in the community. She will be sorely missed.

"Several weeks ago, Maxine began organizing today's fashion-show. Two of her employees—Procne Ellis and Sheila Trust—are following in her footsteps by overseeing the event. The lunch and entire show are dedicated to the memory of Maxine Springer."

Applause again swelled from the audience. When it faded, Rebecca resumed her duty as master of ceremonies and fashion commentator.

"Maxine's two stalwart employees will open the show by modeling smart outfits that are perfect for the Pacific Northwest's casual lifestyle. From Whimsical Woman, Procne is wearing a cheery dress and matching coat. The color and wool fabric will add warmth on those chilly days and evenings in late winter and early spring.

From Upscale Garments, Sheila is adorned in a black, pseudo leather coat, a pair of black wool pants with matching jacket, and a frilly white shirt."

Philomela watched her sister walk up the aisle. As far as Philomela was concerned, Procne could have been walking on a runway in a Parisian fashion house. She gracefully went up three steps on the left side of the stage, reached center stage and stood facing the audience. She turned slowly to show all sides of her red coat, and then she took off the coat and made another three hundred and sixty-five degree turn to display the red dress. Oohs and aahs came from the audience. Procne walked across the stage and down the steps on the right side. At that same moment, Sheila glided up the left aisle. On center stage she repeated Procne's performance then followed her down the steps on the right side. Seeing Sheila start to glide down the right aisle Philomela pushed Selene into the left aisle.

Rebecca resumed her monologue: "The garments in both shops are well designed and are varied enough to satisfy a wide spectrum of tastes. The Valentine theme of the show was chosen in order to combine two seasons—late winter and early spring. The model walking on stage is Selene Hamilton, a seamstress who often clerks in both dress shops and does alterations for customers. Her passion-pink loungewear, made of fluffy fleece, is perfect for those chilly winter days and evenings…"

Philomela watched Selene glide gracefully across the stage. The first two models had performed with elegance and self-assurance. Selene was a picture of peace and tranquility. The audience did not ooh and ahh—they motionlessly sat and watched the ethereal woman show off the loungewear. Everyone seemed entranced.

"Psst."

Philomela turned and saw Procne standing in the

doorway of the make-shift dressing room. She had three models at the ready. She guided one forward as Selene started to glide down the right aisle toward the vestibule. Rebecca proceeded to introduce the new model and describe her outfit. Philomela slipped into the dressing room and hung Sheila and Procne's discarded clothes on the rack at the back of the room. Selene entered the dressing room, removed her outfit, and gave it to Philomela who hung it beside the others.

Rebecca praised the usefulness of dark attire for everyday wear and formal functions as well as for celebrations of life and memorial services. A volunteer from the Center, wearing a black silk dress and black wool cape, started up the left aisle. Another model from the Center, wearing a black and gray outfit, was making her way down the right one. When they returned to the dressing room Philomela and Procne helped them disrobe then left them on their own to don their next outfits. The two organizers elegantly graced the runway for a second time and, once again, were followed by Selene whose pale blue flowing dress made her look like an angel. The sequence continued with Rebecca briefly describing each ensemble. Philomela was pleased that the descriptions she had helped write seemed to enhance the viewing of each outfit. Time flew by quickly.

When the show ended, Procne and Sheila walked amidst chattering women in the vestibule and graciously received compliments. The one exception was Sarah Winston who told them the show was too long and would have been better if Maxine Springer had overseen it. A few people overheard her remarks, shook their heads with annoyance, then praised everything—from commentator and models to garments and organizers—with more vigor than ever.

"It was the best show ever," one lady said to Procne.

"The clothes were lovely and everything flowed so smoothly."

"Thank you," Procne replied. "Maxine trained us well."

As Sheila and Procne readied the racks to be taken to the van, Philomela extended her own compliment. "The show was awesome," she said. "Everyone, including me, was entranced."

"Things seemed to go quite well," Sheila modestly said.

Procne grinned.

"The worst part of organizing a fashion show is getting all the stuff back to the shops." Sheila groaned and started to push a rack toward the stairs.

"The best part," Philomela said, "is that the models from the Center each bought two of the outfits they had modeled and Selene bought one. That makes two from Upscale and five from Whimsical. Seven garments less to lug back in the van."

"Did they pay for them?" Sheila asked.

"Of course." Procne smiled and patted her shoulder bag. "I have the money and receipts right here. I'll give you yours when we get back to the shop."

Philomela, having made three of the transactions herself, experienced a proprietary feeling of satisfaction. It was a revelation—the retail business not only involved a lot of hard work, but it also included many moments of fun and well-earned rewards. She followed her sister who was pushing a rack of clothes out the front door to the stairs. The two of them hung on to each end of the rack and eased it down the six steps. Seeing a broad smile on Procne's face, Philomela knew without doubt that her sister would be capable of managing Whimsical Woman. And she would do it with pizzazz, dedication, and cheerfulness.

Coming back up the stairs, Philomela met Sheila who was coming down.

"Well, this has been my initiation as a dress shop owner," Sheila said.

"A successful one, too." Philomela smiled. Then her smile faded as she wondered if Sheila was disappointed in acquiring only one shop from Maxine. The thought was not uplifting. It prompted her to suspect Sheila may have been willing to commit murder in hope of obtaining both shops.

Pushing the horrid thought aside, Philomela picked up a box of accessories and carried them out the front door. Walking down the steps, she noticed a car glide to a stop at the parking lot exit. She paused mid-step and stared. There was no doubt—the car's color was British Racing Green. She strained her neck to get a view of the driver, but the car quickly turned onto the main road and sped away.

Who was driving that car?

CHAPTER 33

Late Saturday Afternoon:

Sitting in the back seat of the Mazda, Philomela mentioned seeing the dark green car to Procne and Selene. "It turned and sped off before I had a good look at the driver."

"Too bad," Selene murmured.

"Did you see a logo on the car?" Procne asked.

"No. I didn't. Nor did I recognize the car's specific shape."

Procne stared at the sleek black car on the road in front of her. "With all the rules and regulations today, most cars look the same."

Reaching the dress shops on Main Avenue, she parked directly behind the white van. Sheila was already preparing to unload clothing racks so the threesome got out of Procne's car and hurried over to her. They pushed the first rack into Upscale Garments and the other two into Whimsical Woman.

Inside the dressy shop, Sheila and Selene put clothes and accessories in their appropriate display places. Procne and Philomela did the same in the funky shop. Soon both shops were ready for an influx of customers on the next workday, Monday.

"You'd never know the shops had been torn apart before the fashion-show," Procne said. "We tidy things up good."

Philomela bobbed her head in agreement. "I wonder how many members of the audience will purchase something next week."

"Lots, I hope." Procne grinned optimistically. "Right now, I'll dash next door and give Sheila the money for the volunteers' purchases." She returned a few minutes later with Sheila and Selene in tow. Patting her abdomen, she asked, "Anyone hungry?"

"Not really," Sheila replied. "I'm still wound up. But you have to admit, the fashion-show was a bang-up way to start our new ownerships. We really should end the big day with a bite to eat and a celebratory drink."

Agreement was unanimous. Philomela glanced at her sister and noted she didn't deny Sheila's remark about new ownership.

At Fireside Pizza, the foursome sat around a table and sipped local ciders. Reading the label, Sheila said they should be able to handle its low alcohol content. Procne suggested they each have a salad and split the large house special pizza to absorb the alcohol. Amicably the other three agreed. As Philomela took her first sip of cider, she glanced toward the door and, to her surprise, saw Grace and Basil walk into the restaurant.

"The Devonshires just came in." For no apparent reason the muscles of her abdomen tightened, but she sloughed it off, thinking the contraction was caused by a draft from the open door.

Procne turned and waved at the newcomers. Basil responded with a polite nod. Grace avoided eye contact by gazing away from the foursome. She also ignored the young hostess who started to lead her to an empty table adjacent to the three women and instead hurried to an empty table in the far corner of the room. When Basil realized what was happening, he stopped and gazed around as if momentarily confused. Then he shrugged and approached the three women.

"I hear your fashion-show was a success," he said.

"It was," Procne replied. "Everyone seemed to enjoy it."

"Grace said it was a nice tribute to Maxine." He glanced over at his wife who had settled on a chair at the corner table. Then he turned and gazed steadily at Procne. "Hamish said I would need to find a new volunteer for Monday morning. I heard a rumor that both dress shops might have new owners."

"Maybe." Procne grinned but was non-committal. "I'll phone you as soon as the final decision is made."

"Your departure as a volunteer will be a loss to the museum."

"Why thank you, Basil. That's kind of you to say so." Procne beamed at him. As he walked away to join his wife, she murmured, "I think that's the only compliment I ever received from him."

"Good for him." Sheila glanced at his retreating figure. "He's usually a stuffy know-it-all. But I love his wife. She's such a wonderful shopper."

"Yes," Procne agreed, "she is."

Philomela sipped her cider and silently mused on their analysis of Grace—a wonderful shopper. Would that be a good eulogy at a memorial service? Would it stand the test of time as a written tribute on a tombstone? Wonderful shopper or not, there was no question about Grace always looking neat and well groomed. Doubtless, she had other attributes, though, as she herself admitted, being a faith-healer was not one of them.

Philomela glanced surreptitiously at Selene and wondered if she knew more about Grace than she was saying.
Since cleaning up after the fashion-show ended, the
shaman had said very little. Philomela thought she looked
drawn and tired. No wonder, the day had been busy and
she had been a good sport to participate as a model, especially while still recovering from the trauma of the hit-
and-run accident.

And, of course, she was still attending to her psychic
business by sending emails about the Cerulean Moon.

Suddenly, four salads and a pizza laden with cheese,
meat, green peppers, onions, tomatoes, and who knew
what else was set in the middle of the table. "Bon ap-
pétit," the waitress said.

For people who weren't hungry, all four behaved in
an inverse manner. They swarmed over the food like a
horde of locusts and forfeited conversation in lieu of
chewing. After swallowing the last bite of their first slice
of pizza, they each reached for seconds.

"Running a fashion show takes more energy than I
realized, "Philomela said. "Who would think that don-
ning classy clothes could create a big appetite?"

Between mouthfuls the other three chuckled.

After splitting the cost four ways, they paid the bill
and headed for the door. Walking beside Selene, Philomela peripherally noticed her study the two occupants of
the corner table. Philomela glanced in that direction, too,
and saw Grace looking at the wall. By not acknowledging
their existence, she seemed to send all four to outer space.
Philomela found her antisocial action similar to her cool
attitude at lunch. She wondered if Grace's cool behavior
was directed at Selene because of her suggestion that she
get a job.

"Hurry up, Philomela," Procne said. "We have to
walk back to the shop and get the vehicles"

When the Mazda was parked in the townhouse parkade, Selene, Procne, and Philomela climbed out and walked past Sheila's white van. Procne verbalized the obvious. "Sheila beat us home."

"Let's take the stairs instead of the elevator," Philomela suggested. "After gorging ourselves we need the exercise." They walked in single file up the stairs to the open air vestibule. As Selene walked past the door to Trust's townhouse, Philomela said, "Selene, I hope you get lots of rest. Don't forget you're still recovering from the hit-and-run accident. If you have any worries or need anything, just phone us. Procne or I will come right over."

"Thanks, Philomela. I'm tired, but I'm fine. It really has been a wonderful day." She smiled, unlocked the door, and disappeared inside.

Procne unlocked the door to her townhouse. "Well, sis, this has been an exciting start for the new owner of *Whimsical Woman.*"

"It's definite then." Philomela was not surprised. "You've made the big decision."

"I have."

"It's a good one. Even Melvin Springer thinks so." She smiled and told her sister that at the History Café Melvin had said he thought she should do the deal.

In the sitting area, they kicked off their shoes and flopped on a sofa. For almost an hour, they rehashed the fashion-show, discussed the shop, and itemized the many things ownership would entail. Finally, Philomela skirted around to Maxine's murder.

"Procne, you knew Maxine reasonably well. Now that the show is behind you, are you able to think of any reason why one of her customers might want her dead?"

"A few people misunderstood her and some disliked her manner. The majority knew her occasional outspokenness came not from maliciousness but from honest straightforwardness. She wanted her customers to look good. Most of the time, she was diplomatic, even when disagreeing with someone."

"Was she like that when trying to sell a garment?"

"Yes. That was part of her success. If a garment looked bad on a customer, she told them so. Then she'd find something that looked good on them. She had an eye for such things."

"That's an unusual selling approach, isn't it?"

"Not necessarily. But it's a good one. She was always polite and most customers valued her judgment. Though I do recall one woman who took exception at being told an outfit looked less than flattering on her."

"What did the customer say?"

"She had a hissy-fit. She took off the dress, threw it at Maxine, and marched out of the store. The woman, need-less to say, never came back."

"A customer venting her anger by throwing a dress is a far cry from murder."

Procne gazed thoughtfully at her sister. "Sarah Win-ston criticizes outfits all the time. Whether they look good or not. She certainly doesn't have Maxine's unerr-ing fashion sense. She just dislikes everything."

"Are you implying that Sarah's capable of commit-ting a murder?"

"No. I suspect Sarah's incapable of doing lots of things, especially murder."

"Going back to Maxine. Was she generally well liked in the community?"

"She was more admired than liked. She was so beau-tiful, so capable, and had such a gorgeous figure that it was easy to envy her."

"Did you envy her?"

"Of course. Compared to her figure, mine is dumpy,

my hair is a mess, and I don't own two successful shops."

"Did you like her?"

"Actually, I did." Procne nodded her head up and down and then shifted the conversation to Selene's accident. "I wonder if the hit and run had anything to do with the murder. I also wonder if it was targeted as Selene suspects. Or was it just an unexpected accident?"

Philomela gazed pensively at her sister. "The accident could be related to the murder. The guilty party might be afraid Selene intuitively knows who committed the murder. Everyone knows she's psychic and sees things the rest of us don't see. She could easily envision who killed Maxine."

The internet scam suddenly popped into Philomela's mind. Silently she wondered if the so-called accident might have resulted from Selene's internet duplicity. Did an unhappy client choose hit-and-run as a way to seek revenge?

She wanted to discuss the website and weird emails with Procne, but she refrained from doing so. She didn't want Procne to worry about her wayward neighbor.

Not yet.

Perhaps tomorrow.

A short while later, attired in her nightgown, Philomela sat on the edge of the bed and opened her iPad. She read a message from Brent.

Dearest Philomela:

The entire week of helisking was invigorating. The powder snow was great and so were the people. We left shortly after breakfast and John drove most of the way to Calgary. We got no speeding tickets. Our cozy home survived our absence. Tomorrow evening I'll meet you at the airport.

LOL, Brent.

The next message brought her up short. The words expressed such dire urgency.

Dear Rae:
The full moon tonight will help the Celestial Beings work their magic to increase your opportunities for love, success, money, and happiness. Come on now, Rae, act quickly.
This is your best chance to achieve everything you always desired.
Love, Selene

The inevitable blue link appeared and she clicked it—
All your dreams will come true for a mere $99.00.

She started to laugh and stood up, intending to share the joke with her sister. Then she sat down again. No, it would upset Procne too much. After the last few days her sister needed a good night's sleep. Tomorrow morning Philomela would expose the charlatan by showing the website and emails to Procne.

A slight tightening of Philomela's abdominal muscles made her sit up straight on the edge of the bed. The missives, she had to admit, posed a question. The more she saw of Procne's neighbor, the more she wondered whether the ethereal woman truly was capable of spear-heading the email scam. She seemed too kind and too sincere to try and dupe innocent people. Then, once again, Philomela suspected the psychic of being an excellent actress, putting on a show of kindness and sweetness, as well as pretending to be a computer dunderhead.

There was no doubt in Philomela's mind that Selene's psychic abilities were sometimes questionable. Though she had explained her inability to pinpoint the car driver who had hit her, any shaman worth her salt should have made the connection between Rae and Philomela. If Selene suspected Rae's true identity she certainly hid it well. And if she recognized Rae and Philomela as one and the same person, why did she continue to send the money-grubbing emails?

Recalling that Selene's name started with "S," Philomela shuddered.

Could it be possible that Selene had committed the horrendous murder? And was the hit-and-run accident simply a ploy to distract police from the truth?

CHAPTER 34

Sunday Morning:

Sunday began with the peace and calm of a biblical day of rest. Philomela lay in bed and thought of how Christianity and Jews specified one day a week for its adherents to take life easy. Muslims celebrated other traditional holidays but she wasn't sure whether a weekly day of rest was one of them. Buddhism's perfect enlightenment or nirvana would be equivalent to enjoying every day as a day of rest—no matter what happened, life would resemble a peaceful holiday.

Lying on her back, she thought of last night's dream. It certainly wouldn't help her achieve Nirvana. She stared at the ceiling and recalled how the dream had involved her harried search for Maxine's killer. The worst part happened near the end. The back of the murderer appeared, making the person clearly visible. A hoodie, however, hid the face and hair so the person was unidentifiable. She was so close to solving the case and then she woke up. It was disconcerting.

She closed her eyes and tried to bring the dream to the fore of her mind. She wanted to force the killer to turn around. Of course, it didn't work. The dream remained in another realm. The faint second sight she inherited from her grandmother was not strong enough to help her envision the murderer or any other part of the dream. She gave up and climbed out of bed. As water splashed warmly on her body in the shower, she reaffirmed last evening's decision. At breakfast she would tell her sister about the missives that she, Rae, was receiving from Selene.

While they sat at the eating counter enjoying a relaxed second cup of coffee, Philomela broached the touchy subject, brought out her iPad, and placed it on the counter. Though she stressed the messages may be coming from someone other than Procne's neighbor, the expression on her sister's face grew more shocked with each revelation. Philomela brought up the link on last night's email.

Procne read it and exploded. "How could Selene ask you to pay ninety-nine dollars to make all your dreams come true?" She jumped to her feet and her jaw clenched in anger. "This is beyond terrible. I'm going to confront her."

"Don't condemn Selene yet, not until we know for sure she's the guilty party." Philomela was surprised at how quickly Procne's reaction had shattered the Sunday peace and calm.

"I'm going to her place right now and give her a piece of my mind."

"Hang onto your mind, all of it. You might need it."

"Philomela, this isn't funny."

"I know it isn't. But slow down. Let's phone Selene and invite her for coffee. We can ask her about the website and emails in a pleasant, civilized manner."

Procne hesitated then nodded agreement. With her right, index finger, she banged the numbers on the phone.

In a sharp tone of voice she asked Selene to come over for coffee. Then she shut off the phone and banged it onto its charger. "She'll be here in ten minutes."

"Don't forget she's still recovering from the hit and run. She's not back to normal yet. And, for all we know, she may not even be the guilty party."

"Philomela, that's a stupid assumption. Look at the picture on the website. Who else could it possibly be?"

"The old cliché, *seeing is believing,* isn't always correct."

A gentle knock sounded on the door. Procne strode across the hardwood floor and opened it. With an abrupt, "Hello" she ushered Selene inside and silently led her to the kitchen. Philomela could see from Selene's puzzled expression that she knew something ominous was happening.

"Good morning, Selene." Philomela tried to sound cheerful. "Did you sleep well?"

"I slept very well, thank you. And you?"

"Also very well. You're feeling back to normal after the rigors of the fashion-show?"

"Yes. I'm back to normal, whatever that is."

"Great." Philomela filled a red mug with coffee, handed it to their guest, and then led her to the sitting area. Selene sat down on a sofa. Philomela settled in beside her.

Procne sat upright on the other sofa and stared over the coffee table at them. She plunked her mug on the table and her stare turned into a glare. "Okay, Selene, why did you lie about not using the internet for your shamanistic business?"

Selene's body leaned toward Procne and her eyebrows knit together. "What are you talking about?"

"Your messages to Rae."

"Rae? Who's Rae?"

"Rae Nightingale."

Selene glanced at Philomela and then looked back at Procne. "Do you two have a sister called Rae?"

"Don't play innocent with me."

"Procne, are you okay?"

"I'm okay. You're the one who's not okay. You're the one causing trouble."

Selene placed her left hand over her heart and the furrows on her brow grew deeper.

"You're the one who has been asking Philomela for money," Procne said.

Selene sat up straight and placed both hands on her lap. "This is bizarre. Why in the world would I ask Philomela for money?"

"Her second name is Rae. She paid you $49.00 to give to the Celestial Beings. You said your advice to her would be free. Ha, ha, ha." Procne's laughter was as phony as plastic crystal.

"I have no idea what you're talking about. Who are these Celestial Beings?"

"That's what I'd like to know." Procne pursed her lips, stood up, and marched to the kitchen. She returned with Philomela's iPad, opened it to the questionable website, and handed it to her neighbor.

Selene looked at the picture and gasped. "That's me." She read the blurb and clicked the blue link. "Good heavens. This is terrible." She stared at Procne. "I know nothing about this. Who would use my name and picture in such a dishonest manner?"

"Good question," Procne muttered, obviously doubting Selene's reaction.

Philomela, however, suspected Selene was not playacting. She glanced at her sister who was studying Selene, as if trying to verify the psychic's veracity. Then, in a soothing tone of voice, Philomela said, "Actually, the emails could have come from anyone anywhere in the world."

"I don't advertise at all, certainly not on the internet." Selene looked as if she could weep. "I have to stop this. But how do I do it? I know so little about computers."

"Actually, this could be a form of identity theft," Philomela said. "The police should be notified, and the person doing this should be found and punished. There are computer nerds on the police force." For a moment Philomela bit her lower lip, deep in thought. Then she asked, "Selene, do you have any idea who might be doing this?"

Selene shook her head slowly from side to side. "None whatsoever. If this was happening to someone else, I might be able to zero in on a culprit. Unfortunately, it's happening to me, so I'm at a total loss for answers."

Understanding that Selene's psychic abilities did not work for herself, Philomela stared thoughtfully into space. Since her arrival in Saltaire, she had encountered three crimes—murder, hit and run, and now identity theft. As far as she knew, no one, not even the police, had gleaned a clue about any of them.

"I have a brilliant idea." Procne got to her feet and smiled for the first time that morning. "I'm going to phone Shaun. He's a bit of a computer whiz. He'll know how to handle it."

"That's a good idea," Selene said. "Though I hate to trouble him. He's so busy."

"I'll trouble him," Procne said. She made the call and invited Shaun for coffee. It turned out he was free so agreed to join them. Procne brewed a fresh pot, which was ready by the time he came and settled on the sofa across from Selene.

"Shaun," Selene said, getting immediately to the

point. "You may not think this is serious, but we're afraid someone is stealing my identity."

Philomela handed him her iPad and showed him the webpage with Selene's photo and the blurb describing her psychic abilities.

He chuckled. "Selene, you didn't tell me you're an electronic nerd."

"I'm not. I don't know how to do any of this."

Philomela took the iPad from Shaun and, a minute later, handed it back to him. He read the first email from Selene and looked a query at Philomela. "Rae? Why are you getting emails for someone called Rae?"

"That's my second name. I seldom use it." She watched his brows furrow as he pondered her explanation. She waited, expecting him to expound about the use of Selene's name.

"It's terribly upsetting, Shaun," Selene said. "I might have to ask the police for help."

"Oh, come on now, Selene, that won't be necessary." He smiled encouragingly at her. "We can solve this. I'll contact Snopes and let them know it's a scam. We'll email the perpetrator and once she realizes she's been found out, she'll shut down the webpage."

"Do you think so?" Selene sounded hopeful.

"I do."

Listening to Selene and Shaun, Philomela felt her abdominal muscles contract. Was she missing something here?

Could the two of them be in cahoots? Shaun, as always, spoke and smiled with the smoothness of a pan of oil. Selene, on the other hand, was flustered, the epitome of slandered innocence and startling untruths. They illustrated a good cop bad cop scenario—a perfect combination for duping unsuspecting victims.

"Shaun," Philomela said, "you referred to the culprit

as she. Do you think the identity theft is being done by a woman?"

"I don't know," he replied. "It just seems logical that a female would try to impersonate another female."

"Perhaps," Philomela said.

After much discussion, Shaun promised to try and scare the website perpetrator into removing the deceitful webpage.

"If you don't succeed," Selene said, "then I'll contact the police and see what they can do."

Procne got up, refilled their coffee mugs, and brought out some blueberry muffins. She sat down again. "Well, at least we're doing something about the scam. If only we could do something about finding Maxine's killer. It's been five days now. I've been too busy running the dress shop and the fashion-show to focus on it."

"None of us have given the murder the attention it deserves," Philomela said. "I wonder if the police are doing any better. From my point of view, there aren't many clues floating around. I hope the police already have a suspect."

"Then there's the hit-and-run accident." Shaun gazed at Selene. "Maybe the two are related. The driver of the hit-and-run accident could also have murdered Maxine."

"I fail to see a connection," Selene said. "Maxine and I were not close friends. Our arrangements for alterations and relief clerking jobs were casual, but businesslike. If the murderer had a reason to kill Maxine, what reason would he or she have to kill me?"

"The murderer may have feared your psychic abilities," Philomela suggested. "The perpetrator may have been afraid you would receive a vision of the actual crime or get a telepathic message exposing the real murderer."

"I bet that's it," Shaun said. He sat up straight and his eyes glittered. "Find the hit-and-run driver, and you'll have the murderer. Exactly what time did the accident occur?"

"Nine in the morning," Selene replied.

"I was attending a meeting in Victoria at that time." He gazed thoughtfully at Procne then at Philomela. "What were you two doing?"

"Eating breakfast," Philomela replied. "And getting ready to go and have our fingerprints taken."

"We'll have to search around," Shaun said to Selene. "The murderer could have used a car as a weapon to prevent you from psychically revealing who-dun-it." His face broke into a warm smile. "Thank god the murderer failed."

"I concur." Philomela looked sympathetically at Selene. "The alternative is too deadly to think about." She regretted her poor choice of words but did not correct them.

Shaun set his empty coffee mug on the table. "I'll go home and start working on that phony website." He smiled at Selene and stood up.

"How long will it take the culprit to delete the site?" Selene asked.

"I'd guess two days at the max."

Selene smiled. "I appreciate your computer skills and your kindness, Shaun. I feel better already."

"The website may have caused emotional turmoil for many readers," Philomela mused, "and the murder definitely caused loss of life for Maxine. The hit-and-run caused minor injuries to Selene and havoc to the police. I wonder if the website perpetrator, the actual murderer, and the hit-and-run driver are three different people. Or are they one and the same person—three criminals rolled in one?

"I don't know." Shaun lips formed a straight line. Then he said, "Changing the subject, this afternoon there's a big craft show at the Community Center. It's called, 'Arts, Crafts, Etc.' We could snoop around it. Anyone interested in going?"

Procne looked pensive and glanced around the room. "I'd like to go. I might find something that could be of use in my new shop."

"New shop?" Shaun asked. "You've decided?"

"I have." She grinned at Shaun then turned to her neighbor. "Do you want to go to the craft show, Selene?"

"Yes. That would be nice."

"And you, Philomela?"

"Sounds like fun." Philomela was pleased to see the two neighbors behaving like friends again. She hoped it would continue.

They agreed to meet at two o'clock in the open-air vestibule then walk as a foursome to the Community Center.

When their guests were gone, Philomela checked her iPad for messages. There was one from Brent: he gave a weather report and confirmed he would meet her at the airport. There was nothing from her employee and no new message from the phony Selene. She re-read last night's missive.

Dear Rae:

The full moon tonight will help the Celestial Beings work their magic to increase your opportunities for love, success, money, and happiness. Come on now, Rae, act quickly. This is your best chance to achieve everything you always desired.

Love from Selene

Her abdominal muscles contracted slightly. Was she missing something important? She read the message again, but received no enlightening revelation.

CHAPTER 35

Sunday Afternoon:

At the Community Center, Procne, Philomela, Selene, and Shaun paid the small entrance fee and wandered together to a large display of knitted goods. They discussed a few garments then gradually spread out to examine items of individual interest. Shaun zeroed in on portraits hanging on a wall, Selene looked at First Nation dream-catchers hanging on fish-lines between two vertical poles, Procne studied a variety of sea-shells lying in attractive disorder on a table.

Philomela stopped at a display of wooden footstools that would serve as attractive heighteners for short people trying to reach top shelves. The price was right, but the thought of getting one home on the airplane stopped her from digging in her purse for money to purchase one. Just as she made the decision to refrain from buying, she noticed Grace Devonshire stop nearby. She also studied the footstools.

"Hello, Grace," Philomela said. "These attractive footstools would help short people, like you and me, to reach high places."

"Yes, I might buy one for my kitchen. Tall people like Procne have advantages that you and I lack."

"Too true." Philomela noted that Grace was carrying two full shopping bags. "You've obviously found a few items worth purchasing," she said.

"Yes. I found a lovely hand-knit sweater and a purse."

"I'm surprised that a craft sale so soon after Christmas would attract so many people. But the place is packed and people are actually buying."

"We don't get everything we need at Christmas," Grace said.

"I suppose that's true. If I weren't flying home, I'd buy a footstool." Philomela wondered if Grace heard her, because her eyes glazed over and her body stiffened. She clearly was paying attention to something behind Philomela. Curious, Philomela made a half turn and saw Selene walking toward them.

"Hello, you two," Selene said. "Grace, I see you found some items you couldn't resist."

Grace's lips pursed tightly and she deigned to reply.

"Did you enjoy the fashion show yesterday?" Selene asked.

"It was nice," Grace replied. "I must carry on. I need to buy one of these stools." She turned her back on Selene and beckoned to a man behind the counter.

Philomela saw Selene's eyebrows shoot up then lower again. Having been perfunctorily dismissed by Grace, Selene obviously hesitated to say more. Philomela wondered if a footstool warranted Grace's rude brushing off of the psychic. The incident reminded Philomela of the fashion-show lunch and how Grace had responded with an equal lack of grace to Selene's friendly greeting. Philomela smiled at her poor pun. Then she wondered if Grace's actions were based on the healing session she had found so uncomfortable. Or was her behavior a reaction to Selene's suggestion that she get a job to pay for her purchases?

Suddenly Philomela thought of another possibility. Could Grace be hiding something really important? Could she fear that close proximity to Selene would enhance the psychic's ability to envision her secret, whatever it was? Could she be trying to protect the murderer? Her husband perhaps? Or just as bad, could she be the murderer?

Philomela watched Grace discuss the footstool with the man behind the counter, take her wallet from her purse, and hand him her credit card. It seemed that as far as Grace was concerned Philomela and Selene no longer existed.

Selene gave Philomela a weak smile, strolled on, and passed a display of greeting cards. Philomela followed her, but instead of walking past the cards she paused to look at them. They had been painted by a local artist and were scenes of Saltaire, many of which Philomela recognized. She looked up, intending to show them to Selene, but Selene was now chatting with Basil. Philomela took a few steps toward them. Hearing Basil's voice, she stopped.

"I'm at my wits end. I don't know what to do."

"Have you explained the problem to her?" Selene asked.

"Many times. I explained the strain she is putting on our financial situation by indiscriminately using her credit cards. I labored the point when she paid off one credit card with another. And how did she react? By promptly starting to fill the first one again. Her compulsive buying is getting worse every day. I told her Shaun is trying to sell some of our mineral stock so we can pay off her credit card debts. It meant nothing to her. When I finally told her I'd borrowed money from Maxine to pay off her debts, she worried a little, but not enough to stop shopping. I explained about dipping into our capital to pay off Maxine's loan, and she didn't seem to care. She honestly doesn't understand the difference between capital and interest. She thinks money grows on trees, and every year she spends more on stuff she doesn't need. She doesn't even understand that her monthly credit card interest payments are exorbitant."

Philomela was surprised. She had been blaming Basil for problems that had apparently originated with Grace. Here he had been trying to cover up for her. It seemed that Grace's spend-thrift buying was at the bottom of Basil's theft problem and his loan from Maxine. Were these the reasons why Selene had suggested to Grace that she get a job to pay for her purchases?

"She needs help," Selene told Basil. "Shopaholics, alcoholics, and compulsive gamblers have similar problems."

"It's hard to help someone who won't admit to having a problem," Basil said.

"Can you take away her credit cards?" Selene asked. "Or threaten to refuse to claim responsibility for her debts?"

"I hate to do that to her, but I might have to. That will be my last resort. I'd go back to work, but who would hire a man my age?"

Basil looked so downcast that Philomela felt a wave of sympathy for him. His British, stiff-upper-lip manner had disintegrated, making him look like a helpless old man. She averted her eyes from him and gazed down at the greeting cards. The beautiful pictures made the town look lovely and peaceful, a stark reminder that nothing was as it seemed.

She glanced over at Grace and saw her smile at the

man behind the counter then pick up her new footstool. With her footstool in one hand and her two bags and purse in the other, she moved to a counter displaying jewelry.

"Philomela," Procne said, coming up beside her. "Have you bought anything?"

"Not yet. How about you?"

"I'm still looking." Procne glanced over at Selene and Basil and asked, "What's with that unlikely twosome?"

"Leave them to it. They're having a serious discussion about Grace's compulsive buying. I think her shopping binges are much worse than we realized."

"You're kidding."

"No, I'm not." Philomela glanced around then asked her sister, "Have you seen Shaun?"

"Yes. He was busy chatting up all sorts of people. I think he's looking for potential investors. He's doing what is called networking. He's such a smooth talker. You'll never guess who I saw a few minutes ago."

"Who?"

"Dickless Tracy. She was in uniform and looked very smart. She may be keeping an eye out for shoplifters."

Philomela gave her sister a mock frown. "Constable James is her name."

Procne laughed. "I'm going to go and look at jewelry with Grace. Maybe I'll find a local artisan who would like to sell her creations in my new shop."

Philomela nodded, watched her sister walk over and join Grace, and then glanced again at the greeting cards. Surreptitiously shifting closer to Basil and Selene, she felt like a curious snoop. Even knowing this, she leaned her head toward them and unashamedly listened.

"She should be evaluated for depression," Selene said. "The shop-'til-you-drop syndrome gives a depressed person a brief lift, like alcohol to an alcoholic, or drugs to a drug addict. Basil, you have to understand that the Compulsive Buying Disorder is a real illness. It's called *Oniomania.* Eighty percent of people who have it are female. They obtain solace, a lift from depression, by purchasing more and more possessions."

"Depressed?" Basil asked. "She doesn't seem depressed."

"Not all the time."

"Would medication help her?"

"Probably. But side effects of the drug and the threat of developing another addiction are major problems. There's a support group called Debtors Anonymous. It provides a foundation for the basis of a spiritual program. It helps people cope from the insanity of compulsive buying and going deeply in debt." Selene glanced over at Philomela. She smiled and turned to Philomela. "Hello, Philomela. I guess you overheard part of our conversation."

"Some of it, Selene. I confess to listening to you and Basil. I knew Grace liked to shop, but I had no idea it was such a serious problem. Would encouraging her to pay for things by check or by cash help?"

"It would help a great deal. But who is going to force her to do that?"

"Basil could," Philomela replied. Seeing the downcast expression on his face, she regretted her thoughtless reply. Then she came up with a different idea. "Both of you could help Grace if she would let you. But she won't. Besides, you both have to walk on eggshells because you, Basil, have to live with her, and you, Selene, are a sympathetic friend. I, on the other hand, may never see her again. I could be the mean one. I could take the first step right now and shame her into admitting the problem."

"How will you do that?" Selene appeared puzzled.

Without answering, Philomela reached her hand over

the counter and dropped the greeting card she held onto the display. Then she turned to the jewelry area and strode past her sister who was watching Grace take her credit card from her purse. As Grace extended her arm toward the clerk, Philomela reached out and snatched the card.

"Grace." Philomela spoke with the authority of an upstart inquisitor. "Is it true that your other credit card is maxed to the limit?"

Grace glared at her. "It's none of your business, Philomela. Give me my card."

Philomela bent the card and twisted it. "You'll have to pay for the jewelry with cash, Grace."

"You're wrecking my credit card, and I don't have any cash on me."

"Then use your debit card." Philomela bent the credit card back and forth until it snapped in two.

"Look what you've done. I don't have a debit card."

"A check?"

"What are you trying to prove? I don't have a check book."

"Do you really need another necklace you can't afford?"

"You interfering busybody." Grace's voice rose to a yell. "I'm going to call the police."

At that moment Basil and Selene came up to the counter.

Grace, whose eyes glistened with a mix of anger and frustration, stared at her husband. "Basil, do you know what this horrid woman did? She took my credit card and ripped it up."

"Well, Grace, you have another one." His voice was soft and he gazed at her with an expression of puzzled kindness.

"I can't use it."

"Why not?"

Her shoulders slumped forward and tears filled her eyes. She nodded her head as if finally admitting defeat. "It's maxed to the limit," she murmured.

"Grace," Philomela said and her tone was gentle. "I repeat—do you need another necklace you can't afford?"

Grace again glared at her. "I like it. It's pretty."

"That doesn't answer my question. Can you afford it and do you need it?"

Grace lowered her eyes, exhaled loudly, and looked helplessly over at Basil.

He gently shook his head. "You already have a lot of jewelry. You don't need this one. And you certainly cannot afford it."

"Grace." Philomela's voice again became firm and authoritative. "Until you become debt free, it's important to think of what you need—not what you want." She watched Grace fidget uncomfortably and knew the poor woman felt that everyone was ganging up on her. In a manner of speaking, everyone *was* ganging up on her. In a softer tone of voice Philomela said, "Why don't you and Basil and Selene go over there for coffee and relax?" She indicated the nearby eating area. "The three of you could discuss this in private."

Basil jumped at the suggestion. "A cuppa would be lovely right now." He took the stool from Grace and carried it for her.

With Selene at one side and Basil at the other, Grace reluctantly walked toward the refreshment area. Philomela smiled and looked at Procne who, with open mouth, watched the threesome reach a table and sit down.

Procne raised her eyebrows and focused on her sister. "What in the world is going on?"

"I think Grace will be joining Debtors Anonymous. The motive for Basil's museum theft has been solved. So has his loan from Maxine. Basil borrowed from Maxine to pay off Grace's credit card debts. He had trouble repaying Maxine and stupidly took money donated to the museum. He asked Shaun to sell some of his stock. I think he was so upset with Maxine's death and so desperate to get his finances on a level footing that he tried to steal the I-Owe-You."

"Will Grace be able to get over her obsession for more and more stuff?" Procne asked.

"I think so, eventually. But it won't be easy."

"Well, as a saleslady, I promise not to pressure her."

"You never did pressure her, Procne. From what I saw, no one ever pushed Grace into buying anything. She made those decisions all on her own. According to Selene, she could be suffering from a form of depression."

"Depression? Everything's getting more and more confusing." Procne's arms flew sideways with palms upward in an I-give-up gesture. Then she looked around and lowered her arms. "Philomela, I guess we won't wait for Selene. We might as well go home. Is there anything else you want to look at?"

"The outfit I bought at your shop will be a memento of my week in Saltaire. But I should buy something for Brent. Something small that will fit in my suitcase."

"I know just the thing." Procne grasped her sister's elbow. "Follow me." She led the way to a counter covered with miniature cars. "I bet they have Jaguars here."

Sure enough, they found a British Racing Green E-type convertible. Philomela bought it for Brent.

Procne bought a small pot of fresh parsley. "It will improve the taste of winter salads. I also have the name and email address of a lady who makes interesting jewelry. She agreed to sell some in my shop."

Because Selene and the Devonshires were deep in conversation in the eating area and Shaun was nowhere in sight, they headed for the main entrance. On their way to the automatic doors, they met Constable James and stopped to chat. Though the constable was less than forthcoming with answers about the accident or the murder, Philomela hoped that progress was slowly being made. Both sisters promised to phone her if anything new came to mind, no matter how unimportant it might be. They started to go their separate ways when Philomela suddenly stopped and turned back.

"Constable James," she said, "something just came to mind. It's probably unimportant and irrelevant. But here it is." With a weak grin, she moved closer to the constable and described Selene's phony webpage. Then she explained the contents of the weird emails she was receiving with requests for money for spiritual beings. "All this probably doesn't pertain to Maxine's murder," she said, "but Selene is distraught because her name and photo are being used in ways she finds abhorrent. It could be a form of identity theft. Shaun O'Reilly is going to try and get rid of the webpage but if he fails Selene will ask the police to look into it."

The constable nodded her head. "We have technicians who handle such things."

"Good. I also have a question that might pertain to Maxine's murder. Did Hamish MacDonald contact the police department about who he saw on Tuesday morning?"

"No, he didn't."

"Hamish told Procne he saw someone running from the museum early Tuesday morning. Sarah Winston said she saw someone, too."

"Yes, Sarah told us something about that. She was so vague, we couldn't make head or tale of her story. However, I'll talk with her again. And I'll contact Hamish."

"One more thing. And this is rather iffy. The hit-and-run car might be British Racing Green in color."

"Thanks for the information, Philomela." She brought out her cellphone. "I'll have someone look into Selene Hamilton's website right away. And I'll run a check on British Racing Green cars, just in case."

With that they said farewell and parted company.

CHAPTER 36

Sunday Late Afternoon:

Philomela followed Procne out the door of the Community Center and stepped into an eerie cloud of gray. The atmosphere reminded her of pictures of Jack the Ripper skulking through foggy London. The eeriness increased as a ship's fog horn floated through the air, lamenting a lack of visibility. Doubtless, the captain of the ship, like herself, could see no more than a foot ahead, behind, or at each side. Airline pilots would have the same problem. They would be unable to land and take off on local runways, making her scheduled departure for Calgary doubtful.

Walking through the heavy mist on Main Avenue, Philomela felt her sister grab her arm. "Let's get out of this pea soup and stop for coffee. Who knows? Jean might have some breaking news."

"Good idea." Though the eerie mist felt soft on Philomela's skin, its swirling lack of visibility disconcerted both her thinking and her balance.

Entering the bright, bustling cafe, she blinked twice then looked around for an empty table. There weren't any. Seeing Shaun sitting across a table from Melvin Springer, she nudged her sister and nodded toward them.

"I see them," Procne whispered.

Buying two mugs of coffee, the sisters quietly quizzed Jean about the murder.

"To be honest," Jean said, "I don't think the police have a clue. Constable James came in this morning. While getting her a coffee and a sticky bun, I asked if she had any leads. She said there were a few people of interest, but nothing definite."

"I just saw her at the craft sale." Philomela nodded optimistically. "Let's hope they find a prime suspect soon."

"I hope so," Jean said. "It's disappointing the way things are shaping up, or should I say *not* shaping up. Everyone's nervous about having a murderer wandering around town. Who knows when or where the culprit will strike again?"

"At the moment, we can only hope Maxine's death was targeted. It's bad enough if someone killed her for personal vengeance or greed, but a terrorist, a mass murderer, or a serial killer would be worse." Philomela tightened her lips, picked up her coffee mug from the counter, and glanced around. Seeing two elderly ladies preparing to vacate a corner table, she said, "Thanks for the coffee, Jean. I'm going to grab that table before someone else does."

Walking toward it, she watched the two ladies put on their raincoats. Peripherally, she saw Shaun grin at her and raise his hand in greeting so she stopped beside him. Melvin, she noted, ignored her by continuing to stare down at his coffee mug.

"Philomela, did you buy anything this afternoon?" Shaun asked.

"As a matter of fact I did. A Jaguar convertible."

"Come on now, you've got to be kidding. Or did I miss seeing the cars at the craft sale?"

She smiled and reached inside her purse. For no apparent reason her abdominal muscles gave a faint twist, but she ignored the feeling and dramatically brought out the model car. "Here it is. A gift for my husband."

Shaun burst out laughing. Melvin looked up at the small car and chuckled.

Procne, carrying her creamed and sugared coffee, stopped beside her sister. "What's so funny?"

"Philomela bought a Jaguar," Shaun replied.

"I know. Lovely, isn't it? Did either of you purchase anything at Arts, Crafts, Etc.?"

"Biscotti." Shaun grinned. "They're like stale cookies, but I like dunking them in hot coffee." He held up a package of long hard biscuits and looked around. "What happened to Selene?"

"She's back at the Community Center having tea with the Devonshires."

"Really?" Shaun's eyebrows arched in surprise. "I didn't know she and the Devonshires were friends."

Procne shrugged. "They are now, I guess."

"You didn't attend the craft sale, Melvin," Philomela said, trying to include him in the conversation.

"No, that's not my thing. But Maxine would have liked it."

"Do you have any hobbies?" Philomela continued to try and include the widower in the conversation. "Or does your accountancy office keep you too busy?" Though her questions were general and polite, she truly was interested in the new widower.

"I golf and putter in the garden," he said. "But I'm not dedicated to either."

"The gardens here are spectacular, even in January. Working in them must be gratifying."

"Sometimes growth is too good. It makes for a lot of pruning."

She nodded and smiled at Melvin then strolled over to the now empty corner table. She sat down, sipped her coffee, and wished her iPad was in her purse. A slowly developing suspicion was filling her mind, and she wanted to check a few emails from the phony Selene. It seemed serendipitous that she hadn't deleted the emails. Though she hoped to find the killer, she didn't want it to be someone she knew.

Procne placed her coffee mug on the table, sat down, and gazed at her sister. "Shaun is trying to get Melvin to invest in an up and coming mining company. A big financial deal. To me it sounds risky." She shook her head. "But what do I know about stock markets?"

"Is Melvin interested?"

"I don't know. But he asked quite a few questions."

"Melvin is an enigma," Philomela said. "I must admit my original impression of him was dreadful. But he is improving, probably getting over the initial shock of his wife's horrid death. I suppose Shaun figures Melvin's money is as good as anyone's."

"Maybe Shaun is being sympathetic, trying to help Melvin get on with his life."

"Perhaps."

"They must have struck a deal," Procne said. "They're leaving and they're both smiling."

Several minutes later the sisters finished their coffee and left the crowded, brightly lit History Café. They walked out to a world that Philomela found dimmer, foggier, and thicker than when they had entered the café. Fog horns sporadically sounded from across the water and a set of shrouded headlights passed by them on Main Avenue. The headlights disappeared and the world grew eerier and spookier than ever. Nervously, almost expecting

Jack the Ripper to stalk them, she automatically walked faster. So did Procne.

After opening the metal gate and entering the open-air vestibule of the townhouse, Philomela wondered if Selene was home yet. She hoped the Devonshires would drive her from the Community Center so she wouldn't have to walk alone in the fog. Philomela scooted past Procne's and Trust's doors and peeked through the glass of Selene's door. A light was on, but she couldn't remember if Selene had left it on before departing for the arts and crafts sale.

She turned, gazed through the metal grill and watched fog swirl around a corner streetlight. "I may not be able to fly home tonight," she murmured. "No airplane can take off in this fog."

"Yeah, it's thicker than pea soup." Procne unlocked the door and walked into her townhouse. "Instead of pea soup," she said, "I'll serve homemade lentil soup tonight. Is that okay with you?"

"Perfect. I'm not very hungry. I'll help you, but first I want to check my emails. If the fog doesn't lift, I'll have to let Brent know so he won't drive to the Calgary airport."

She hurried to her niece's bedroom, anxious to confirm her new suspicion about the phony emails. She picked up her iPad, opened it, and checked the last email. She found what she was looking for. Then she checked a few other emails and found the same word combination. She carried the iPad to the kitchen and placed it on the eating counter.

Procne stood at the cook-top stirring a pot of soup. "Would you like a glass of wine or juice?" she asked.

"Nothing, thanks. But I would like your opinion about a certain verbal expression."

Procne turned to her sister and frowned. "Pardon?"

"Do you associate the expression, *Come on now*, with anyone in particular?"

"No. A lot of people use that expression."

Philomela looked down at her iPad and read aloud, "*Come on now, Rae, act quickly. This is your best chance to achieve everything you always desired.*"

"Is that an email from the phony Selene?" Procne concentrated on stirring the soup.

"Yes."

Procne stopped stirring. "At the moment I can think of someone who occasionally uses that expression."

Philomela leaned expectantly toward her. "And who might that be?"

"I think I've heard Melvin Springer use it."

"Oh." Philomela's brows knit together. "I don't recall hearing him use it. Nor have I ever heard your psychic neighbor use it. But the so-called Selene often used it in her emails."

"So we have to listen for someone to say, *come on now*. Then we'll be able to pinpoint the cyberspace criminal?"

Philomela nodded. "I heard it used this afternoon in the History Cafe."

"You did?

"Yes, when I was chatting with Shaun and Melvin."

Procne's eyes resembled two full moons. She opened her mouth, but no words came out. Finally she whispered, "Melvin."

Philomela pensively shook her head. "Shaun."

"Oh, no, not Shaun."

Philomela nodded her head. "I suspect Shaun and Selene are in cahoots. Shaun has the computer skills and Selene has the psychic abilities."

"Selene and Shaun in cahoots." Procne threw her hands up in the air. "What next?"

"I'd liked to solve the email puzzle before I leave Saltaire." Philomela glanced at her wristwatch. "If the fog clears so planes can fly, I'll have to be at the airport in two and a half hours. Not much time to solve the sordid email scheme. If we ask Selene specific questions, we'll be able to tell if she's involved. I suggest we go to her place right now, provided she has returned from the Community Center."

Procne paid more attention to immediate food needs than to solving the email scam. She stared at her sister. "What about our soup?"

"Turn off the burner. We can eat after we visit Selene."

CHAPTER 37

Early Sunday Evening:

Selene opened the door and her mouth formed a circle of surprise.

"Oh—Procne—Philomela. Hello. Um…come on in." She stepped aside and ushered the two sisters into her entrance hall. "Pardon me if I seem a bit flustered—but to be honest, I really am flustered."

"Are we interrupting something?" Philomela asked.

"Not really. It's just that right now I'm overwhelmed."

At that moment Philomela saw Shaun appear at the other end of the corridor. Her shoulders sagged as if weighted by a sudden burden.

"Shaun just proposed to me," Selene said.

The burden on Philomela's shoulders increased in weight and a dark cloud surrounded her head. The people beside her became shivery forms of darkness.

"You mean he proposed marriage?" Procne's voice screeched loudly and jarred the dark cloud off to the left side of Philomela's head.

"That's right," Selene said. "I'm so surprised and so flattered I hardly know what to say."

Say no, a voice thudded inside Philomela's left ear. Her lips didn't repeat the words and the dark cloud swirled away. As her blurred vision returned to normal, the sight of the psychic's happy face should have made her feel joyous. Instead, she felt sad and nervous. It came to mind that Selene's ability to see the best in everyone made her oblivious to danger.

Watching Selene from the corner of her eyes, Philomela doubted she would knowingly participate in an internet scam. Though intuitive, Selene seemed incapable of recognizing that psychopaths and sociopaths could affect her life. She seemed unable to understand that they lacked empathy yet could superficially imitate the appropriate actions of others.

"Selene," Philomela said, "before we bring out the champagne, I'd like to hear how Shaun is doing with regard to the phony website and emails."

"He's already contacted the website person." Selene smiled, obviously confident the problem was under control.

Philomela was puzzled. "You mean the website has been removed?"

"I don't think so—not yet. But it soon will be."

Shaun wandered nonchalantly up to the three women and smiled. "Nice to see you two ladies again. Anything new?"

"We're still concerned about Selene's phony website," Philomela said. "And the emails. Have you discovered anything?"

"I sent a message to the perpetrator of the website. I'm confident it will disappear in a couple of days. If, in three days' time, the website's still there, I'll take more drastic steps." He cleared his throat, lightly shrugged his shoulders, and widened his smile. "Quite a coincidence. Two psychics with the same name."

"Isn't it, though?" Philomela's lips curved upward but the smile failed to reach her eyes. "Do you think the picture on the internet is Selene's identical twin sister?" She gazed questioningly at Shaun.

"I don't have a twin sister," Selene interjected.

Philomela ignored Selene's remark and continued to stare at Shaun. "Do you know who is taking illegal advantage of Selene's good name and reputation?"

"Illegal advantage? Come on now, Philomela." Shaun, unaware of Procne's loud gasp, said, "That's a bit far-fetched."

"Does the phony Selene live here in Saltaire?" Philomela asked.

"I haven't determined that yet. She could live anywhere in the world."

"The scammer knows a lot about Selene Hamilton and how to take advantage of her insights. There are a lot of sharks out there looking for gullible fish. Didn't that circus man say, 'There's a sucker born every minute?'"

"Philomela, you have a suspicious nature," Shaun said.

"Perhaps. Do you?"

He shrugged. "When I have a good reason to be suspicious. I confess to having wondered about Melvin. But now I'm not so sure."

Recalling how Shaun had bad-mouthed Melvin, Philomela pretended to direct her own suspicions at the new widower. "I suppose he could be guilty of the hoax."

"He's good on computers." Shaun looked thoughtful for several seconds as if contemplating the idea. "But then again, his accountancy business is successful and he doesn't need more money. In fact, a few months ago Melvin planned to invest with me. He promised to try and convince Maxine to do the same. Unfortunately, she died before any money changed hands."

Philomela's gut feeling told her the failure of money changing hands may have been unfortunate for Shaun, but doubtless was fortunate for Melvin and Maxine.

"I confess to wondering about Basil, too." Shaun shook his head as if finding the topic distressful. "Basil has serious money problems. But I wouldn't accuse him of being desperate enough to commit murder. He might have been responsible for the website and emails. Personally, though, I think it's the work of a computer-savvy female."

"Do you have anyone in mind?" Philomela asked.

"Sheila Trust is computer literate." Shaun shrugged again. "But so are lots of other women."

Philomela waited, hoping his soliloquy would incriminate himself, but no obvious blunder materialized. She concluded he was too smooth by half to get in such an awkward position.

"Selene." Procne looked a query at her neighbor. "What do you think? If you didn't set up the website, have you any idea who might have done it?"

"None whatsoever." Selene rubbed the tips of her fingers on her forehead then shook her head from side to side. "I find it terribly distressing."

Shaun moved over to her and, in a proprietary manner, put his arm around her. His hand grasped her shoulder and pulled her toward him in what looked to Philomela like a rough hug. "Don't worry, Selene," he said. "I'll get rid of that webpage, one way or another."

He spoke with such confidence that Philomela almost believed him. Of course, if he were the website's instigator, he could easily remove it, and later he could just as easily re-establish it. Surreptitiously studying him, she wondered why he wanted to marry Selene. Had his love for her been long standing or had it appeared quite suddenly? Somehow the idea of him being in love with anyone but himself seemed impossible. He was an outgoing social charmer, and she was a gentle, reclusive person. They were as different as chalk and cheese. How could they live happily together? Even though opposites might attract, Philomela suspected he had an ulterior motive for instigating the ringing of wedding bells.

"Let's forget about the webpage and drink a toast to our engagement." Shaun's voice rang with enthusiasm. His hand released its grip on Selene's shoulder, his arm dropped to his side, and he stared at his new fiancée as if expecting her to automatically bring his suggestion to fruition.

But Selene didn't move. She stood as immobile as a petrified tree trunk. Philomela noticed a blank expression on her face and wondered if something weird was happening to her. Was she getting a message? Was she still in shock over Shaun's marriage proposal? Or was she in the initial stages of developing a cold or a more serious illness?

"Selene." Procne stepped toward her neighbor. "I'll help you pour some champagne."

"Oh…yes." As if puzzled, Selene glanced at Shaun then stared at Procne. "I'd like your help, but I have no champagne. Only wine." In wooden-soldier fashion, she walked toward the kitchen and Procne followed behind her.

Watching Selene's movements, Philomela was reminded of a battery-run robot she once saw in a toy shop. She followed the two women to the kitchen and watched the psychic slowly set four glasses on the counter beside a large bowl full of fruit. Procne quickly inserted a cork screw into the wine bottle and popped out the cork. Philomela glanced back at Shaun who had followed them to the kitchen. She felt uneasy because his manner had shown unconcern with the false website. Worse, he had been oblivious of his fiancée's sudden distress. She suspected he was too self-centered to recognize that the person he supposedly loved had developed some sort of problem.

Once again, she wondered why Shaun wanted Selene to be a permanent fixture in his life. To cook his meals and wash his clothes? To clean his domicile? To participate in hot sex? Or to manipulate her psychic talents in underhanded ways that would enhance his personal advantage?

Philomela shuddered. She suspected that having Shaun as a husband would be the undoing of the sensitive woman. His demanding superficiality would dismay her, his selfish insensitivity would wear her down, and his mental and possible physical abuse would be hurtful. Could the psychic not see such a future for herself? Was she so unaware of her own needs?

The doorbell rang and Selene glided over to the intercom. She pressed the button, looked at the camera, and said, "Good evening."

CHAPTER 38

Philomela stood bedside Shaun and Procne and watched Selene stare into the screen of the intercom. Through the little box on the wall Philomela heard the newcomer clearly reply.

"Constable James here. Could I see you for a minute, Ms. Hamilton?"

"Certainly." Selene pressed a button and Philomela heard a buzzing sound. "My door's unlocked, so just come on in." Selene continued to stare at the tiny screen.

Shaun moved off to the sitting area and Philomela watched Procne scurry along the corridor toward the front door. She disappeared from sight but Philomela heard her greet the newcomer.

"Hi, Constable James. Come on in."

"Oh—Procne." The constable's voice registered surprise. "I didn't expect to see you here. I hope I'm not intruding—or interrupting something."

"Not at all," Procne replied. "Just a neighborly get-together."

"Is it convenient for me to talk with Ms. Hamilton?"

"Of course. Is something wrong?"

"Not really. You'll be pleased to know we're making progress with the murder case."

Philomela heard the good news and edged with interest from the kitchen toward the corridor. She paused and watched her sister and the constable walk toward her. A melody rang in the air and Constable James unhooked the cellphone from her belt.

Holding the device to her ear, she moved slowly toward the kitchen. "I'm at Selene Hamilton's townhouse right now and a few of her neighbors are here...Yes, he is. So is Procne Ellis and her sister...Yes that's a good plan." She shut off the cellphone, re-hooked it to her belt, and walked over to Selene.

"Nice to see you, Constable James," Selene said. "I was going to give my guests a drink. Shaun and I are celebrating our engagement to be married. Would you join us?"

"Married? My goodness. That's a surprise. Congratulations. Thank you, no drinks for me. I'm on duty."

Philomela edged close to the policewoman. "Are you gaining any headway in solving Maxine's murder?" she whispered.

"Thanks to your suggestion this afternoon, we questioned a new witness and re-questioned an old one." She paused and looked seriously at Philomela.

"I don't suppose you can tell us any details."

"Sorry, Philomela, not at this time."

"And the webpage?" Philomela asked. "Have you found out anything about the webpage fiasco?"

"Yes. Quite a bit as a matter of fact."

"Good." Philomela smiled. "So have I."

"You know about the webpage set up in my name?" Selene looked with surprise at the constable. "Is there really another psychic with my name?"

"No," Constable James replied. "The webpage is definitely a scam. Your name and photo have been stolen and maligned."

"Do you know who did it?" Philomela asked.

"Yes. And I also know who the hit-and-run driver was. Your tip about the green car was the clue we needed. Grace Devonshire was driving, and it was an accident. She should have stayed at the scene, of course. There will be repercussions about that."

The doorbell rang and Selene again went to the box on the wall. She spoke into it and Corporal Stinson gave his name. Selene pressed the button to let him into the open-air vestibule. "My townhouse door is unlocked. Come on in."

When Corporal Stinson entered the kitchen, Shaun left the sitting area and walked up to him. He warmly greeted both the constable and the corporal.

Then with a flourish, he raised his left arm and glanced at his watch.

"I'm afraid I have to leave this jolly gathering," he said. "I have a meeting in fifteen minutes with a new client."

"I think you should stay," the corporal said. "We have a few questions to ask you."

"Ask away." Shaun gave him a friendly smile. "The quicker the better."

"How much money have you made from Selene's webpage?"

Selene gasped. Open mouthed and wide eyed, she stared with surprise at Shaun.

Feeling a surge of self-satisfaction, Philomela bobbed her head up and down.

"That's a baseless accusation," Shaun snapped.

"No, it's not baseless." Corporal Stinson studied him a few seconds. "We have backup—your email messages, your PayPal and credit-card receipts." He turned to Selene. "I gather you know nothing about how that webpage got started."

"I first learned about the page this morning. Procne and Philomela showed it to me on Philomela's iPad. But you must be mistaken. Shaun wouldn't do such a thing, not to me. An hour ago he even asked me to marry him."

"That would be convenient." Corporal Stinson snorted sarcastically. "In court, a wife cannot be forced to testify against her husband."

So, Philomela thought, *that's another reason Shaun wanted to marry Selene. Not only could he make illegal use of her sensitive abilities, but she could not be forced to testify against him.* Philomela looked over at the psychic and saw her eyes fill with moisture.

"So the puzzle of the phony webpage has been solved." Procne nodded at Philomela. She glanced warily at Selene then turned and focused on Constable James. "What about Maxine's murder? I heard you say that Philomela's suggestion was of help."

"She suggested I compare Sarah Winston's story with Hamish MacDonald's, which we did."

"Hmmph," Shaun grunted. "Sarah's as reliable as a horsefly."

"Shaun's right," Procne said. "Sarah even spread a rumor that my sister had murdered Maxine."

"Our second witness is more reliable," Corporal Stinson said. "Hamish MacDonald was out walking his dog on Main Avenue about seven o'clock Tuesday morning and he met Sarah. She pointed to a man hurrying away from the museum and Hamish recognized you, Shaun. But he didn't think anything of it, not even when he recalled that Basil had mentioned he was having trouble getting you to sell his mineral stock because he needed the money. After talking with Hamish, we visited Melvin. He checked Maxine's personal files at home and discovered an I-Owe-You from Basil. We then talked with Basil who confessed he was in financial trouble and Maxine had come to his aid with a loan. She wanted him to repay it so she could wipe the loan from her books. The only way he could repay it was to sell stock that Shaun had bought for him.

"Selling stock sometimes takes time," Shaun said.

"Especially when Basil's money went into your pocket instead of into the purchase of mining stock." Corporal Stinson briefly studied Shaun then cleared his throat. "I also learned from Melvin that you and Maxine grew up in the same town. She knew you had been involved with a few shady business dealings. She also knew you had dumped a pregnant girlfriend. She didn't trust you, so she advised Melvin to watch his step when dealing with you. It wasn't until Melvin admitted having invested with you that she hit the roof. She phoned you immediately and threatened to expose some of your less-than-legal past dealings if you didn't refund the money to Melvin. That was when you spread more than one false rumor about Melvin being loose with his sexual favors."

"You mean Shaun projected his own sins on Melvin?" Philomela asked.

"Exactly," the corporal replied. "After that, Shaun saw only one way to save his reputation. Silence Maxine. Forever."

Speechless, Selene looked from Corporal Stinson to Shaun. Philomela glanced at Shaun just in time to see him plough his fist into Corporal Stinson's face. Not expecting the blow, the corporal staggered and fell backward on the floor. Selene screamed.

Constable James pulled a gun from her holster and pointed it at Shaun. "Stand with your hands in the air," she ordered.

He ignored her and ran toward the door, apparently

confident she wouldn't shoot. Feeling the same confidence, Philomela picked up the heavy blue fruit bowl from the counter and ran after Shaun. As he fumbled to open the door she reached up and smashed the bowl against his head.

For some reason the bowl remained in one piece, but fruit and vegetables flew everywhere. Apples hit the wall, bananas landed on the floor, and tomatoes splattered on Shaun's shoulder. His eyes rolled backward and his knees gave way. He slid to the floor like a sheet of fabric. His stunned state lasted long enough for Constable James to grasp both his hands, pull them behind his back, and snap on handcuffs.

Philomela felt a delayed reaction of weakness. But she took a deep breath, gathered up the scattered fruit and vegetables, and replaced them in the intact bowl. She carried them toward the kitchen and stopped beside Corporal Stinson who was sitting up.

"Are you okay?" she asked.

He gave his head a shake, obviously trying to remove visions of stars and cobwebs. Then he scrambled to his feet. "Yeah, I'm fine."

"Constable James handcuffed Shaun," Philomela said. She inclined her head toward the front door and added, "Everything is under control."

Several minutes later the police were ready to leave. Corporal Stinson told Selene he would be in touch with her after the phony webpage was removed. He and Constable James then guided Shaun out the door and departed.

Feeling dazed, all three women stared at the closed door. Then they looked at each other and without a word trooped to the living area and plopped onto Selene's two blue and white loveseats. Selene and Procne sighed loudly. Philomela leaned back and stretched her legs out in front of her. The turn of events had happened so quickly she could hardly comprehend it.

"Selene," Philomela finally asked, "did you have any inkling that Shaun might not be on the up and up with you?"

"No. I trusted him completely. But when Shaun suggested we celebrate our engagement with a drink of champagne, something about the way his hand grasped my shoulder bothered me. Suddenly, I heard words float near my left ear—*this engagement is not for you*. The words were clear and they came as a shock—never before had my spiritual guides given me any personal advice. I didn't believe it at first. After all, Shaun has always treated me with kindness."

"Why wouldn't he be kind to you?" Philomela said. "Using your good name on the internet was a great meal ticket for him."

Selene's eyes were wide and slightly moist.

"Well, neighbor," Procne said, "it's a good thing you learned all these ugly things before you married the jerk." She turned to her sister and giggled. "Philomela, I had no idea you were strong enough to knock someone cuckoo."

"Neither did I. It's a good thing Maxine wasn't murdered by a museum board member or volunteer. Simon Fraser will be relieved about that." She glanced out the window, sat up straight, and leaped to her feet. "Look, the fog is lifting. I see stars."

EPILOGUE

Sunday Evening Later:

Sitting in the 737-600, Philomela looked out the window at the night sky. A few clouds shifted position and exposed the gibbous moon. It reminded her, not of the mythical Greek moon-goddess, but of her sister's real-life-neighbor whose blue-gray garments, wispy fair hair, and silver jewelry created a delicate but showy appearance. At the same time, her gentle manner, aura of peace, soft voice, and words of optimism enhanced her innate sensitivity. If she wasn't already a true shaman, she soon would be.

Philomela was glad her kid sister had such a kind and honest neighbor. Selene, on the other hand, was fortunate to have a neighbor as cheery and well-grounded as Procne. Their symbiotic friendship would probably endure for years to come.

A cloud hid the moon as the airplane started its descent. Philomela looked down at the lights of Calgary as they came closer, brightening the darkness. After getting off the plane, she walked to the airport's arrival area and spotted Brent sitting on a bench near a carousel. She noticed that his jacket fit poorly and something white covered part of his upper body. Coming closer to him, she realized a white sling was holding his left arm across his chest.

He looked up, saw her, and leaped to his feet. "Philomela." He quickly threw his right arm around her shoulders and his face nuzzled her hair. She snuggled close to him. No words were necessary.

She leaned back and saw that inside the white sling his lower arm was encased in a cast. "What happened?" she asked.

"Nothing much. Just a broken wrist. I'll tell you about it in the car."

"How in the world did you drive to the airport?"

"With one hand, slowly. Yesterday, John drove all the way home from the mountains. So that was good."

They got her suitcase from the carousel and walked to the parkade. Philomela automatically climbed into the car behind the steering wheel and Brent, with the sling supporting his arm, sat contentedly in the passenger seat. On the way home, he explained how he had injured his wrist.

"I must have been tired and going too fast down the steep hill. I simply fell and my hand landed on a hard surface, a rock I think. A guide made a temporary splint out of a tree branch. It held everything in place until I got to the hospital. Apparently, the break was clean and easy to set. So here I am—imperfect but alive."

"Luckily, the accident happened at three o'clock on Friday afternoon—your last day. So you didn't miss much skiing time."

He stared at her, his facial expression registered amazement. "How did you know?"

She gave him a sardonic grin. "You were uppermost in my mind on Friday afternoon when I experienced a sharp pain in my left wrist. I looked at it to see what was wrong and noted the time on my wristwatch. Three o'clock." She nonchalantly added, "Then the pain left me and I forgot all about it—until now."

"Coincidence."

"Or mental telepathy."

"Hmmph."

Philomela smiled and concentrated on the flow of traffic. It was much busier and much faster than the traffic in Saltaire.

"You know, Brent, Saltaire is a charming, seaside town. The climate is temperate, the people are interesting, and there's hardly any traffic. It's a reputable resort area with many marinas and restaurants. The terrain near the ocean is flat which makes for easy walking. I certainly understand why a lot of people retire there."

"Hmm."

"When we start thinking of retirement, we should keep the town in mind."

"I'm not ready to quit working yet. But speaking of work—your emails said Procne is pleased with her new dress shop."

"She's thrilled. And for good reason. The deal was dandy and the shop is splendid. With Procne's pleasant personality and her flare for fashion, she'll do well."

He grinned but didn't mention her overuse of alliteration. "Procne deserves a lucky break. And I'm glad you two had a good time." He paused. "Dare I ask what you did to help solve that poor woman's murder?"

"I made a couple of suggestions to a police constable."

"Hmm. Did you have any contact with the murderer himself?"

"A little bit." She thought of her chats with the perpetrator and of how a few hours ago she connected the blue fruit bowl with his head.

"So, generally speaking, Saltaire is a quiet town."

"Yes, nothing much happens there." *And that*, Philomela thought, *is the understatement of the year*.

The End

About the Author

Benni Chisholm grew up on the Canadian prairies and, while a student earning a BSN, started writing light verse. Later, in the shadows of the Rocky Mountain foothills she worked as a public health nurse, helped four wonderful children raise themselves, and saw the publication of a few poems, a biography, an anniversary booklet, a newsletter (eight years as editor), and several articles and short stories. Chisholm's fondness for travel is apparent in her mystery novels: *Stained Sand*, which is set in Hawaii, *Odd Odyssey*, where the protagonist finds adventure on a trip around the world, and *Showman or Shaman*, set in the Pacific Northwest.

www.ingramcontent.com/pod-product-compliance
Lightning Source LLC
Chambersburg PA
CBHW062136170626
46813CB00002B/712